To my parents

HOW A
GUNMAN
SAYS
GOODBYE

Also available in the
Glasgow Trilogy

THE NECESSARY DEATH
OF LEWIS WINTER

HOW A GUNMAN SAYS GOODBYE

MALCOLM MACKAY

MANTLE

First published 2013 by Mantle
an imprint of Pan Macmillan, a division of Macmillan Publishers Limited
Pan Macmillan, 20 New Wharf Road, London N1 9RR
Basingstoke and Oxford
Associated companies throughout the world
www.panmacmillan.com

ISBN 978-0-230-76972-4

1 3 5 7 9 8 6 4 2

A CIP catalogue record for this book is available from the British Library.

Typeset by Ellipsis Digital Limited, Glasgow
Printed and bound by CPI Group (UK) Ltd, Croydon, CR0 4YY

Visit **www.panmacmillan.com** to read more about all our books
and to buy them. You will also find features, author interviews and
news of any author events, and you can sign up for e-newsletters
so that you're always first to hear about our new releases.

CHARACTERS

Calum MacLean – A young gunman, a big talent. He killed Lewis Winter and he killed Glen Davidson. Did a good job. All it got him was deeper into an organization that he wants no part of.

Peter Jamieson – A growing empire, but is under attack. Shug Francis thinks he can take what Jamieson's built. So long as there are no distractions, Jamieson will strike back hard.

John Young – Organizing, scheming and doing all in his power as second in command to keep the Jamieson organization growing.

Frank MacLeod – He was the best gunman in the city. Now he's back, with his new hip ready to see action. Been a while since he worked, but you never forget.

Emma Munro – A student, her life ahead of her. Her new boyfriend, Calum, is a good guy, she thinks, if he would only open up a little.

DI Michael Fisher – Moves are being made in his city. He can nail those behind it all, but he needs the right contacts. Information is king.

Hugh 'Shug' Francis – His first move against Jamieson was a failure. Winter dead; Davidson following him to the grave. Restock, plan and get it right.

Tommy Scott – Starting from the absolute bottom, but he's going to make it to the top. Dealing drugs for Shug is just the start.

Andy 'Clueless' McClure – Where Tommy goes, Clueless goes; everyone knows that. He will help his mate to the top, if that's where he's going.

Kenny McBride – Peter Jamieson's driver. Near the bottom of the food chain, but even those at the bottom have plenty to worry about if things look like turning sour.

Shaun Hutton – He's Shug's new gunman, replacing Davidson. Hutton's smart, he knows you need to be on the winning team.

George Daly – Muscle for Jamieson, a friend for Calum. Always fighting to avoid better things. Be happy with what you have.

Nate Colgan – A scary, powerful, smart man. Employed to be all of those things, principally by Jamieson.

William MacLean – Always worrying about his little brother. Always willing to do what it takes to help protect Calum.

PC Joseph Higgins – He works so hard, he does his best, but it's tough. Sometimes you just don't know who the good guys are any more.

David 'Fizzy' Waters – Shug's right-hand man, always has been. Proud of his friend, happy to be the buffer between Shug and those lower down.

PC Paul Greig – So he talks to criminals: is that not a part of policing? He can justify what he does to himself, just not to others.

DC Ian Davies – If you learn one thing working closely with Fisher, it's that keeping your mouth shut and staying out of his way lead to a lot less work.

Lewis Winter – He had twenty-five years of one failure after another. Then Calum MacLean killed him. Well, he was a drug dealer, so there aren't many mourning.

Martin 'Marty' Jones – If he didn't make so much damn money, Jamieson would never let him hang around the club.

Adam Jones – Manager of the optimistically named Heavenly nightclub and, like his brother Marty, a great lover of profit.

Glen Davidson – He was a freelance gunman. Then he tried to kill Calum with a knife. He slashed Calum, injured him, but it was Davidson dead on the floor in the end.

Mark Garvey – Selling guns is dangerous, dirty. You need all the protection you can get, and informing to a strong DI is one safety net.

Kirk Webster – He's well placed, working for a phone company. That's his one redeeming feature.

Bobby Peterson – Has a nice little printing business. Jamieson owns a little share of it. Making money from legitimate businesses is important.

Ian Allen – Works with his cousin, Charlie, running a strong drug network just outside the city. They need new suppliers, though – someone reliable.

Charlie Allen – He's Ian's cousin, not his brother. People often make that mistake. Not that it bothers them; their lives are about money, not identity.

John 'Reader' Benson – It was such a long time ago that Reader gave Frank his first job in the business as muscle. Forty-four years. Things have changed.

Barney McGovern – Another piece of Frank's past. Barney employed Frank in the Eighties, went to meet his maker in the Nineties.

Anna Milton – Emma Munro's best friend. She takes a little getting used to, sure, but she's not a bad person.

Colin Thomson – It hasn't been an easy life for him. Living in a grotty flat, his health in decline. Then there's shooting in the flat above.

DCI Anthony Reid – Give your detectives the freedom to do their work. He gives Fisher a long leash, despite the Winter investigation going nowhere.

Jamie Stamford – Muscle for Alex MacArthur. Everyone has a vice, and Jamie's is gambling. You should never have a vice that gets in the way of work.

Neil Fraser – Muscle for Peter Jamieson. A short temper and a small brain get a man into trouble, no matter who his boss is.

Alex MacArthur – One of the leading men in the criminal world for decades now. Controls just about the biggest organization in the city.

Elaine Francis – She's been married to Shug long enough to know what he does for a living. To know when to turn a deaf ear and a blind eye.

Dennis Dunbar – Dennis has been dead a long time now, but he sent plenty to the grave before him. He taught Frank the important lessons of life as a gunman.

Donnie Maskell – More than thirty years since he was a leading gangster and employed Frank. Stay in the business as long as Frank, and you rack up all sorts of employers.

DI Douglas Chalmers – Retired now, but he spent years chasing Frank MacLeod. The Fisher of his day, perhaps.

DCI Richard Whyte – Retired twenty years ago, died five years ago. Always had a bee in his bonnet about catching Frank. Never caught the bee.

Derek Conner – Used to run a mediocre drug network in the city. Then had the dubious honour of being the first person Peter Jamieson killed.

Donall 'Spikey' Tokely – Used to run in a gang with Tommy and Clueless. He's grown up now, so he sells guns instead.

1

Careful on these stairs. That would be some return, falling flat on his face the first day back. Not the first time he's been to the club since he had his hip replaced. He's been haunting the place for the last two weeks. Letting everyone see he's back. New hip, same old Frank. Someone got the message. Frank had a phone call this morning from John Young. Young's the second in command, Peter Jamieson's right-hand man. When Young calls you up and invites you to the club, it's usually because Jamieson wants to see you. For some people, that could be very bad news. For Frank, it's good. The recovery, the holiday – that was all fine. Enjoyable, for a while. It's nice to put your feet up and not even think about work. It got boring, though. When your work is your life, a long holiday is a bad thing. He's been itching to return to work. To be back in the loop. It's taken a couple of weeks to convince people, but it seems to have worked.

In through the double doors at the top of the stairs. Into what's known these days as the snooker room. The club and dance floor are downstairs, but they're for customers. People in the business, people who know what the club's really about, tend to stay upstairs. There's a bar to your right as you

1

come in the door. The main floor is taken up with snooker tables. They became Jamieson's passion a couple of years ago. He has plenty of little hobbies. Harmless things to pass the time and relieve the pressure. He'll get bored of snooker eventually and drift along to something else. Golf, probably. Right now, it's snooker and horse racing. Not too many people in the snooker room at this time of day. A couple of hardy alcoholics at the bar. A few recognizable faces at the tables, killing time. One of them's a loan shark that Frank's seen at the club in the last couple of weeks. Seems to be hanging around a lot. Kenny McBride, Jamieson's driver, is there too. Nobody that could be mistaken for important.

At the far end of the room is a short corridor. Rooms on both sides, offices, but only one that matters. Bottom of the corridor on your left-hand side, Peter Jamieson's office. The room in which he runs his organization. He has a number of legit businesses, like the club, but they exist only to serve their illegitimate counterparts. Money is cleaned through the club; people like Frank are given fake jobs here to explain their income. He's the security consultant for the club, apparently. The security consultant is walking along the corridor, making sure he hides the last trace of his limp. He's fit enough to work, but he has to prove that to everyone. If they see the slight limp that remains, they'll think he's still an old cripple. He's sixty-two now, which is old enough. But he's no cripple. He's quite determined about that.

Knocking on the door and waiting for a response. Someone's calling for him to come in. He's opening the door, seeing the familiar scene in front of him. Jamieson's sitting behind his desk on the far side of the large room, facing the door. There are a couple of televisions behind him, usually showing horse racing. Not today. Today they're both switched off. John Young is sitting on the old leather couch to Jamieson's left. He's always there. It's a little trick they pull. Means that when someone sits opposite Jamieson, they can't see Young, but he can see them. They're a sharp pair, these two.

'Frank,' Jamieson's saying, and standing up. 'Good to see you, pal.' This is more of a greeting than he expected. He was in the club a couple of days ago, saw Jamieson then. This is different, though, and they both know it. This is the official return.

He's shaken hands with both Jamieson and Young, very uncharacteristic, and is now sitting in front of the desk.

'It is good to have you back, Frank,' Jamieson's saying. 'A relief, to be honest with you.'

Frank's nodding politely. Better not to look too pleased with yourself. Better to remember what's happened in your absence. Things change, even in the space of three months. They hired Calum MacLean, for a start. That was Frank's recommendation. Calum has talent, and he's smart. He's young, too; Frank can't remember if he's even turned thirty yet. Jamieson would never say it, but Calum is Frank's long-term replacement. Right now, he's his backup, but he can't even play that role. Injured on a job, both hands badly cut up. Frank hasn't seen Calum for a while. Not since before the trip to Spain. It's probably past time to pay a visit. Keep up to date. Things change, and you have to know about it to stay fresh.

'You'll take a glass of whiskey,' Jamieson's telling him. 'You driving? Och, you can still have one.'

He's filling two celebratory glasses. Celebrating the return of Frank MacLeod.

'Oh, you know, I think your tan is fading,' Jamieson's saying with a smile. He sent Frank away for a couple of weeks, to stay in his little Spanish villa. Frank's first foreign holiday in twenty years. A lovely relaxing break, if you like that sort of thing.

'Good,' Frank's saying. 'Hard to blend into a crowd round here, looking like a fucking Oompa-Loompa.'

Jokes out of the way, down to business. 'Good to have you back, because we're in need of your talents,' Jamieson's saying. 'We need to send out a little message, and you're the man for the job. I might have used Calum, but he's out of action. That's meant things running longer than they should have. Made us look a little weak.'

'How is Calum?' Frank's asking. Making it sound like genuine concern for the boy. More concerned about the state of play within the organization. He respects Calum, but this is a cut-throat business. A boy with Calum's talent doesn't stay as backup for long.

Jamieson's taking longer than expected to answer the question. Puffing out his cheeks, glancing at Young. Frank's watching carefully. He knows Jamieson's not convinced of Calum's loyalty. That's why Frank went to see Calum before flying to Spain. Tried to persuade him that organization-work is the way to go. The old head, winning round the young freelancer. Didn't quite work.

'Honestly? I think the boy's still swinging the lead. Only one of his cuts was serious. It's been patched up long enough for him to come to me and tell me he's ready to work. I sent our doc round to have a look at him a couple of days ago. I don't want to push him too much, but he reckons the boy's good to work.'

Frank's nodding. It all makes sense. Calum was a free-lancer. Never worked for an organization before. He was brought in for the Lewis Winter job. Kill Winter, a dealer for Shug Francis. He did the job well, by all accounts. Shug worked out it was Calum who killed his man. Stupidly decided to strike back. Sent big Glen Davidson to kill Calum. It didn't go well. Davidson's knife may have slashed Calum's hands, but it ended up ripping a hole in Davidson's side. Another one of Shug's men dead.

'Best not to push him,' Frank's saying. 'He's not used to

being in an organization. Freelancers get to run wild. Give him time.'

Frank might not want to be replaced, but it'll happen eventually. When it does, it should be Calum who takes over. For Jamieson's sake, it needs to be someone like Calum. Someone who lives the job, respects and understands it. There are far too many silly little buggers running around thinking they're gunmen. They're not. They're just men with guns. He was thinking about this a lot in Spain. Thinking that he might just be the last of his generation. Frank, Pat and Bob are being replaced by Kyle, Conner and Jordan. Kids doing grown-up work. A talent like Calum is rare. Always was, but more so now. You have to handle him with care, make sure you don't lose him to someone else.

'I'll speak to him again, if you want,' Frank's saying. Hoping Jamieson will be smart enough to say no.

He's grimacing. 'Nah. You can only pass off that conversation as friendly once. Any more and he knows it's me putting the squeeze on him.' Jamieson's sharp all right. 'Never mind the boy,' he's saying, 'it's you I want to talk about. How's the hip?'

'Hip's good,' Frank's saying with a smile. 'Much better than before I went off.'

Jamieson's nodding. This is what he wants to hear. 'Good. I have a job for you.' Lowering his voice now, getting more serious. He's about to order a man's death – it seems right that it should be solemn. 'Shug's been hard at work trying to get networks set up. He has more than one supplier. I think he's getting his supply from down south. Can't find any locals he's using. We've managed to put a stop to a few of the networks, but one of them's become a problem.'

This is what Frank expected to hear. It tallies with the rumours. Shug getting a little desperate. Word is Jamieson's hired Nate Colgan to make sure no network gets off the ground. Intimidation and beatings. Stops anyone becoming enough of a problem that they have to be removed. Obviously one got through.

'There's a kid called Tommy Scott,' Jamieson's saying. 'Wee bastard of a thing. We didn't think much of him. He used to be a peddler. Street stuff. Ran with a gang, sold to them – shit like that. Used to do deliveries on a bicycle. A fucking bike! I guess I underestimated the bastard. I've been getting complaints. The kid cutting into our market, up Springburn way. I tried sending a warning, but the little bastard's tough. Determined, too. Got one of his gangs providing security for his peddlers. Only has three or four guys delivering for him now, but a couple of months ago he had none. He's growing fast, and stepping on toes. I'm fed up of hearing people complain. I need my people to know I'll protect their patch. I need Shug-bloody-Francis to know his men aren't safe.'

No great surprises here. Shug tries his luck with a bunch

of ambitious young men in the business. One proves to be better than the rest. Now Frank has to deal with him. It's bad luck for the kid.

Before he leaves the office, Young is showing him a photo of Scott. Telling him the address. A tower block, second floor from the top. Well, that's just bloody brilliant. Very few places worse than that. Having to make an exit from a tower block is never ideal. You're always a long way from your getaway. But location apart, it's a soft job. They're breaking him back in gently. Jamieson will be preparing a big move against Shug Francis. He must be. Should've done it by now. Shug's been targeting Jamieson, so Jamieson must squash him or be considered feeble. This may be the first strike in that squashing. Scott looks like a typical council-estate kid. Greasy hair, tracksuit, probably a bunch of silly tattoos up his arm. It should be easy. He has one little mate who hangs around with him a lot, according to Young's info. Andy McClure. Known as Clueless.

Frank's walking out of the club now. A few little butterflies beginning to stir. Three months away. His last job had been a couple of months before that. It's a long time idle, especially at his age. He's nodding a polite goodbye to a few of the familiar faces on his way out. He's dropping into the driver's seat of his car. Those who know his business will understand that he's back. A visit to Jamieson without stopping at the bar means work. Jamieson said it was a relief for him. He has no idea. When you live the job, you realize how empty life can be without it. Those three months began to drag. Spain was nice, but it's not Frank's style. Sunshine retirement is for other people. He wants the rain of Glasgow. The tension of the job. The thrill of it. That's his life. Oh, it's so good to be back.

2

A typical day in the life of Tommy Scott. Out of bed about ten o'clock. Used to get up late because he'd been drinking and partying late the night before. These days it's because he works late. Out of bed and into the shower. Didn't used to shower every day, but you have to make an effort now. Presentation is important. They taught him that at one of the workshops the job centre made him attend about six months ago. He didn't care then, didn't listen. Stuck in a room with a bunch of junkies and no-hopers. Tedious embarrassment. He remembered that advice when Shug's right-hand man, Fizzy, made a little remark suggesting that he looked like he'd just stumbled out of a tower block. He had. Point was, he needed to look like he hadn't. So now it's a shower every day, and a new wardrobe. Nothing fancy, just new and clean. Then breakfast. Then work.

He used to hate his work. Walking the streets, trying to compete with the other peddlers. Hell of a job. The things he had to do. He used to go around the estates on a bicycle to save time. You can't be credible on a bicycle. On reflection, it was an embarrassment. He understands better now. He's done with the bike. Done with all the low-grade shit he had to do. All the mistakes of the past will stay in the past. There's a lot back there. Even at the age of twenty-six he's managed to drop the ball a good number of times. A victim of the lifestyle. Started out as a teenager who liked to party, then became a teenager who lived to party. Weekends. Then all week long. Did some drugs. Slept around a lot. Had a kid at nineteen that he's seen twice since it was born. Had another at twenty-one. Never seen that one. Hasn't seen the mother since she was six months gone. Mistakes of the past. Can't carry them with you – too much weight. Hasn't had a girl-friend for a couple of months, too busy with work.

Breakfast time. A bowl of cornflakes with a sprinkling of sugar and some milk that's on the borderline of whiffy. Gulp it down; he has more important things to do. A meeting. A business meeting. Who would have thought, three months ago when he was pissing about on a bike, selling badly cut coke and any other garbage he could lay his hands on, that Tommy Scott would have a business meeting. Back then, it was house parties through the week, clubs at the weekend. Now it's work. Just work. Nothing else matters, not until he has what he's looking for. That's money, by the way. Real money. Not just enough to live on. Not just enough to see him through a wild weekend and pay the bills. Enough to buy a car. Enough to buy a house. He's going to get it too, he's convinced.

It was a fluke, if we're being honest. But then, it usually is, isn't it? He'd heard a few stories on the street about Shug Francis. Word was that he was trying to force his way in. Trying to take territory from Peter Jamieson. Tommy had done work for Jamieson before, peddling. Didn't last. The prick running the network for Jamieson didn't like Tommy's lifestyle. Shug was struggling to find anyone to deal for him. Peddlers he could get. Easy to find a halfwit to stand on a street corner and hand out sweeties for money. He needed better people. People further up the chain. Someone who could build and run a network, not just be a part of it. The word going round now is that Jamieson had Lewis Winter rubbed out. There's a counter-rumour that says it was Winter's girlfriend and her bit on the side, but that sounds too much fun to be true. Winter's death scared people away. If that's what happened to the last guy running a network for Shug. Another guy was beaten senseless before he could even start. They say Nate Colgan did the beating. Scary bastard, that one. A couple of other guys were bought off; they're both working for Jamieson now.

So Shug's severely short-handed. Beginning to look like his attempt at muscling in is going to peter out, like so many others. Then Tommy bumps into David 'Fizzy' Waters in a petrol station. Completely random. Fizzy was filling up his car; Tommy was buying a lottery ticket. You have to dream, don't you? Fizzy was on his way out. Tommy abandoned the magic numbers and chased after him. Fizzy had no idea who he was, but Tommy introduced himself. How often will a chance like this come along? He told Fizzy he was interested in helping Shug out. Told him he knew the streets well, which was true. Told him he was connected, which was less true. Gave him his number, told him to call. Couple of weeks went by – nothing. Then the phone call. A couple of crappy, menial jobs peddling and delivering, proving your worth. Then they stepped it up.

Initiative. That's what they were looking for. Someone who could think for himself. Act without having to run to them all the time. People in charge don't like you running to them with every little problem. So he did things for himself. He used the clout that working for Shug gave him, to get new contacts. In no time he became the employee he had told Fizzy he already was. Now he's much more than that. Now he has a list of good contacts to sell to. He has a number of people working for him, too, as peddlers and couriers. He set up the sort of local network in a couple of months that Shug expected to have to build himself. Would have taken Shug six months, easy. And Tommy's making the money he wants.

They didn't trust him at first. They didn't say so, but he's not daft, he could tell. They thought he was another dimwit from the estates. A peddler and nothing more. Actually, his background has helped him out. His years partying, hanging around in a street gang, throwing time and opportunity away. That's become useful, because he knows useful people. He's

13

close enough to one of the street gangs to use them. They've carried out a few beatings for drugs. They've done some peddling for money. Mostly small-scale, but it helps that people know they're backing you up. They have to be handled carefully, they're volatile and untrustworthy, but good PR. Your own little battalion of thugs. Very useful.

Used to be Tommy and his best mate from childhood, Andy McClure. Just the two of them. Tommy and Clueless, to use his unfortunate but accurate nickname. Partying together, working together and, when money trouble dictated, living together. They shared everything. Money, needles, women. They still do. Tommy understands the importance of having someone he can trust. All these new contacts, all these new colleagues, only interested in him because of cash. Same reason he's interested in Shug. They'd throw him over the first chance they got. Not Andy – he'll be by his side to the end. You need that. Just someone you know you can turn to. Doesn't take Clueless to big meetings, though; he has nothing smart to contribute.

He's thinking about that as he leaves the flat and makes his way out of the building. Clueless is going to be pissed off that this is another meeting he's not at. He thinks he should be there. He sees himself as the right-hand man, a key player. But he's not. Not bright enough to be a useful right-hand man. Besides, Tommy isn't important enough yet to need one. He's still a low-scale dealer, although he's rising fast. He has a good number of peddlers; he's pushing into good areas. He's sending the right messages. But he's not a big player. Important to Shug, sure, but not to anyone else. This meeting might help change that. A couple of guys who control the patch on a few large estates in Lanarkshire. Big area with big demand. They're known, but not important to the big organizations. They have ambitions too. Good to have on board. Men of ambition should stick together.

They're eyeing him up as he's walking into the pub. Trying to decide if he's serious or not. They've heard he's a rising star. They need a new supplier. A rising star with good connections would be ideal. They're cousins, apparently. Ian and Charlie Allen, although he doesn't know which is which. They don't look like family to Tommy as he's walking over to them. Both middle-aged. One of them's tall, has a mop of fair hair, pockmarked cheeks. The other one looks short and tubby, with a shaven head and glasses. None of that matters, although the age can be an issue. Tommy's young, and he looks young. Middle-aged men don't like that. They want someone with their own experience level. Makes them feel comfortable, thinking they're working with someone like themselves. But they can live with discomfort, if the deal's good.

Shaking their hands. Smiling to both. Introducing himself and sitting opposite. Projecting confidence. He's nervous, but he knows how to hide it now.

'I've heard you're looking for a new supplier,' he's saying quietly, the pleasantries out of the way. People like this don't play about. Get to the point – they respect that. 'An operation like yours needs someone reliable, consistent and with good variety. I can offer that. I can match your need.' He's been thinking those words over on the way here. They sound good to him. They sound like what the Allens will want to hear.

'We've been let down by our last supplier,' the chubby one's saying. He won't say more than that, no detail. You don't bad-mouth a supplier publicly, even if he's let you down. If he finds out you've blackened his name, he might choose to do something about it. Suppliers tend to be dangerous men. 'How big is your operation?'

'Bigger than you need,' Tommy's telling them.

That's true. Shug has a deal with a major supplier, but the supplier's getting tetchy. Shug isn't moving enough gear yet, that's why a deal like this will impress the boss. Tommy isn't supposed to know that they're struggling to shift gear, but it's obvious. A big supplier doesn't want someone small on his books. Shug needs to increase deliveries or lose supply.

'We have everything you need,' Tommy's telling them, 'and then some. We can match your demand with ease. If your demand increases, which I'm sure it will, then we'll have no trouble with that. We only provide quality product. Your customers will like what we provide.' It's good sales patter. Ingratiating. A little bit creepy.

'Good to know,' the chubby one's saying, and nodding. 'We'll be in touch in the next couple of days.' They're getting up and leaving. Business meeting over.

It went well. They were never going to commit one way or the other just yet. They wanted to meet him, hear what he had to say. See if he was a serious kind of guy. They heard what they wanted to hear. No need to discuss money. Both sides will know what the market price is when the transactions are being done. It'll vary, deal to deal. Tommy's convinced they're going to call and agree to the hook-up. They won't get a better one. This'll be a big boost with Shug. Such a rare opportunity. Shug, struggling to get people on board. Tommy could be his most important dealer. He could become senior. Not just have good money, but be truly rich. Powerful too. That's what he's thinking as he's walking back home. Get some lunch. Check on some of the peddlers. Only a couple should be running low. It's a Wednesday, sluggish demand. Top them all up tomorrow, before the weekend burst. Keep business ticking over nicely. His business.

3

Sitting outside a tower block, watching the rain bounce off the windscreen. Waiting and watching. Making sure you're not seen. A boring but necessary part of the job. The most boring part of this job tops the most interesting part of a normal job. People would think him odd, sitting in his car like this. Any passer-by could see you and remember your face. Take your registration. A couple of days later they hear about a man being murdered nearby; they do their civic duty and report you to the police. Frank's heard every story there is to hear. All the different ways people are caught out. The sob-stories of a hundred halfwits, locked up because of one mistake.

Frank long ago learned how to be careful. You sit, and you watch, and you wait. You are patient. You scout a location properly. Then you move quickly. The speed at which he does his work, from order to completion, has always been his trademark. It's one of the things that will separate him from Calum. Calum's good, but he's slow. Ponders the job. Takes too long in scouting. It reassures people like Jamieson to have things done quickly. Makes them think it was nice and easy.

Watching the clock. Watching the door. He doesn't know if it's the right door to watch. Doesn't even know if he's on the correct side of the building. Scott could be tucked up in bed already. Or he might have a squad of spotty-faced little mates in there with him. Better to wait, play it safe. He's thinking that he should probably have parked further away from the building. His eyesight isn't perfect, less so in this rain. Better to be close enough to see the door. Better to reduce the amount of walking he has to do as well. Sort of dump where the lifts could be out of order. That might be too much for him. Climbing all the way up there and back down again. Nope, that wouldn't do. Even if he were young and fit, that would mean too long an exit time after the kill. Something else to worry about. Still, that's what scouting is for.

It's nearly two o'clock in the morning now. Enough waiting around. Nobody's used the door he's watching. There isn't a single light visible on this side of the building. Many of the flats are empty, Frank knows that. One by one, they're ripping these monstrosities down. Good riddance. They seem like horrible places to live. They're certainly horrible places to do a job. As people move out, their flats are left empty. When there's only a handful occupied, the council moves the occupants. The fewer people living in the building, the more unpleasant it becomes. Other people start using the building for their own ends. Homeless people. Junkies. People dump things there. Can't be a nice place for a guy like Scott to live.

No wonder he's taking the stupid risk of working for Shug. Taking the risk of following in Lewis Winter's footsteps. Living like this is a reason to be desperate.

Frank's getting out of the car and pressing the button on his key to lock it. Hip's a little stiff. Sitting in the car like that isn't good for it. Doctor told him that. Told him he needed to be careful with it for a little while. Don't overreach, that's what he said. Frank told him he was a security consultant. The doc smiled, said something about an office job being a good thing. Frank nodded along. Now he's walking towards the door of the building, pulling up his hood. It's raining, but there might also be CCTV. Most of the cameras don't work, but you still take the precaution of pulling up your hood. And it is raining, after all.

He's in the doorway. There's a camera up in a corner, but even with a brief glance he can see it's useless. It looks like some little scamp has decided he doesn't like being watched and has smashed the thing. It makes this a good door to enter through. A useful bit of scouting. Into the lobby, confronted by two lifts. Neither seems to be out of order. More good news. Nobody around. He's pressing the button to call the lift. Nobody inside when the doors open. Inside and pressing the button for the second-from-top floor. It's a long way up and a slow lift. Watching the lights tick up, praying they don't stop on another floor. Other people out and about, bumping into him. The lift stops on the thirteenth floor, second from the top. Out into the cold corridor. Silent and empty, just how he likes it. Now he's looking at door numbers. Trying to find Scott's, so that he'll be able to get to it in a hurry for the hit. Trying to work out what side of the building it's on, so that he can watch for the lights.

Towards the end of the corridor, on his right, he finds what he's looking for. Flat 34B. Door closed, silence inside. He's checking the surroundings. Nothing of note, except the flat opposite. Flat 35A. The door is directly opposite Scott's front door. Would be nice to know if there was anyone living there. He might have to check that out tomorrow morning. Find out who lives where, and who's likely to hear suspicious noises. Frank's not dumb enough to stand right in front of a door with a peephole. He's up against the wall that the door is on, taking sideways glances at it. Looking for signs of security. Certainly no cameras up here. Door doesn't look like it has any unexpected locks on it, either. That might become important, but hopefully not. He's seen all he needs to for now. He's smiling to himself as he's walking back towards the lift. It all looks as simple as he'd hoped. He's looking back along the corridor as the lift doors open for him. There are a couple of places where you can see wet foot-prints. He'll have to remember that if it's raining tomorrow night.

The job will be tomorrow night. He's decided on that as the lift's returning to the ground floor. A simple job with no complications. No need to delay it any longer than that. Out of the lift and through the lobby. Out to his car. Still raining. Rain's a mixed blessing. More chance of leaving footprints behind. More chance of falling on your arse, if you need to move quickly. But it does give an excuse for a hood. And it keeps people indoors. There's much to be said for that. He's in the car, starting it up and pulling away. Driving through the city at night, as he has so many times before. Changing city, though – lurching from an industrial past to a shiny future in one ungainly bound. You have to know the place. Every nook and cranny, as the old ones would say. It takes a second before his memory reminds Frank that he is one of the old ones.

He's outside his house. Closing the car door quietly and heading up the garden path. He'll be using a different car tomorrow. Leaving the house earlier, too. Still, you develop the habit of carefulness, and you stick to it. He's through the front door, closing it quietly. Locking it. He won't put a light on. He knows where everything in the house is. He can move about in the dark just fine. The need for silence has gone, though. There's nobody to wake up. Nobody to hide from here. There's never been anyone in his life. Well, nobody close enough that they would live with him. Been a few women over the years, but he never let it get serious. When he was in Spain there was an Englishwoman. Mid-forties, funny, presentable. She was there visiting her son. She kept saying how silly it was that people their age were having a holiday romance. Didn't stop her enjoying it. All Frank's ever had were short romances. Holiday romances, you could call them. Holidays from the life he's chosen for himself.

4

There's no escaping the fact that Clueless is a moron. A complete clot of a human being, truth be known. Tommy Scott's always known it, but he's a loyal friend and he tries his best. Sometimes, though, sometimes Clueless shows signs that he's learning. Like right now, for instance. He's coming in the front door of the flat. Scott sent him across the hall with a bag of gear. They stash a lot of stuff under the floorboards in the empty flat opposite. Less chance of it being found there. Scott doesn't keep big amounts near him for long – he's smarter than that. He picks it up from Shug's supplier, then moves it on to his peddlers in quick time. Common sense says you can't hold it for long. Anyway, that's just the routine they go through. Clueless has gone across the hall to hide the stuff. Taking longer than usual to come back. Now he's coming in the front door, and there's a strange look on his face. He usually specializes in a fine line of vacant expressions. This look is more baffled.

Clueless has come in the front door and closed it behind him. 'I just saw some guy in the corridor,' he's saying.

'Yeah?' Scott says. He could feign interest, but it's usually better not to encourage him.

'Yeah. I looked through the peephole before I came out, like you said to. There was this guy. Old guy, he was. Looked old, anyway. Had a big jacket on. Had the hood up. He was against the wall like that,' he's saying, mimicking Frank's stance. 'Looking at your door.'

Okay, now he's interested. 'Yeah? Did he just leave?'

'Aye. I waited for him to get in the lift, and then I came in here.'

The only light in the flat comes from the TV in the corner. The sound's down low. Scott's over at the window, peeking out through the gap in the curtain, looking down at the car park. 'Switch that TV off,' he's saying to Clueless. Waiting a few seconds for complete darkness, and watching as a figure moves across the car park. Down towards the road and into a car.

He left, which is a good thing. Means he's probably not going to try anything tonight. Silly old bastard. Oh, this is a chance. This is a big chance.

'Who was that guy anyway?' Clueless is asking him. 'Should I have done something?'

'No, you did the right thing.' Pausing. How much does he tell his friend? He'll need him, so he has to tell it all. 'I think that guy works for Peter Jamieson.'

'Jamieson? Shit, you think that old guy was after us?'

'I reckon he was. And I reckon he'll be back. See, if I'm

right, that old fart was here to try and kill us. Only, when he does come back, we're going to be waiting for him.'

'Are we?' Clueless is pausing, thinking about this. Takes a while. 'Isn't this the sort of thing we should be telling Shug about? Let him deal with it?'

'No,' Scott's saying. It would be the easy thing to do, but not right. Initiative. That's what they want. Use your initiative. Deal with it yourself and really impress them.

There's no prospect of sleep tonight anyway. Not with the worry in the back of his mind that Frank MacLeod might come right back. Might not have been him, but who else? Fizzy, that's Shug's right-hand man, warned him. Said that Jamieson was a tough bastard, that he has gunmen on his staff. The most dangerous one is Frank MacLeod. Old guy that's killed loads and always got away with it. Bit of a legend, it seems. Would be a big blow to Jamieson if he ended up dead. Big boost for Shug, if one of his men did it. What an opportunity! Shit, something like this only comes along once in a lifetime. They have to grab the chance. Kill him. Kill a man. Shit, never done that before. Never even thought about it. Scott's thinking about that as they get ready to go out. Killing a man is something else. It's crossing some sort of line. But he has to. Doesn't have a choice. Kill or be killed. And it's such a great chance for him.

Out into the rain and the cold, looking for a gun. Any sort of gun. Anything that's capable of doing the job. There are

26

places you can go, professional gunrunners. They sell any time, but only to the right people. They have to know you, know that they can trust you. They won't sell to the likes of Scott, and he knows it. One day they'll be desperate for his business, queuing up, but not tonight. They're bloody expensive too, and he doesn't have much cash on him. So they're going for the cheap option. They won't get such a good gun, but who cares? As long as it goes bang and Frank MacLeod falls down and doesn't get back up, then it's good enough. Might not be clean, either. Scott knows all the parlance. Clean is when a gun hasn't been used in any other crime that can then be linked to you, if you're caught with it. They won't get a weapon that can guarantee them that. Cheap and available – that's what matters.

His name's Donall Tokely. Everyone calls him Spikey, for reasons most people have forgotten. Seems to have had something to do with a childhood hairstyle. When Scott and Clueless ran with a gang in this area, Spikey was in there with them. A year or so younger, but a tough little bastard. He and a few of the other gang members ended up in jail. Got three years for robbery. The day he got out, he stole a charity collection tin from a newsagent's. In the last year he's got closer to people at the serious end of the business. Made connections through his mother, of all people. She sells counterfeit clothes from her house. Spikey got pally with some of her suppliers, and he's gone up in the world since. The rumours said he was handling weapons. People were bringing old stuff across from Northern Ireland, and Spikey was selling it for them. He showed a handgun to Scott a couple of months ago. Told him if he was serious about setting up a network, then he should buy one. Scott said no thanks. Not now, anyway. Well, this is the new now, and now he wants to buy that gun.

They're banging on his door, waiting impatiently. So what if he's fast asleep? They need this done quickly. This is life, death and business. Scott wants all the preparation time he can get. He doesn't actually know what he needs to do, but it seems obvious that he will need time. They have to be careful with this one. Frank MacLeod is, amongst other things, a very dangerous man. Banging on the door again. Scott's trying to remember if Spikey still lives with his mother. He's far more afraid of that beefy old witch than he is of Spikey. Heard a few stories about her that made him sick in his mouth. The sound of a latch being pulled back; now the door's opening.

'Tommy. Shit! Tommy. Do you know what time it is? Are you off your face or something?' Spikey's staring at him through half-closed eyes. Scott always liked Spikey. They seemed to have similar ambitions. He always thought of Spikey as a cut above most of their other friends. Now, something's changed. Scott understands that. His ambitions have far outgrown Spikey's. Scott's moving on to a different level, and leaving mediocrity like Spikey behind.

'Listen, mate,' he's saying, making sure to get the 'mate' in there. 'I need a gun. Like, right now. Nothing fancy, just something that works. I don't have much cash on me, but I'll pay what I've got and owe you the rest. You know I'm good for it. I can pay you either in cash or gear – your choice. We can probably make a good deal on gear, as it happens.'

Spikey's looking at him with a frown. Too many words to process at this hour. 'You want a gun. I thought you didn't want one.'

'I do now.'

'Uh-huh. But I don't have any. Not just now. I can get you one, if you want, but it'll take a few days. You should have said. When I had them, I mean.'

'How can you not have guns?' Scott's asking. There's a bit of anger in his voice that Clueless and Spikey have both noticed. 'You sell the fucking things for a living.'

'Yeah, okay, back off a wee bit, huh? I do sell them. I sold a shitload of them a few weeks ago. Made a good pile out of it. Sold the lot to the one buyer. Same people I got them off, actually. They wanted them back. Paid up to get them, too. Nice profit for nothing. I've got more coming, though, if you'll wait.'

That was the go-to option. Where the hell do they go to now? The only other people with guns that Scott knows are people who probably won't sell to him. Spikey's such an idiot. Scott knew it as soon as Spikey told them about selling the guns back to the previous owners. He doesn't seem to get it. They sell the guns to him, and then buy them back at a higher price. Only one reason why you throw money away like that. They have someone willing to pay a much higher price now. If Spikey had anything resembling a brain in his head, he'd have turned down their offer and gone looking for the better offer himself. Nope, he took the quick profit. No ambition. No initiative. That's why he'll never get anywhere.

'Do we have to use a gun?' Clueless is asking.

'If he has a gun and we don't, we're fucked. Even two to one. This guy's a professional, and we're not. We have to do this right. So that we can show Shug that we know how.'

Mark Garvey. Nasty piece of work. Sells guns, though, everyone knows it. Sells to some of the worst people. Seems to be able to keep himself off the police radar, God alone knows how. Must be one lucky bastard, because he's in it up to his armpits. Robbers, gunmen, dealers, pimps – the whole nine yards. Some people say he shut up a couple of his own suppliers before they had the chance to drop him in it. Might be bullshit. There's a lot of it about. Scott knows where he lives, or at least where he used to live. If he's moved, then they're about to wake up the wrong guy.

Knocking on another door. A nicer area this time. The door's opening. Attractive woman in her thirties, short night-dress.

'Erm, we're looking for Mark Garvey,' Scott's saying. A

light's gone on behind her. Hmm, maybe not quite so attractive now. Bottle-blonde, crow's feet, not the best skin. Would still look good with a bit of make-up on.

The woman's gone. Garvey's standing in the doorway now, frowning. Early fifties, bottle-brown hair, trying to look young for the wife, no doubt. Hard to keep up with a second marriage.

'What do you want?' Garvey's asking. Looking at Scott, paying Clueless no attention. At a glance, he knows who matters here.

'We need a weapon,' Scott's saying quietly. Maybe Garvey doesn't tell the little wife everything. 'Anything usable will do us.'

'Will it now? Good for you. I think you got the wrong address.' He's moving to close the door.

'I think we got the right address,' Scott's saying, sticking his foot in the jamb. 'I know you don't sell to strangers. Fair enough. I have an organization behind me. I can either pay you cash or set up a good deal on gear. Your choice. This could become a standing arrangement.'

'No, it couldn't,' Garvey's saying. 'Now get your foot out of my door before I lose my rag.'

'We're in a hurry here. Helping us out won't be forgotten.'

'You listen to me,' Garvey's saying, leaning forward aggressively. He's not a big man, but the movement does the trick. Scott's pulled his foot away. 'If you're in a hurry for a piece and you got an organization behind you, then you go to the organization. That's what it's there for. You don't go waking me up in the middle of the fucking night, understood?' He's closed the door. Not with a slam – that might be heard by the neighbours, and a guy like Garvey doesn't want the neighbours knowing he's had visitors.

Plodding the streets again. They've tried two more dealers. Ignored by one, door shut on them by the other. Scott doesn't know any others. The old gang probably have something, but he's not so close that they'd give it to him. They protect their valuables jealously. He could go to Shug. Would probably get a gun from him. But that would render the whole thing pointless. Shug would almost certainly send someone else round to do the job. Then they'd only get credit for reporting it. Credit doesn't go far.

Plodding back to the flat, Clueless complaining. He's been no bloody use. They're back where they started, and Scott's thinking hard. Trying to work out how you bring down a killer like Frank MacLeod. How two men stop one man and his gun. This is the initiative that matters.

5

Doing the rounds. Nothing special, just putting in an appearance. It matters. People need to see that you're active, that you're keeping an eye on them. Puts a little pressure on. John Young's had one meeting already this morning. Went to see one of their two main suppliers. Had to be particularly careful with that one. Suppliers are a tetchy bunch. They need to be wary, fair enough. Police operations against the big importers tend to be better funded, better run. The better funded and run they've become, the harder suppliers have become to deal with. This was a casual meeting. A little business, mostly just getting a subtle message across. Young's heard rumours about people that matter switching suppliers. People falling out like bloody school kids. That's dangerous for everyone. He's a little more reassured now. Supplier says it's small stuff. Contained. A couple of people squabbling over money. Won't turn violent. Isn't contagious.

First little concern calmed. Now on to the next one. There are always plenty. This one's closer to the business. People really aren't very bright. It surprises Young every day how stupid people can be. People who really should know better. It's money that does it, you know. Greed makes people stupid. Stupid to a point where they're willing to risk vastly more than they stand to gain. Marty Jones runs a dirty little operation that makes money. He's basically a pimp. Nobody likes him much, but he does a job and he makes money. He cuts the organization in, and in exchange gets the benefits of being part of the Jamieson group. Marty supplies a product that people want to use, and he makes good money. But that's never enough for people like Marty. They can't just be happy with what they've got. Not until they learn.

Young's had Marty watched this morning. Just got a call that he's gone to the nightclub that his brother runs. Perfect. The scene of the crime. Young's pulling up outside the club and getting out of the car. Huffing and puffing. Could do with losing some weight, he's realizing. Into the club. Unfamiliar. Asking a woman mopping the floor in the foyer where he can find the manager. She's pointing along a corridor. He would laugh at the lack of security, if it didn't remind him of their own. Along the corridor, finding a door with 'Manager' written on it. Not knocking, just going in. Poky little place. Grim. Marty sitting on a chair in front of the desk, his brother Adam in the chair behind it. They're both looking at Young and neither knows what to say. Just the start he wanted.

There's an old chair at the side of the room. Young's taking his place in it.

'I think you both know why I'm here,' he's saying. No smile, no jokes, no playing the smartarse. This is business and they need to understand how serious it is.

'I'm not sure . . .' Marty's saying, and stopping. He's not sure what to say.

'I know that you two have been running private parties out of this place. I know that you've been using merchandise provided by us. I know that you've been making a tidy profit from it, and not passing that profit on. I'm not going to tell you to stop the parties. I've come here alone, as a gesture of my goodwill. You're making money. Good. You cut us in. You're making connections with other organizations through these parties. Good. We can all benefit from that.' He's looking at Marty now. 'In the next couple of days you're going to come round to the club and show me the books on these parties. You're going to provide the back-pay of our cut. We're going to make an agreement that works for both of us. If not, I'll come round here again and I won't be alone.'

He's getting up and leaving. Neither of them says a word. They've been caught red-handed. Marty's just smart enough to know that he has to play this straight. He'll cut them in. He knows what the price will be, if he doesn't. The threats were all a little clichéd, but it's what they understand. Young isn't the sort to go in and be violent from the start. That would ruin any prospect of profiting from this. On the other hand, you can't be too subtle with them. They need to understand what will happen if they don't clean up the mess they've made. The money isn't huge, but it was worth Young making the appearance himself. They need to know they can't ignore the organization. Everyone needs to know that. But it's more than that. These parties have potential. It was when he found out who was attending that he became most interested. People with important roles in some big organizations. People it would pay to be close to. People with information – Young's favourite weapon.

One quick meeting before lunch and then back to the club. This one matters most. No role is more important than defending themselves from their enemies. Only way to do that is to find out what your enemies are up to. He's at a flat he uses a lot. Small place, but secure and neatly positioned to make it impossible for an observer to see who's coming and going from which flats. Good place to meet people that you don't wish to be seen meeting. He has been using it for a while, though. He's already keeping his eye open for a suitable alternative. His contact is there before him. Long-term contact, not entirely reliable. That's why he has to do the waiting. Young will be last in and first out. The contact will wait for him to arrive and give him time to get away before leaving.

'So you're working nights,' Young's saying, taking a seat at the kitchen table. It's a sparsely furnished flat, always cold.

'This week and next,' Greig's nodding. PC Paul Greig. Rather too enthusiastic a contact. Young's known him for years. A cop in his late thirties destined never to rise from the bottom of the heap. Seems to have talent as a cop. Also has a reputation. So bent that even the criminals can't trust him. But occasionally he delivers.

'Tell me what I need to know,' Young's saying.

'I think the Lewis Winter investigation is almost as dead as he is. Pretty much only Fisher working on it now, and even he has other things to do these days. People have lost interest.'

Young's nodding along. Trying to make it look like he doesn't already know this. Just let the contact talk. Don't annoy or scare him.

'Fisher's problem is that he can't put the pieces together,' Greig's saying now. He's experienced. He knows what Young wants. 'He has all the names that matter, just can't put them in order. He knows there's something between Shug and Jamieson. He knows Glen Davidson was involved and that he's disappeared. He knows Lewis Winter was involved and he's dead. He knows Davidson called this guy MacLean just before he disappeared. He knows MacLean moved house the day after. Doesn't take much of a genius to piece it together, but you need evidence. I don't think he'll find any, either. Too many professionals involved.'

Young's looking at him. The mention of Calum is always a worry. They've tried to keep him off the radar for as long as possible, but it was never going to last. That's the business.

'So Fisher's putting all these pieces together, is he?' Young's asking. Making it seem like he doesn't much care. Fooling no one.

Greig's shrugging. 'He's got the pieces, but it would take one hell of a leap to make a case with them. Maybe a better cop could. Get one of those bolts of inspiration. Fisher ain't that kind of cop. He won't let go, sure, but he won't go anywhere with it.' Another shrug.

Young's nodding, not believing. Fisher's dangerous enough. Takes an idiot to underestimate someone so tenacious. Respect your enemy.

Into the car and driving through the city. Heading back to the club, but taking a detour. Fisher's house is twenty minutes out of his way. A journey worth taking. Not to do anything. You don't do anything to a cop. But you need to know what they're up to. You find out about them and their family. Find out about their friends. Their lifestyle. Any little detail that might have value later on. All for defensive purposes, not attack. He doesn't need to drive past the house, but he finds it easier to work things out with a clear picture before him. See the house – imagine the man inside. No family worth speaking of. Few friends. There has to be a weakness. Has to be. They've checked his emails and phone, but found nothing. There are other things they can do. Get a key to the house. Have a poke about inside. Check his browser history. Information. If you find nothing of value, create it. That's last-resort territory. However much a pain Fisher is, he's still a cop. And you don't provoke a cop.

6

Frank had a good night's sleep. There was a day, rather a long time ago, when he would be nervous in the hours before a job. Not any more. Having a routine settles you. It becomes familiar and enjoyable. Takes the edge off the preparations. Once the job's actually started, it's easy. Your focus becomes the dominant emotion. No room for worry. He's up and showering, having his breakfast, checking the newspaper. He needs to find out about the occupants of the flats, but that's easy enough. One early phone call to a contact. He'll get the info through a third party. Probably more than a third party – fourth or fifth. Anyway, somewhere down the line you get to some old woman working in an office for the local postal service. She'll never hear Frank's name, never know that the information is for criminal use. She'll get a small payment and share the information about who occupies which flats. It's the best Frank can do at such short notice. Hardly the most reliable info. Chances are there'll be people crashing in an empty flat or two in that building. That's the risk you take. You can only work with the best information to hand.

Reading the paper, then heading out to the shop. Walk a

little every day. Exercise the hip, build up your strength. Also, be seen in the community. Frank's spent years playing a part locally. Looking like the slightly sad ageing gent, living all by himself. He's never been close to his neighbours, but he makes sure they see just enough of him to prevent them getting nosy. He's heading to the corner shop at the bottom of the road. A short walk, but it means he'll be seen acting normal on the day of a job. That's what this is about. He doesn't need the pint of milk and packet of biscuits he'll buy. He just wants to be seen being his normal, ordinary self. If anyone round here knows what he does for a living, then they've never mentioned it. Never even suggested that they know. Maybe they're just smart enough to keep their mouths shut.

The shopkeeper's seen him. A couple of other people were in the shop, too. Now he's back at the house, wasting the afternoon away. It's the one downside of the job. When you're working, you have to stay away from all your colleagues. It's a strange thing. The older he gets, the more he enjoys going to the club and seeing people there. Shoot a frame of snooker, waste a couple of hours. He goes along two or three times a week when there's no work on. Ostensibly to play the role of security consultant, make the job seem convincing. In truth, he enjoys the company. You stay away from the person who hires you for a job. You keep your distance for at least a few days afterwards, sometimes as much as a week.

Depends on the heat. There probably won't be much for someone like Scott. It'll be a gang-related death. Not likely to get a lot of traction with the media, not unless it's a particularly slow news day. The police won't make a big play of it, either. Better not to scare the locals with talk of gangland killings.

The afternoon has gone. He's cooking his dinner. Nothing too heavy, and nothing exotic. You don't want your innards to trip you up. There will be some nerves at the time. Not a lot, experience deals with that, but there might be something. The nerves can come in a rush. If everything goes well, no surprises, then he'll be fine. When everything happens quickly, and exactly as expected, he can go through a job without feeling the slightest flutter. That's not healthy, he knows it. You should have some nerves. Keeps you on your toes. If a surprise comes along, then the nerves come with it. They can come in a wave, race up on you and consume you. It's how you handle those that matters most. Experience helps, but it's not everything. You can have no experience, but a calm mind. You can have a mountain of experience, as Frank does, and the nerves can still cripple you. It's happened. People get surprised by something and freeze. Never happened to Frank.

It's dark outside now. He's starting to prepare. Getting the plain clothing on. A little bit of a cliché to dress in black. The colour doesn't matter much, but when you're working in the night it's a reasonable precaution to go dark. The most important factor is making sure the clothing has no distinguishing marks. You wear nothing that can be accurately described. You make sure that the police can't find replicas and show it to the world. Utterly plain, worn only once and then destroyed. He'll cover his face. He doesn't on every job. If you have a job where there's no prospect of witnesses or cameras, then why bother? Sometimes you have to be ultra-careful to get close to someone. That can mean no covering your face because that makes you stand out. These days it's balaclavas more and more. The good old days – no such thing as CCTV. Back then, he wouldn't have worn one for this job.

He's leaving the house at ten minutes past ten. He'll be at the flats before eleven, but he'll spend a while sitting and watching. Give it as much time as possible. Make sure everyone's fast asleep. Makes a job so much easier. It's not raining tonight, which is something. He's parked a little further away from the building tonight. He knows roughly which windows to watch now. No lights on in the flat that he's sure belongs to Scott. There are two lights on in a flat three floors down, but he's not worried about them. The key to his calm is the information that was put through his letter box in the afternoon. There's nobody in the flat opposite. Nobody in the flat next door, either. Only one other occupied flat on that entire floor, and it's at the opposite end of the corridor. The flat directly beneath is occupied, and that's the one concern. The man who lives there might hear the gunshot. Might be too deeply asleep to hear it. Might hear it and not realize what it is. With a floor between them, it shouldn't matter. Frank will be out by the time anyone hearing the shot has clambered from their bed.

He's sitting watching the door. The hip's starting to grumble a little. It's these moments when he wishes he still smoked. Used to. Used to smoke thirty a day. Right up until Peter Jamieson told him the rough tobacco he smoked smelled terrible. That didn't matter. He then told Frank that he could always recognize the smell on his clothes. That mattered. You can't have a distinctive smell as a gunman. No more than you can have a distinctive look, mannerism or sound. You see many kids in the business today covered in tattoos. Morons, every single one. Marking their bodies with immediately distinctive designs. Stupid. So he was worried about the smell, especially with fewer people than ever smoking. Back in the day, the smell blended in. Not any more. So he quit smoking, and began munching through a packet of extra-strong mints every day instead. That might have been a great leap forward for his lungs, but not for the smell. The minty-fresh gunman. Still too distinctive, so he quit the mints, too.

Nothing, and more nothing. The last lights in the building going out. It's twenty past midnight when the door opens and a figure emerges. A young man. Hard to get a good look from here. Definitely too short to be Scott. Could well be his mate, though. Looks like the kind of little oaf that Clueless McClure undoubtedly is. He's walking along the side of the building and round the corner. Out of view. Going home for the night. Frank's smiling to himself. One less thing to worry about. It'll be Scott alone, and that's a job he can deal with. Okay, he's honest enough to accept that there isn't a whole lot of glory in this job. When he was away, Calum did the Winter job cleanly. Then he handled the Davidson attack. Glory in that. They might think he's milking his hand injuries, but they admire the job he did. Brave and smart, they all say. Kept his head clear throughout. This is nothing like that. A simple job to send a message. There was always that thought in the back of Frank's mind when he was away. People forget about you. Forget that you're capable of doing a good job as well. The flavour of the month gets all the attention. You need to do something to grab it back. Even something simple, like this.

He's waited another half-hour in the darkness. Waiting for any sort of movement. Any sign of a light. Giving it a little more time. The clock's reached one. Enough waiting. He's out of the car. A little thing he's never driven before. Nippy and uninspiring. He'll switch back to his own car as soon as he's done here. This'll be the only time he'll ever be near this car. No one could possibly link it to him. Pulling on his balaclava and walking across the car park. Nobody in sight. Cold, but dry. Walking briskly up to the door. Suppressing that last hint of a limp. It's a recognizable feature. In through the door, confident the camera doesn't work. Pressing the button for the lift and stepping in as the doors open. A slight twinge of nerves in the pit of his stomach. Someone else could be calling the lift. Maybe he should have left it an hour later. Too late for these thoughts now. Kill the nerves and focus. You're past the point of no return.

The lift's opening on Scott's floor. Frank's stepping slowly out, looking left and right. The lights are on all night in the corridor, but there's no sign of life. All doors closed. Silence reigns. Walking softly to the left, along the corridor. Reaching into his inside coat pocket for the gun. A small thing he picked up from his supplier. He has three suppliers that he rotates, so none realizes how much work he does. Been working with them all for a long time. There's trust there now. Still better not to let any of them know your work schedule. The gun isn't powerful, he can see that. Good enough to guarantee a kill at short range. That's all it needs to be. Checking around him as he reaches the door. Knocking twice. Loud enough to wake Scott, but not a dramatic thump that might make him wary. Frank's standing slightly to the side. Just out of view of the peephole. A man in a balaclava with a gun at his side is not a man you open the door to. Waiting. Ready to knock again. Then something strange. It sounds like a crack in the distance. Things are going white. He can feel his legs give way. Is it his hip? No, he's realized as he's falling forward against the door of Scott's flat, it's worse than that.

7

Everything's blurry. Dark around the edges, with an uncomfortable light in the middle. Closing his eyes again, that seems easier. It's taking a few seconds, fuzzy moments of discomfort, but now he's remembering where he is. He's keeping his eyes shut anyway. The sooner he opens them, the sooner he has to confront the situation. Better to be silent. Better to listen.

'I think he moved, Tommy, I think I saw him move. Definitely.'

A nasal exclamation. So much for lying still and listening. Stay still. You're not dead yet. You can still retrieve this. As long as you're breathing, things can turn around. He can hear them both walking up and down the corridor. They're not doing anything. Pacing the floor, trying to work out what to do with their prize. They have Frank MacLeod where they want him. They just don't know what to do next.

He's opening his eyes now, looking at them. Look for the detail that matters. Tommy Scott's holding the gun. He has it down at his side. He looks pained. Looks like he's trying to work something out. The expression of a kid who's in over his head. The corridor's dimly lit. Lamplight, it looks like. Scott's little mate, Andy 'Clueless' McClure, is standing beside him. He looks excited, lost in the thrill of the moment. Adrenalin controlling intelligence. Not that there was much of that to begin with. Scott was always the brains of this little operation. Frank's in no place to judge, though. He's the one lying on the floor, just inside the front door. Everyone's more intelligent than him right now. The dingy corridor he's lying in opens into the kitchen at the bottom. There are two closed doors on his right and one on his left. The front door's behind him. The only way out.

He can't even remember it happening. He remembers knocking on the front door. Just after one o'clock in the morning. Feeling the reassuring gun in his right hand, out of view of the door. Ready to step inside, and shoot. Quick job, in and out, leave the body. So simple. Now he's waking up inside the flat. The front door didn't open first, he's sure of that. Someone got him from behind. Must have come out of the flat opposite – two steps and they were right behind him. Knocked him out, dragged him into the flat. He didn't hear them, didn't expect them. Now Tommy Scott's walking up and down the corridor with Frank's gun in his hand. What a disaster! Humiliation. Forty-four years in the business, since the day John 'Reader' Benson paid him buttons to beat the snot out of a scrawny racecourse bookie. Been in some tight spots since then. But nothing like this. This is too tight to move.

Tommy's just noticed that Frank's awake. Might as well try to sit up. Tommy's marching back along the corridor towards him. Twenty-six years of age, skinny, dark-haired and always tired-looking. Used to be a peddler. A street dealer. Used to go round the estates on a bicycle selling wraps to kids. A bicycle, for Christ's sake! Of course nobody took him seriously. How Shug Francis saw anything in him is a mystery. Nevertheless, he did. Desperation maybe. Anyone willing and able was welcome, regardless of ability. Jamieson's stamped on all of Shug's other efforts. Shug brought Tommy on board. Gave him a strong supply. Scott took it and set up his own little network. Frank's underestimated him. He's seeing that now. Judging him on what he's done before. Not judging him on what he's doing now. Still thinking of Scott as that greasy kid on the bike. Now Scott's standing over Frank, pointing Frank's own gun at him.

'You're gonna keep your mouth shut, okay. You're gonna keep it shut.' He sounds nervous. He should do. He's moving away, trying to think. He doesn't know what to do with Frank. If it was up to his dippy mate, Frank knows he'd be dead already. Scott's just smart enough to realize this requires more thought. He needs to make the best of this. A chance has fallen into his lap. A chance to impress Shug, to move one step further up the ladder. Take your opportunities when they come, kid, they won't come often. Scott might not realize it now, but he might never get another chance like this.

Frank's shaking his head. Don't think of this like a pro, think of it like a victim. That's what you are now. He's become the kind of person he's always destroyed. How do you get out of here? There isn't an answer. Forty-four years in the business. Probably the best gunman in the city for thirty. Yet there's no answer.

Tommy's under pressure like never before. Clueless is watching him, standing in the corridor. He's not going to say or do anything if he can help it. He knows his place. Stand guard. If the old man gets up, knock him down. If Tommy asks you to go do something, then you go do it. That's his level. They've been best mates since they were kids. Tommy's always been smarter, the stronger personality. Tommy always looked out for Clueless, protected him. Made sure he shared Tommy's successes. Now Tommy's dragging Clueless to the top with him, and it's fun. This is exciting. Lying in wait for the old guy. Holding the door of the flat opposite shut from the inside, but off the latch. Pulling it open slowly as the old crock's knocking on Tommy's door. One long step and a swipe. Hammering him on the back of the head with a metal pipe. It's the sort of thrilling thing this life is all about.

Doesn't look like much, old Frank MacLeod. Short, grey-haired, lined old face. Some geriatric that Tommy reckons is after them. Peter Jamieson's gunman. Would have been cool to have a gun for it. Tommy was smart, though. He knew exactly what the old man would do. Read him like a book. The flat opposite's been empty for months. They use it all the time, hide stuff there, dump stuff there. Nobody's going to move in – the place is dripping with damp, the walls are black with it. The old guy made it easy for them. Clueless went out the front and walked away from the building so that Frank would see him go. Then he snuck round the back and returned to the flat. All exciting stuff. Outwitting a hitman. Tommy doesn't know what to do now, though. That's a worry, but Clueless has confidence in him.

Tommy's been thinking about this moment all day. This is an opportunity. He's looking back down the hall at Frank, watching the old man watching him. Got Frank's own gun in his hand. Seems obvious. Kill him, get rid of the body. Common sense, surely. But what if there's more? What if the best thing is to let Shug know that Frank's here? Maybe Shug could learn things, important things. But maybe he would want Tommy to handle all that himself. You ask the questions, you get the information. Do it without letting anyone know. Get info, and then kill Frank. Then go to Shug with the info. Taking the initiative. That's the thing they love. He'd be impressed with that. And pleased that he was kept out of the thing until the danger had passed.

Frank's watching. The kid has no idea what to do now. This pair set him up nicely, fair play to them for that. They just didn't plan this far ahead. Failing to plot your moves is inexcusable. Unprofessional. The boy can do all the mental gymnastics he likes; Frank knows what the problem is. The next thing they have to do is kill him, and Tommy Scott's never killed a man. Big step from being a peddler to a killer. Big step from cracking his skull to putting a bullet in it. They're the scariest steps you can take in this business. You do it once, and people want you to do it again. There's no going back. Scott knows there has to be a killing, but he doesn't have the guts for it. Not yet, anyway.

'Why don't you just hurry up and do it, boy,' Frank's saying to him. Surprising himself; he didn't mean to provoke. 'You're embarrassing yourself.'

Scott's turning and glaring at him. Frank could have gone one of two ways. Could have tried to be nice, in the hope of keeping himself alive, but that seems pointless. Nice might buy time, but not life. Or he could try to goad the younger man into a mistake. That's what he's doing.

'He's right, we should shoot the prick,' Clueless is saying suddenly. Voicing an unwelcome opinion.

'Shut up,' Tommy's snapping back. 'We do this in my time, not his. You shut your fucking mouth, old man. Won't tell you again.' Make the decision. You have to make the decision. Make the phone call.

8

David 'Fizzy' Waters is lying asleep in his bed, as any civilized person should at this hour. Something's pushing at the edge of his awareness. A noise. Faint. He's opening his eyes, sitting up. A mobile, ringing in the bottom drawer of his bedside cabinet. There are two phones in there. Both pay-as-you-go, both only used by contacts. He's pulling open the drawer, picking out the old phone with the lighted display. Some random mobile number he doesn't recognize. Not usually a good thing. Getting out of bed, creeping out of the bedroom. He doesn't want to wake his girlfriend, if he can avoid it. Out into the corridor, answering the phone. Could be anyone on the other end. You never know these days. Since Shug decided to fight his way into the drug trade there have been more unsavoury characters in his world than ever.

'Hello.'

'Hi, Fizzy, Mr Waters – it's me, it's Tommy Scott.'

Speaking of unsavoury characters. A peddler with big ambitions. One of the few who was willing to try working a network for Shug. Lewis Winter taking a bullet to the skull scared most people off. Not Scott. He was enthusiastic. Ambition conquered fear and common sense. Thank goodness for that. Turns out he's good at the job. It was unexpected, but he hasn't put a foot wrong. Yet. He has a network of peddlers up and running and making money. Now he's calling at ten past one in the morning, which suggests he may just have lost his footing.

'I have a problem, but it might be a good problem.' Scott sounds a little breathless. Sounds like he's trying to keep the volume down. Fizzy's closing his eyes. He's never yet heard of a good problem.

It used to be cars. Nothing else. Shug owns a collection of garages across the city, runs a solid, legitimate business. Makes enough money to be comfortable. Apparently, these days, comfortable isn't enough. Started out stealing cars. Now there's a network, the only meaningful one left in the city. Maybe the last large car network in the country. Car security gets better, making money from them gets harder. Someone steals the car, someone else resprays and retags it, someone else deals with electronic tracking, someone else creates a false history, someone else moves it south and someone else sells it. That's a lot of someones to pay. Any more and there wouldn't be a profit left for Shug. You can't move the high-end cars that would yield bigger profits. Too distinctive. You can sell those abroad, but it's a very specialist market that Shug has never quite cracked. So moving drugs around became attractive. Already moving vehicles, why not put something in them? But it's hard. Just establishing yourself, getting credible, is treacherous. It brings a lot of challenging people into your life. People like Tommy Scott.

'What's the problem, Tommy?' Fizzy's asking in a whisper.

'Frank MacLeod. You know Frank MacLeod? Well, he came after me, but me and Clueless were able to set him up. We've got him. He's here. At my flat. He's lying in the corridor.'

'Dead?' Fizzy's asking with hope.

'Nah, not dead. He's alive. We cracked him on the head. Thing is, I thought you or Shug might want to see him. Might want to talk to him. Could be a good opportunity to get some information from him.'

And this is supposed to be a good problem. What the hell sort of information is Frank MacLeod going to give them? How could they ever trust a word that came out of his mouth? Any information from an old pro like MacLeod is useless. Guy like that, he's loyal if he's anything. Fizzy's about to say something, but it's dawning on him. Scott isn't calling because he thinks they'll want to talk to Frank. He's calling because he wants someone else to come and kill him.

He should be angry, but he's not. Fizzy doesn't blame the boy for wanting someone else to do that job. Ugly work for ugly souls. He's thinking of Glen Davidson, and the night he went to kill Calum MacLean. Fizzy drove him there, waited outside. Davidson never returned. Instead, one of Jamieson's thugs turned up with a van. He and MacLean drove off with Davidson's body. Maybe, professionally, Scott should take responsibility for Frank. Maybe he should pull the trigger himself, prove that he can. He caught him, he kills him. Fizzy wouldn't do it, though, and he's not going to force someone else.

'Listen, kid, you've done well, getting him there. He's at your own flat?'

'Yeah.'

'Right. I'll get someone round. Won't be me or Shug. It'll be someone to take care of him. Someone to get rid of him. You sit tight. Don't let him move.'

He's thinking that he should have been more enthusiastic towards the boy. Too late now – he's hung up. Getting rid of Frank MacLeod, that's a coup. Jamieson's gunman. One of his closest allies. If Frank went to kill them, and they got the better of him, then they've done something noteworthy. Something many others have tried and failed to do. Have to tell them that later. The first people to get the better of Frank MacLeod. First he knows of, anyway. If anyone else had bettered Frank, he'd be dead by now. Nature of the work he does. Would be preferable if there was a way of doing this without contacting Shug. This is why Fizzy ought to know more about the business. Especially about the people they're using. He knows Shug's using Shaun Hutton as his gunman now, although he hasn't had a job for him yet.

He likes Hutton, seems a better option than Davidson was. A more pleasant person, anyway. Not that that's how you judge a gunman, but still. Shug knows Hutton's number, Fizzy doesn't. Shug is keeping a lot more secrets than he used to.

The phone's ringing. It'll take a while for Shug to answer. His wife will wake first, and then wake Shug. Then he'll spend thirty seconds bitching into thin air. Then he'll answer his phone. They're too old for this. This is the first time it's occurred to Fizzy. If they were going to do this, they should have done it ten years ago. They were in their twenties, they had fewer responsibilities, and the market would have been easier to get into. They had the energy and the ability to take risks. Starting in your thirties has more disadvantages than advantages. More money to start you up, but less of everything else.

'Fizzy – Jesus, have you looked at a clock lately?' Still sounding groggy, not happy to be awake. Shug's not an instinctively aggressive soul, and he doesn't hold grudges, but he can be tetchy.

'We have an issue.'

'What sort of issue?'

'A little bit good, bigger bit bad.'

Fizzy's explained what's happened. He's told Shug that Frank MacLeod is lying on Tommy Scott's floor, waiting for a bullet. Someone needs to deliver it. Shug's said almost nothing so far.

'What about Scott? He's got MacLeod's gun.'

'Scott's not a gunman,' Fizzy's saying, digging the boy out of a hole. 'This is a great chance to get rid of MacLeod and weaken Jamieson. We get rid of one of Jamieson's best – think how that'll look. If Scott and his halfwit pal do the job, God knows what might go wrong. We need a pro round there. Someone who can do the job and remove the body cleanly. Get this right and we get rid of the old man without anyone knowing.'

There's silence on the other end. Shug's thinking. Fizzy can hear him moving around. He'll be out of the bedroom by now, into his den. Doesn't want to keep Elaine awake.

'Okay. You're right. I'll make a call.'

Shug's hung up; he's going to call Hutton. This is just horrible. Fizzy's sitting in his living room now, his phone in his hand, and he doesn't know what to do. Nothing. There's nothing he can do. His part in this is over. Wasn't much of a part. Hutton will go there and do the job. The phone traffic will stop, so as not to link people to the scene any more than they already are. The proper and professional thing to do is nothing. Never used to be like this. Not back when they started. Best mates, running a small business, making a bit on the side with stolen cars. A few times the owners caught them in the act. Had to fight their way out. One was quite badly injured. That was unpleasant. Still, nobody ever died. They never crossed that line. Now they're leaving that line a long way behind.

9

Phone calls are waking a lot of people tonight; Shaun Hutton isn't the last. Like many in the business, he's a multiple mobile-phone owner. He's now searching for one of his work phones. He has three. All cheap models, pay-as-you-go. Nothing smart about them. He's always kept his work schedule to a minimum. It's one reason why he doesn't carry much respect in the business. People think he comes and goes when it pleases him. They don't think he's reliable because he's not always available. They see him as being half in the industry, half out. That's a dangerous thing to be. They want you all the way in. Makes them feel comfortable. He works enough to pay his bills. No more, no less. He has a nice little house, where he lives alone. He has a nice little car. He has a nice little version of all the things he wants. That's the way it's going to stay. No rush to riches. He has the right phone, at last.

It's Shug Francis. At this time of night, it means there's either a warning or a job. Hopefully the latter; a warning usually means unpredictable work with little reward.

'Hello, Shaun speaking.'

'Shaun, it's Shug, how are you?'

He still doesn't have the hang of this. Asking how a guy is

when there's probably some emergency that needs address-ing. Too civil. Too much of a normal civilian, still. 'I'm fine. What's up?'

'Got a job for you. Right away. You know Frank MacLeod?'

Stupid question. 'I know of him.'

'You know Tommy Scott?'

'Eh, no, should I?' he's asking, but he sort of knows. He's buying time while he thinks. He knows Scott is a dealer work-ing for Shug. He's heard that Scott's been making a point of stepping on a lot of toes. Toes better left alone.

Shug's explaining what happened. Hutton's listening, taking it all in, twisting it backwards and forwards in his mind, and finding the right angle. Old Frank MacLeod. Took a long time for someone to catch him out. Kind of sad it was a punk like Scott, but that's the way the wind blows. Kids are coming through street gangs and turning into pros. They're hard before they even get started. Maybe Frank took him too lightly. Maybe he's just getting too old. Young man's game, and all that. Shug's still prattling on. He's given an address, and Hutton's mechanically memorized it. Top of a tower block – well, that's bloody brilliant. Couldn't be worse for a removal. Two other people there as well. Two strangers that he might not be able to depend on. This just keeps getting better. Shug keeps calling one of them Clueless, which is apparently his nickname. He's going to have to find himself a new tag. That's not inspiring at all.

'So, what do you think?' Shug's asking.

He shouldn't be asking. He should be telling. He's the boss. He gives the orders; the gunman follows them. Hasn't quite got the hang of leadership yet.

'I think the removal is going to be the hardest part. Could be a nightmare, up there. I think there's going to be fallout from this as well. Most of it will fall on Tommy Scott.'

'He can handle it,' Shug's saying.

'Uh-huh,' Hutton's answering, not so sure. Scott's going to need to learn to lie very low after this. He's inexperienced, he and his mate. High chance of one of them making a mistake and paying for it. 'I'll need to go get a car; I'm not using my own. If they've got Frank's gun, then I can use that when I get there. I'll need to get some equipment as well, to get rid of the body. It'll take me,' Shaun's saying, and pausing while he pretends to look at his watch, 'the best part of an hour. That'll be twenty past two. Can your man sit on him until then?'

'He can. Come and see me tomorrow, when it's done.'

'No, better to wait longer than that. You won't hear from me for another week, unless there's an emergency.'

It's three minutes since he hung up on Shug, and he's still deciding what to do next. You pick sides in this business. You don't have to like the politics, but doing a job for one person inevitably means pissing off another. You choose your jobs based more on who you can afford to piss off than who you want to work for. It's okay if you're in an organization; there's no choice to make. You work for the organization and piss off whoever the boss wants to piss off. If you're freelance, you have to plot a careful course. You have to make sure you leave enough friendly future employers. He's putting the phone down and going into the cupboard in his bedroom. There's another mobile there. Hasn't switched it on for a couple of months. Might not have any battery power. The screen's lighting – there's still some power in there. One bar. That'll do. It'll be a short call. Dialling a number he memorized a long time ago. There's no sense of guilt in it. This is a business. You pick your sides. You always have to make a living.

'Hello?' He doesn't sound sleepy at all. That's because John Young's always been a night owl. He was up and about when the phone rang.

'John, this is Shaun Hutton.'

'Shaun, what's up?' There's already a note of caution in his voice. Young knows Shaun wouldn't call unless it was an emergency. John Young knows how this business works. He's known Hutton for six years. Used him on a handful of jobs in that time, nothing major. Threw a few things his way because he was a useful contact to have. Put some money his way, too, just to buy a little loyalty. Then Shug started courting him to be his new gunman. That was a godsend for Young. Six years secretly cultivating a contact finally paying off. Now this late-night call from Shug's gunman. Hutton's wondering if Young's already connected the call to Frank. He must know Frank's out on a job, working against Shug. He'll know what to expect.

'Listen, John, you have a situation. Frank MacLeod went to hit Tommy Scott, but the kid jumped him. I got word that Frank's knocked out in Scott's flat. They want me round there to finish him and get rid of the body. I told them it'll take me an hour to get a car and the tools I need. You have an hour to send someone round and get Frank. If he's still there when I arrive, then I have to do the job. I can't back out. You got an hour.'

He's switching the phone off and shoving it back in the cupboard. Young's been good to him, always kept him onside. A desirable future employer. He owes him a warning, but he doesn't owe him any more. Backing out of the job would put his own neck on the block. He won't do that. The first priority is keeping yourself alive. Young's been good enough to buy himself an hour. You get a job and you go do it. If someone just happens to beat you to it, that's too bad.

10

As you might imagine, there are many thoughts swirling round Young's head. The first is always the paranoid instinct. Is this a set-up? Is Hutton trying to lure another Jamieson man round to the flat so that he can double his money? It would make sense. An ambitious gunman might try his luck. Make it a double celebration for Shug. No way of finding out. Probably not a set-up anyway. Most gunmen are more cautious than that. Most good ones, anyway.

He's angry with Frank now. How the hell do you get jumped by an overgrown scrotum like Tommy Scott? A man of Frank's standards. His first job back since he had his hip replaced. Maybe he's gone over the hill. Maybe he rushed back, insisting he was ready. Young's angry, but Peter Jamieson won't accept losing Frank. He's always seen Frank as some sort of kindly uncle. Looked after him. Sent him to the villa in Spain to help him recuperate from the operation. The gnarled old veteran with more talent than anyone, who helped Peter establish his organization. Frank gave them credibility when Jamieson was just another pretender, and Young his unproven right-hand man. People know Peter and Frank are close. They can't lose Frank. It would be terrible PR.

Call Jamieson. You have one hour. If you're going to do this, then you can't waste a second. Is an hour enough? Not under normal circumstances. This could just be sending someone else to fail. Throwing away a second gunman to try to rescue an already-doomed first one.

'Peter, you awake?' Calling Jamieson on his regular phone, while trying to find his damned car keys.

'Uh, yeah' is the uncertain response.

'Listen to me, we have a problem. You listening? It's Frank. That little prick Scott jumped him on his way to the job. They've got Frank in Scott's flat. They called in Shaun Hutton to do the job on him. We have one hour before Shaun gets there. What do you want to do?'

Sometimes you see a man like Jamieson, messing around with horse racing and marathon snooker sessions, and you doubt his ability. He can give the impression he's too laid-back, doesn't take his work seriously. Not a leader. Then a moment like this arrives.

Without a second's thought Jamieson's talking. 'I'll call Calum MacLean. You get to the club with a gun for him; he won't have one of his own. I'll get Kenny as well. He can drive Calum to the flat; Calum and Frank can come back in Frank's car. I'm on my way to the club as well; I'll see you there. Let's be quick about this.'

Jamieson's hung up. Not a moment of indecision. In a way it almost doesn't matter if his decision is right or wrong;

by being quick he's giving them a chance. It's a hellish risk, though. Putting Calum at huge risk to save Frank. Maybe losing them both. Calum's good. He can handle the unpredictable better than anyone – the Davidson incident proved that. Young doesn't doubt his ability to do the job, just the value of making him do it. All this risk to protect Frank, and for what? How much can they rely on the old man after an incident like this?

Out of the house and into his car. It's turned into a cold night. Windscreen's frosted. Pulling away with the heater at full blast. Young has to move fast, but not so fast that a speed-camera picks him up. Moving around at all at this hour of the night can make you stand out. Everything about this job is wrong. Everything. Glancing at the clock on the dashboard: twenty-eight minutes past one. They maybe have fifty-five minutes left to beat Hutton to the flat. That's if Hutton takes the full hour, which he can't guarantee. Young's not going to beat himself up about Hutton. If he'd kept him closer, given him more work and more money, then Hutton might have been willing to back out altogether. Then they could handle this their way. Their pace. That's still a maybe. A freelancer doesn't want a reputation as a guy who stabs his employers in the back. Then again, Hutton might not want to be a freelancer. He might be looking for employment with an established organization. Backup to an established gunman. If Young had offered him that over the phone tonight . . . No, don't dwell on it. Maybes kill progress. You can't plan for something like this. You can't keep everyone close. There isn't room. If Shug had hired anyone else to be his gunman, they wouldn't even have this hour.

On the road to pick up a gun. There's a few places you can go, if you know the right people. Gunmen typically use dealers they know and trust. Young doesn't have those connections. He's never fired a gun in his life, but he knows where a few are stored. He knows, because he stored them. He's the only person who does know. You can plan this much. He's driving to a building that Jamieson owns, has owned for a few years. It now has a third-rate travel agent on the ground floor and two flats above. They leased it out, but Young still has a key. About a year ago Jamieson had one of his men pick up a bagful of handguns that were on the market. There were four, apparently clean. Young stored three of them for a rainy day. In the middle of the night he hid one behind panelling in a cupboard that was once a coal cellar, beneath the travel agency.

A part of the job he hates. Having to creep around. It's not something he has any talent for. There are people who do it for a living, housebreakers. Very few pros left, these days. Most burglars are junkies. Young needs to get into the building, get the gun and get out without making a noise. He's legally entitled to be here, he thinks, but someone in the flats could hear him, panic and call the cops. Then he'd have to explain what he's doing here in the depths of the night. That's a hard conversation to have with a cop, whilst holding a gun. There are two other guns hidden in better locations in the city, but this is the closest, and time matters more than convenience.

In the back door, pressing the code on the alarm box. Thing probably isn't active anyway. The couple who run the travel agency are a pair of swindlers, and not good ones. They won't be paying running costs for security. Along the corridor and down the bare concrete steps to the cupboard. Pitch-black. Feeling carefully, taking a step inside. He's found the panel. It's stiffer than he remembered. He's pulling at it; it's scraping against the brickwork at the side. Noise. Horrible noise. He's reaching out a hand. A plastic bag with something bulky inside. That's what he's here for.

Moving faster now. Pulling the door quietly shut behind him, across the street and back into his car. Opening the bag, unwrapping the cloth, looking at the gun and a little cardboard box of ammo. Exactly as he left it. There's a cold feeling tingling away in the pit of his stomach. What if it doesn't work? What if you provide the gun that doesn't work, and Calum dies because of it? Don't think about that. Just get it to the club. The gun looks fine. Every gunman takes a risk with their weapon when they go on a job. It's the nature of their work. Their risk to take. Your mistake, their punishment. He's starting the car, pulling away from the side of the road.

He's taking a quick glance behind him as he goes, making sure none of the lights in the flats above the travel agency have come on. They haven't.

He's looking at the clock again as he's pulling up outside the club. It's one thirty-four. A quarter of their time has gone already. This could easily all be for nothing. Calum could turn up when it's too late to save anyone. Or he could turn up and confront Hutton. That would be even worse. Calum's sharp, though, he won't get into a fight if he doesn't have to. Nor will Hutton. He knows how to play this, too. Young's out of the car, walking briskly along an alleyway to the side of the club, holding the bag tight to his side. There's nobody about. They'll replace the CCTV that the club has covering the area with repeat footage from another night. Every precaution taken.

Neither Jamieson nor Calum is at the club yet. Young's unlocking the side door and ducking inside. Pitch-black again. Moving in a dark world – sort of thing gunmen are supposed to be very good at. Young does most of his work in the daylight. Making his way carefully along what should be an empty corridor, but you never know. The cleaners will have left less than an hour ago. Wet floors and a stink of detergent. He's found his way to the bottom of the stairs and he's making his way quickly up. Awkward stairs, each step shorter than you think it'll be. A lot of people fall on them, but he knows them well enough. Through the snooker hall, along the corridor and into Jamieson's office. He's pulling the blackout blinds shut and switching on the little lamp on the desk. It's not much light, but it's enough. He's put the bag on the table and he's pulling the cloth out. It's a long thin strip, and he's not going to take any chances with it. He'll burn it along with the plastic bag. He hasn't touched the gun itself, and he won't. He's not putting his prints on it, given what it could be about to do.

Now he's sitting on the couch, in his usual position. Two more minutes have ticked by on the clock since he got here. This is starting to look hopeless. What is Frank doing, right now? Maybe he's already dead. If he tried to do something, tried to make a run for it, they'll have shot him. It's not impossible that he might find a way to escape unaided. If Scott's armed, but they still need Hutton to do the job, then Scott obviously doesn't have the bottle to pull a trigger. That might give Frank the opportunity to do something. It isn't much to cling to. The odds are that Frank's alive, but not for much longer. They should leave him there to die. Horrible to think, but true. Young hates being in the club at this hour. It's the silence. He feels exposed. You can hide behind people. You can hide behind noise. The only protection now is the darkness, and he's in the light. A car door. Someone arriving outside. Wouldn't usually hear that. So exposed.

11

The second Young said there was a problem, Jamieson was awake. He knows Young doesn't exaggerate. One of the great things about him. He can sort out most trouble without ever involving Jamieson. The ideal right-hand man in that respect. He only makes a nuisance of himself if it's big. This really is. Frank. One of the few he can respect. One of the few he really trusts. It was such a relief when Frank said he was fit to return to work. A good feeling to give him a job. To have him back. He won't lose Frank. You judge a man by how he protects his people. The people who matter to him. He'll go as far as he has to for Frank's sake. Not just to impress others. It's also to impress yourself. Convince yourself you have an organization that can rescue its own. No matter the trouble, you're strong enough to sort it out. You can deliver another blow to Shug-bloody-Francis.

This trouble with Shug has been going on way too long. People are talking. He hears the rumours that nobody wants to tell him about. They think he's weak. They think Shug might have the better of him. He doesn't. Jamieson knows that, and so, probably, does Shug. Shug's bitten off more than he can chew. He manages to keep holding on by his fingernails. Bloody awkward target. A pest that's difficult to swat away precisely because he is small. Most of his money is legit. Most of the people who work for him are outside the industry. Targeting them would bring greater police involvement, which he needs to avoid. Have to stamp on his criminal business. Have to see it to stamp on it. Tommy Scott. A public face. Make an example. That could still happen.

Jamieson's walking downstairs with his phone in his hand. His wife might have woken up beside him, but she didn't show it. She won't say a word. Won't even ask him about it in the morning. She's been in this life long enough to understand the value of silence. Away from the kids' bedrooms, too. They don't understand the value of silence. They're old enough to understand the nature of their father's work, but they mustn't hear things they shouldn't. Things they might repeat. The chore of fatherhood. Into the living room, closing the door, sitting on the couch. The first number he finds is Kenny McBride's. Kenny's his driver, has been for a few years. A good boy. A little nervy around people that matter, a little mouthy around those that don't. There are still lessons for him to learn. Reliable, though, that's the key.

'Kenny,' he's saying quietly. 'Get round to my house right away, pick me up, okay.'

There's a slight pause while Kenny processes the order. The latest in the chain to be woken. His mind moves at a gentle pace at the best of times. 'Yes, on my way.'

That's it. That's the conversation. Jamieson gives the order and Kenny accepts it without question. Jamieson never needs to justify himself. Kenny never needs detail. Others might ask for more. People like Frank and Calum. That's because the work they do matters. It's because they can afford to ask. They've earned the right to question. But drivers are ten a penny. Kenny's expendable. Good drivers aren't so common, but Kenny rarely needs to be good. Chauffeur and delivery boy aren't taxing. Tonight may be a night when Kenny needs to prove himself. That's something else to worry about.

The job formed in Jamieson's mind as soon as Young told him what had happened. He could picture it all. The way they'll have to do it. They supply Calum with a gun because he won't have time to go and get one himself. Kenny drives him to the flats. He leaves him there. Calum's on his own. He gets to the flat and does what he does so well, with Scott and his bum-chum. He gets Frank out and they leave in Frank's car. Without realizing it, Jamieson is slapping the seat of the couch. It's a bloody nightmare job. He's closing his eyes tight. Justify it to yourself. Go on. Find a justification. Anything. Reverse the roles. Would you send Frank in to rescue Calum? Would you take this risk with a friend's life to rescue an employee? No, you hypocritical prick, you wouldn't. You'll risk an employee for a friend, though. Even if the employee's more valuable.

He's standing up now, in the darkness. What would happen if you lost Frank? No, it's still not justification enough to risk Calum. Frank's not a young man. The end has been creeping up on him for a long time. He deserves a better end than this. That's no justification, either. Most people deserve a better ending than the one they get. Certainly in this business. Very few get to pick the door they leave by. The thought of Frank lying on the floor of some shitty flat, with those bastards standing over him. Two little scumbags, goading him, thinking they're better than him. The thought of Hutton putting a bullet in him. Dragging him out of the building and dumping his body somewhere. If it were Calum, Jamieson would leave him. It's the risk a gunman takes. They don't expect someone to come and rescue them if they botch it. They don't expect people to risk their lives for them. They certainly shouldn't.

Sitting down again. Another minute wasted. Not too late to back out. Let Frank suffer his fate. The price of botching a job. It's the same for everyone, why should he be different? It's a hopeless mission. Calum would have to get into the building and up to the flat. High up. Scott lives near the top of a tower block; Jamieson remembers that from the research. Get inside. How do you do that? That would be his problem. Get in. Kill two men. Has to be both of them. One will have Frank's gun. Him first. Then the other one. He's a witness. He's a danger. He'll have to go. So a double hit.

That's rare. Raises eyebrows with the police. Gets them all excited. Invites trouble. Then Calum has to get Frank out of the building. What if he's injured? What if his hip has gone again? Frank might be a dead weight. How does Calum get him safely out without being seen? Oh, it's a shitty job to send one of your own into.

But he will send Calum to do it. Jamieson knows it already. Has known it all along. Right now he's sitting on the couch and he's wasting time. He knows that, too. He knows he's making Calum's job harder with this pointless agonizing. There's little enough time. He's squandering a little of what there is. Just call Calum. Tell him nothing yet. Get him to the club. Too late for him to say or do anything when he's there to collect the gun. He's a pro. He'll do the job. He's one of the few capable of doing it well. Jamieson's shaking his head. Calum will try to do the job. He'll try to do it well. Another fucking cripple. Frank with his hip, Calum with his hands. Stabbed by the now-silenced Glen Davidson. Calum handled that well. Hasn't done a job in the months since. Calum doesn't want to work for an organization – that's been obvious from the start. Jamieson has suspected for a few weeks that Calum's swinging the lead. Time to change that.

12

It only takes one ring to wake Calum. The last man woken on this wakeful night. He's never been a good sleeper. Not because he's waiting for a call – he never worked so often that he got regular calls. It's just his nature. Cautious, unsettled, preferring to live in a small, controllable world. His sleeping is worse now than ever. He's been waiting for a call like this. Knowing it would come. Dreading it. He's supposed to be a professional. He's supposed to set standards for himself. Make the sacrifices. He's made an unprofessional error. The error is lying next to him. She's asleep. Calum's reaching out and grabbing his mobile from the bedside table. At a glance he can see that it's not Young's number. Young calls if there's a job to do. It's a local number he doesn't recognize. That could be good or bad.

He's already out of bed by the time the phone starts its third ring. He's answered it, but he's saying nothing until he's out of the room.

'Hello,' he's saying. He's trying not to whisper. There shouldn't be anyone in his flat that he needs to hide this conversation from. A good gunman is available to talk freely whenever the call comes. Calum's uncomfortable, trying to cover up his error. He's along the corridor and into the kitchen now.

'Calum, this is Peter. I need you to come to the club. Right away. I mean right away.'

There is no answer to that. Jamieson can't possibly expect him to say anything. He tells you in no uncertain terms to come. Peter Jamieson is the boss; it's his organization. You do what he tells you, or there are consequences. He tells you to come, you come. You don't have the freedom to refuse.

'I'm on my way.'

'Good,' Jamieson's saying, sounding a little depressed as he hangs up.

Calum ought to be worrying about this job. No other thought should intrude upon him at this moment. A middle-of-the-night emergency. He's hardly thinking about it. It hasn't struck him yet how odd it was that Jamieson called. In normal circumstances, that would be his first thought. Why Jamieson, and not Young? It's always Young. It's part of Young's job. It's obviously something worth being concerned about. If he was thinking clearly, he might have thought that Young himself was in some sort of trouble. He hates emergency jobs anyway. They're rushed. Mistakes are easy and sometimes inevitable. He's a planner. Meticulous and patient. Slow, some would say. Let them say it. His quality comes from his patience. He's not even thinking about that, though. He's thinking about her instead.

Her name's Emma. Emma Munro. In a sense, she's Jamieson's fault. She's awake now. She's put the lamp on and she's sitting up in bed. He's in the bedroom doorway. She's rather short, but she carries it well. Short black hair, round face, a stud in her nose that he finds cute, and a tattoo on her wrist that he hates. He hasn't told her yet that he finds tattoos vulgar. It hasn't felt like the right time. The right time to pick a fight. It's unusual for Calum. The whole scenario is. Emma's the first proper girlfriend he's had in nearly ten years. He's always held women at arm's length. They don't rush towards him often; he's, at best, a below-average-looking guy. Any time they've threatened to get close he's found a way of repelling them. Like telling them he finds their choice of body art vulgar and unattractive. Pick a little fight. Let it burn out of control. Let them walk away because he's unreasonable. You have to do it early in a relationship, though, before they get forgiving. He should do it now. Do it. Pick a fight.

It's a warm little flat; she's pushed the duvet down. She's wearing a vest that's too small for her, and her underpants. She's yawning. It's the second time this week that she's stayed the night. He likes it – let's not pretend otherwise. He likes it a lot. It feels normal. It feels the way he assumes all normal relationships feel. Can't have normal. Not with his job. He's not normal. She's a liability. There's no way of doing the job without her finding out what he's up to. Or at least realizing that he's up to something. He can't have that. No good gunman takes that risk. It's why most of the good ones are single. Why most of them aren't a kick in the pants off being loners. It was stupid letting her get so close. It's weak not to push her away. It would be doing her a favour. She shouldn't be dragged into his life. She's only here because of Jamieson. Well, George can take some of the blame.

George Daly is a good friend, a good guy. It's not like him to turn up out of the blue and start trying to play best buddies, though. Calum has carefully created a life for himself where nobody turns up unexpectedly. A reliable, solid sort of life. Then George shows up. Calum had just moved from the safe house to a new flat. Jamieson pulled strings on his behalf; he was getting a nice little flat, decent sort of area. Nothing too fancy, he didn't want to stand out. Jamieson was making every effort to win him round. Iron fist in a velvet glove routine. Doing plenty of nice things to make you want to work for him, now and then dropping in a reminder that you have no choice. Making Calum realize that he's part of the organization now. Jamieson has a good relationship with Frank MacLeod, but he knows Frank won't last forever. Needs a long-term replacement, needs backup. That's Calum's role. But Jamieson's obviously worked out that Calum doesn't want that role, so the pressure's on. Send George round to pal up with him, make him feel closer to the organization. George works for Jamieson too – his best muscle. Entangle Calum in the Jamieson world. Create emotional bonds.

They were friends already. They've done jobs together. Lewis Winter and Glen Davidson. Two in quick succession. George is always good company, so Calum agreed to go to a club with him. Not into clubbing. Never dances. Sweaty, unpleasant places, full of sweaty, unpleasant people. George was out there, throwing shapeless shapes and drawing attention. Calum hung tight by the bar. Two girls, young, student types. A boringly pretty blonde and an entertainingly pretty brunette. They were right next to him, but Calum said nothing. Just sipped at his orange juice. No alcohol, ever. Keep control. The new flat, being a part of an organization now, it was different. Made him willing to do things a little differently, but not a lot differently. No getting blitzed and chatting up random women in bars. Then George came back.

'Ah, I hope Calum's being keeping you entertained,' he grinned, sticking out a hand towards the blonde first. 'My name's George.'

It hadn't occurred to George that Calum wouldn't have spoken to them, and nobody ever corrected him. The four of them stuck together that evening. George and the blonde – Anna or Annie something-or-other – disappeared together at the end of the evening. Calum didn't make a move. He was saying goodbye when Emma gave him her number and asked for his.

'You really are the strong silent type,' she said with a mocking smile. It was cute.

'Mostly just silent,' he shrugged. He gave her his number. Just seemed rude not to. She called the next day. He answered. Now here they are. Behaving like a normal couple, three weeks later. It's just fun. Good, innocent, dangerous fun. Innocent for her. Dangerous for him. Maybe dangerous for her too, if the wrong people find out. He's known a return to work was coming. That butcher with a medical certificate and a pill problem that works for Jamieson was round to check on him a few days ago. Sent by Jamieson, no doubt. Said the stab wounds to each hand and the right arm had healed nicely. A little healing still to do in the left hand, but mostly fine. Davidson's knife shouldn't leave permanent damage. This call's been coming since then.

She's only twenty-one. Nine years his junior. Still a student. Finishing her last year of politics at Strathclyde University. Finished in three months. She's said she'll probably end up in Edinburgh or London. Seems to think she has an in with a research organization that'll take her on. Unlikely she'll stay in Glasgow. That would solve it. A short-term relationship, fun while it lasts. Three months is still too long to hide a secret like this. If she doesn't already know. She's a smart girl; she might have worked it out already. Not as serious as Calum, but every bit as sharp. He's spun a yarn about his hand injuries. Said he worked for a printing company and the machinery chewed his hands. Said he's not sure he has a job to go back to. She nodded along, and hasn't said anything about it since.

She looks adorable, sitting there. She must know something. Must at least know that he's been lying to her about working for a printer. Her friend had a night of fun with George, hasn't seen him since. How much did the friend glean from George? He wouldn't have told her anything incriminating, he's not so daft, but he might have given something away. If she knows and she's turning a blind eye, then that's positive. She won't know that he's a gunman. If she can live with the fact that he's a criminal, then it would seem okay. But it's not. He's not concerned about her finding out and dumping him. His concern is much more selfish than that. He's concerned that she might find something that gets him into trouble. That she might make his job harder. That she might be the very thing that trips him up.

Hard enough doing a job you don't want to do, without having her there. Having to think about her, factor her in to every decision. How to avoid her knowing anything she shouldn't know. Tell her to go. Just tell her it's over. It was a bit of fun and it's run its course. He's looking at her, and he's hating himself. Too weak to tell her. Enjoying her too much. It's unprofessional. Hard to admit, but he wanted this. He wanted her. Not specifically her, but a girlfriend, someone to be with. Loneliness was catching up with him. That's why he let this happen. She's not Jamieson's fault or George's fault. She's his own fault. He chose to let things happen that he should have stopped. A year ago he would have stopped it. He hasn't sent her away. Hard to admit, but he's unprofessional. First time that's happened.

'Well,' she's saying, staring at him with a bemused smile, 'who was it?'

He's been standing in the doorway looking at her for nearly twenty seconds. The phone's still in his hand. 'Oh, it was William,' he's saying, referring to his older brother. This is a lie he's been preparing for a while. From the moment he realized he was going to let her spend the night at his flat. It's thin, but plausible enough. 'He's stuck without a lift. Sounds a bit pissed. Has no money for a taxi. I said I'd go and get him. He's always a good sport for me.' Don't give too much detail – that would be unnatural. Just tell her what she needs to know. Sound a little put out, but forgiving towards your brother. Not so annoyed that it prompts her to make something of it.

'Huh,' she's saying. 'I hope you give him what for, dragging you out at this time.'

He's smiling and nodding as he's pulling on a plain hooded top. Someone's going to get what for.

Does she know? It seemed like a knowing smile was threatening to break out, when she said that about giving William what for. He's out on the street, getting into his plain car. A car incapable of drawing attention to itself. He knows what's going to happen. He'll go to the club, there'll be some sort of emergency and he'll have to go and work a job. She must know. She's too smart not to have realized that he's up to something. As long as she only suspects that he's a criminal. As long as she doesn't know he's a gunman. If she thinks him no more than a rogue, then she might keep mistaking him for a decent human being. He's pulling away from the flat. There's still a little discomfort in his left hand when he grips things. The steering wheel, for one. Presumably a gun too, although the last time he handled one was when he killed Lewis Winter. More than two months ago. Feels a lot longer.

13

Sitting in the boys' old flat. Perched on the radiator in the living room. It's dark in the flat – electricity's been cut off. No curtains over the windows, though; plenty of street light and moonlight to show the scene. It's the second time Detective Inspector Michael Fisher's come here. Calum MacLean is involved. That much he's sure of. All he has are phone records. It's his investigation, but he can't make it move. The phone records show that Glen Davidson called Calum MacLean. Davidson made the call from the home of Shug Francis. Within twenty-four hours Davidson's gone missing and MacLean's moved house. Now put that together to form a coherent investigation. Can't do it.

The Lewis Winter murder. Make Glen Davidson number-one suspect. He's a gunman, Fisher knows that. He made the call from Shug's house. So let's say Shug hired him to hit Winter. A deal gone wrong. Makes sense so far. Conjecture, but believable. So who the hell's MacLean? And where the hell's Davidson? The first question Fisher can answer to some degree. MacLean's nearly thirty, no police record, from the city. No record of work. Fisher hasn't found his new address yet, but that's only a matter of time. Found out that he has a brother and a widowed mother. No point questioning either of them yet. Don't let MacLean know he's on the radar until there's something to throw at him. Brother's name's come up in a couple of investigations before. Owns a share in a garage that's been under suspicion previously. Nothing major, but worth noting. If big brother's involved in the criminal industry, it's not a huge leap to suspect little brother is, too.

If Calum MacLean works for anyone, it's Peter Jamieson. It's become slowly obvious that Shug Francis and Peter Jamieson are at war with each other. It was one of his own men that brought him that suggestion. Turned out to be sound. The rumours around the city are that Shug's making a pest of himself. It's still Jamieson's fight to lose, but Shug's at least making him work for it. That would suggest Shug making multiple moves against Jamieson's men. Was Winter Jamieson's man? Not according to rumour. Closer to Shug, if anything. So let's stick to the theory of a deal going sour. MacLean, on the other hand, he may well be one of Jamieson's. So, what are we saying? After getting rid of Winter, within a week Shug sent his gunman to try and take down one of Jamieson's men? Hmm. Not so likely. Not so soon after Winter. Something happened here, though. Right in this flat. It's why Fisher's back.

MacLean had been gone a week or two by the time Fisher tracked him down. The landlord wasn't helpful. Shifty bugger, that one. Didn't want to say anything. Fisher got a forensics team in, got them to look around the place. The flat had been deep-cleaned. Not a fingerprint in the whole place. Furniture and carpets were gone. Fixtures had been cleaned to a high standard. Walls, too. Damaged the wallpaper in a couple of rooms cleaning it, but they didn't seem to care. Cleanliness the priority. Checked the light sockets. They'd been cleaned too. Even the damned ceilings. Forensics checked the bathroom and kitchen for signs of hairs or skin. Came away with nothing. A professional clean. The kind that a large criminal organization can carry out to cover tracks. The kind Peter Jamieson would be smart and careful enough to order.

Something happened here, but what? He needs to tie MacLean to Jamieson. Needs to find out what exactly MacLean does for Jamieson. Has to be something important, otherwise why target him? There's one theory that ties things together. Winter does a deal with Shug. MacLean then lures him to work for Jamieson. Shug finds out. Punishes Winter for being a traitor and tries to send a message to Jamieson. That might work. Not the greatest theory, but the best he has right now. If he could locate Davidson, that might help. Did he do a runner or was he removed? Running is the most likely. Maybe he was screwing Shug, too. No loyalty amongst these people. So Davidson tips off MacLean. Davidson lies low, MacLean makes a hasty move.

Fisher's rubbing his eyes. It's late. Too late for this. Too late in the day, too late in the investigation. Standing in an empty little flat, trying to work out where the fuck your investigation went. Not one convincing option. It's tied him up in knots and left him hanging. The Winter case has run away from him. Winter was never important enough to get a lot of attention. When it became clear that they didn't have enough information to arrest anyone, the team started moving on. Fisher's DCI didn't want resources wasted on a dead end. Might have been a different story if the victim wasn't someone so overwhelmingly pathetic. Winter was a low-level dealer. A failure all his life. Too guilty for sympathy. Too small to lead to a big conviction. So all they get is a four-month jail term for his ex, and a suspended three-month term for her one-night stand for perverting the course of justice. Fast-tracked because it was such minor stuff.

Fisher's leaving the flat. He's always thought it helped to be at the scene. Walk the criminal's path. See what they saw; judge how they would have reacted. That's fine, when you know what the crime was. When you know a crime has even happened here. He doesn't. It's a guess. One he has no solid evidence to back up. It's that nagging feeling. The sense that this is a chance and, if he misses it, there won't be another one for years. A chance for a crack at Peter Jamieson and his organization. Shug Francis too, but he's smaller. Jamieson would be the big prize. The biggest prize of Fisher's career. The biggest arrest in organized crime in the city for years.

He's out of the flat now, into the corridor. Putting the front-door key in his pocket. He'll keep a hold of that, just in case. He's shaking his head as he walks out into the cold. A lot of cops wouldn't even know this was a chance. Maybe wouldn't care. Would decide it was too tough, and wait for the next one. He's a good enough cop to know that this is a chance he ought to take. Just not good enough to take it. Fisher's under pressure from above. They want him to move on to other investigations. If anything else comes along relating to Winter, then he can go back to it. Until then, get on with more productive things. Dropping into the driver's seat and turning on the engine. Glancing at the clock on the dashboard. One forty in the morning. Hanging around empty flats at stupid o'clock looking for inspiration. Getting desperate. He knows it, so does everyone else. Go get some sleep. Start again in the morning. Nothing's going to happen tonight.

14

The door to the office has burst open and Jamieson's marched in. Kenny has stayed behind in the snooker hall; he knows this isn't his place. The office is for important people only. Jamieson can't hide his disappointment that Calum's not here yet. He always takes everything so bloody slow. Careful is fine, but tardy is annoying.

'You get a piece for him?'

'Top drawer of your desk,' Young's saying to him. He's relieved that someone else is here. He feels less vulnerable. The silence is broken, the emptiness chased away. 'I haven't touched it, obviously.'

Jamieson's nodding, but not listening. He's standing behind his desk, showing no sign of wanting to sit down. 'Jesus Christ!' he's saying under his breath to nobody in particular. Now he's shaking his head.

Two minutes have passed. Another two. Jamieson just standing there, Young sitting on the couch. There's been no warning. Just a sudden knock on the door.

'In,' Jamieson's saying loudly. The door's opening and Calum's stepping inside, closing it behind him. Typical of him to be able to sneak in without anyone hearing, Young's thinking. Probably a good sign. Jamieson's sitting down now. Time to look professional, even if you don't feel it. Calum doesn't know what he's walking into. He won't enjoy finding out. 'Sit down,' Jamieson's saying. 'How's your hand?'

'Right one's fine,' Calum's saying as he's sitting down opposite Jamieson, 'left one's still a little stiff when I grip things. I'm right-handed, so . . .' he trails off. It has a curious feel, being in the office in lamplight. Feels like they're sneaking around Jamieson's own office. Usual routine, though. Facing Jamieson, Young off to the side, just out of view.

Just come straight out and tell him. He has no opportunity to back out anyway; you've drawn him too close for that. 'I need you to go and do a job,' Jamieson's saying, and glancing at his watch. Twenty to two. This is cutting it. 'Frank went to hit Tommy Scott. Scott and another guy jumped him. They've got him at Scott's flat. They're waiting for . . . another gunman to turn up and finish him. You've got about half an hour to get there first, turn the tables.'

Calum's not saying anything. Sitting there, listening, taking it all in. Work out what it really means. Read between lines. They jumped Frank. Shouldn't happen. Someone's tipped Jamieson off. Seems odd. Must be the gunman who's going round to do the job. He's sold them time. Now they want Calum to go and rescue Frank. There's little worse than a rescue job.

Jamieson can see that the wheels are turning. Give him

detail, and then send him on his way. Tell him only what he needs to know. 'Kenny's going to drive you there. He'll drop you off outside the building – he knows where it is. You're looking for flat 34B. Second-from-top floor of a tower block. Thirteenth floor. Should only be two people there with Frank. Get rid of them. You and Frank can get away in Frank's motor.' He's reaching into the top drawer of his desk, taking out a bag. Calum's already guessed what's in there.

'I need gloves and a balaclava,' he's saying matter-of-factly.

Jamieson glances across to Young. He'd thought Calum would take these things from home. He should have. If Emma hadn't been there, he would have. He's not going to give them an explanation; they also get only the details they need. Young's getting up. There's a couple of balaclavas in a box in the storeroom. The box marked 'Lost and found', in case an inquisitive officer of the law happens across it. There's a few boxes of clear surgical gloves that the cleaners use.

'You need to be damn quick about this,' Jamieson's saying, as Young hurries out to the storeroom. 'You need to get Frank. I want Scott and his mate dead. Mostly Scott. The mate's a dickhead, a hanger-on, but he'll be a witness if you leave him. Scott's been a fucking nuisance. Get rid of him.'

'And the other gunman?' Calum's asking.

A brief pause. Hutton is Young's contact. They should protect their useful contacts. They're hard enough to come by. Too bad. Hutton knew what he was getting involved in when he called and gave them the warning. He shouldn't expect favours in return. 'If he turns up and you have to deal with him, then you deal with him. Hopefully he won't show up. Play it by ear. Do what you need to, nothing more.' That doesn't need saying.

Young's bounding back into the room. He's not a natural runner, a little too chunky. He's placing a black balaclava and a box of gloves on the desk.

Calum's stuffed the balaclava into his pocket and quickly pulled on a pair of gloves. 'How clean is the gun?' he's asking, taking it out of the cloth.

'We've never used it,' Young's saying. 'Been in storage since we bought it.'

Calum's nodding. Might not be exactly clean, but clean enough. If the police link it to other people, then that's other people's problem. As long as it's untraceable to Calum or anyone near him, he doesn't much care. He's checking the clip – it's full. Now putting the gun into his pocket. 'Don't need those,' he's saying, nodding to the box of ammo. He doesn't want to fire more than two shots. More than four and he's in disaster territory. An entire clip and he's in the middle of a fucking nightmare. Spare bullets should not be required. 'Right. I'm off.'

Jamieson wants to say something. He wants to encourage Calum. He'd like to tell him to bring Frank back to the club, but that's not professional. None of this is professional, but that would be crossing a line. 'Calum,' he's saying as Calum is pulling the door shut behind him. He's stopped to look back at Jamieson. 'Text me when it's done. Has it been successful? Yes or no.'

Calum's walking along the corridor. Jamieson would never usually ask for a text. He shouldn't be asking for it now. Calum's not happy, but he hasn't a choice. The boss asks, you do. The boss takes stupid risks because he's emotional about the job, you suffer the consequences. Welcome to organization-work. Out into the snooker hall. He had nodded to Kenny on the way in, sitting on a table. Still there, hanging around in the dark.

'You know where we're going?' Calum's asking him.

'Aye, I know,' Kenny's saying, getting up and walking briskly towards the door. It's a rare opportunity for him to shine. Not often a driver gets any sort of real responsibility. Deliver this or that. Go and pick up this fellow. You need to know the city; you need to know how to drive without drawing attention to yourself. A short drive, but he's looking forward to it.

15

They're in the car. Kenny doesn't know what to say, whether to say anything. He's relaxed, he'd like to talk, but he's not what counts. Whatever job this is, it's obviously big and obviously hurried. He might never find out. You do the job and you don't ask questions. You hope people recognize that you've shown restraint by not asking. It's like that for most people in the business. If you're not very near the top, then it's hard to draw praise. If someone ever does praise your work, you're not likely to hear it. Would be nice to get a few more compliments, a little recognition. Gunmen do. Importers do. People with stature. There aren't many of them. Kenny just keeps on driving in silence. Some guys don't like it when you make conversation, especially when they're on a job. Calum seems like the sort who would resent someone else breaking his silence. He's quiet even when there's nothing going on. I'm just a glorified taxi driver, really, Kenny's thinking. That's how they all see him.

'It's up on the right here,' Kenny's saying as they approach the flats. 'How close do you want me to get?'

'Not too close. I need to get in unseen.' Ideally he'd like to get in on the opposite side of the building from Scott's flat, but neither of them knows which flat is his. Lack of preparation. Calum should know these things before he goes in to do a job. It's going to be hard to creep up on the flat unseen, when you don't know what you're creeping up on. He might not actually need to creep. If Scott doesn't know who he is, then there's much less risk. If Scott doesn't know what Shug's gunman looks like, either, then he could get right inside the flat unchallenged. Too much to hope for.

'I'll go past the building so you can see it,' Kenny's saying. 'See what lights are on, I mean.'

There are no lights visible on the second-from-top floor. Not on the side of the building they're facing, anyway. Doesn't mean much. If Scott has an ounce of sense, he'll have made sure no lights are visible. Kenny's pulling up at the side of the road, an equal distance between two lamp posts. It's a good effort, but meaningless. The street is bright; anyone who chooses to look will see them. Now the balaclava question. Do you wear it from the moment you leave the car, or put it on outside the flat? In theory, he might not need it at all. If he can get in without bumping into anyone, get to the flat, kill Scott and his accomplice and get out with Frank, maybe nobody will see him. Nobody who's going to live to tell the tale. Big maybe. There could be CCTV cameras around. The sort of place a local council would put them up, to look tough on crime. Put the balaclava on now.

He's pulling it over his head. It always feels uncomfortable – an unnatural thing to have your face covered up. He's feeling the shape of the gun in his pocket, and turning to Kenny. 'Okay,' is all he says, and he's getting out of the car. As soon as he's closed the door, Kenny is pulling away. He'll have more work to do tonight. Take the car to a garage, have it made safe. They'll change the colour and the plates anyway. Calum has to trust them that it was a safe car to begin with, that nobody can trace it back to them. They're all forced to trust each other to do a good job. You trust that they wouldn't have reached this far in the business if they weren't reliable. Surely people further up the chain would have spotted the lucky but useless before now.

Across the road and down a small grass embankment. It's slippery, the grass is wet and he has to be careful. Don't fall on your arse – it's embarrassing even when your face is covered up. Not a soul around, brightly lit and empty streets. He's against the edge of the building now, walking briskly along the pavement towards the corner where the door is. A glance at his watch. It's going on for two o'clock now. Another gunman on his way. This could be fun and games. Scott and his buddy will be work enough. Scott's obviously more tuned-in than they realized, and he and his mate will outnumber Calum, no matter how hopeless the friend is. If both men have weapons, this goes beyond the usual risk of the job. You accept that the other man might get the better of you when it's one on one. Two on one and you're starting to look suicidal. If Shug's gunman shows up in the middle of it all, then it will take a miracle to get out.

There's one thought that's been playing in his mind for the last few minutes. He's thinking about it as he's coming in the door of the building. The hallway is lit up and he can see two lifts on his left-hand side. The thought, as he's walking across to the lifts, is that Frank may already be dead. Better than fifty–fifty chance that he is. Shug's gunman sold them time, but no guarantee. There's no guarantee that Scott hasn't already done the job, and that the gunman is only heading here for a removal. Calum knows how these things go. Tense waiting. Someone snaps. Says or does something stupid. Scott reaches for the gun and puts a premature end to it. If he is dead? Calum goes up there and finds himself in a mess. He can kill Scott and his friend, but he doesn't have the time or the ability to get Frank's body out of the building. So he leaves him. What a confusing picture that leaves behind. Three bodies. Two young men who belong in the flat, one old man who doesn't. Throw Shug's gunman in there, and that's four bodies for the police to play with.

The lift doors are sliding open. Calum's watching, worrying. Nobody there. Thank the good Lord for that. Stepping inside, looking at the buttons. They go up to fourteen. He's pressing thirteen, and hoping Jamieson's information is sound. If he has to go searching for flat 34B, then he can forget about saving Frank in time. The doors are closing, the lift shudders and is starting to move up. It's slow; not quiet, either. Maybe half the flats in the building are empty anyway, which is a bonus. The council is demolishing a lot of these tower blocks, getting rid of the eyesores. No new tenants coming in. Communities in the sky. A horrible place for a community. Even worse place for a job.

A ping and the doors start to slide open. The corridor in front of him is brightly lit, but thankfully empty. He's stepping out of the lift, still nobody visible. He's found the focus he needs. A shadow has fallen across the rest of the world. All that exists right now is this corridor, that flat, Scott, his mate and Frank. There is no Emma, no Jamieson, and no concern beyond this one challenge. Professionalism dictates. Walking along the corridor, not just looking, but listening. Any chattering voices, any doors creaking, any sound that doesn't belong in the corridor of the thirteenth floor of a tower block at two o'clock in the morning. There's no sound at all. He's checking the door numbers as he's walking, making sure he's going the right way down the corridor. There's a 33, but no sign of a 33B. Straight on to 34, then 34B.

The door to 34B is on his right, 35A is directly opposite on his left. Good place for an ambush – might be how they did it. If they're still in there, still alive, then they'll be waiting for a knock on the door. Probably nervous, ready to jump out of their skin. If they see something they don't like, they'll react hard and fast. It all comes down to them knowing what Shug's gunman looks like. If they don't, he gets inside without a fuss. If they do, this goes the ugly route fast. He's lifting up his balaclava; Shug's man wouldn't wear one going into the flat. He has it on the top of his head, it looks non-threatening. He's knocking on the door, two quiet taps. Nothing loud enough to wake the neighbours. Not yet. Loud enough to be heard by someone who's listening. Now he's turning to look the other way, making sure his face isn't the first thing they see. It might buy him a few seconds.

16

They're so nervous. They were bad to start with, but they're insufferable now. It makes Frank want to provoke them, get it over with. The waiting is the worst part, embarrassing somehow. He's been beaten by people who don't even know how to kill him. They're waiting for a gunman to come along and do the job they don't have the balls for. To think of all the pros he's beaten over the years, and these two are his undoing. Humiliating, not embarrassing. The gunman will come, do it clean, get his body out. They'll get away with it. There's only one other flat occupied on this floor and it's at the opposite end of the corridor. If their gunman uses a knife, then nobody's ever going to hear it. They'll go unpunished. If he can get them to fire the gun, that might change things. Okay, he dies, but he's going to die anyway. Get them to make a stupid mistake. Sort of thing that puts them behind bars for ten to fifteen. It wouldn't take much of a push, not with these nerves.

Scott started out cool enough. He made his phone call, he was keeping it together. It's the other one. Clueless they call him, easy to see why. He's been riling Scott for the last half-hour. Provoking his friend and making a hard job harder. He's like a little kid.

'It shouldn't take this long,' he's saying for the umpteenth time. Frank's still sitting inside the front door; Scott still has the gun. Clueless has been standing in the corridor, making a lot of useless noise. 'They call the guy, he comes straight round and does it. They don't waste time. These guys are professionals, they don't fanny about. He wouldn't fuck around when he's got a top target waiting here. It's taking way too long. Something's wrong. I'm telling you.' Talking like he's the expert in the room.

The real expert in the room is sitting on his arse in the corridor, looking down the barrel of his own gun, listening and waiting. Frank hears these little squirts talking and he has to wonder how he ever managed to botch this. The gunman will be here any minute. They didn't call Shug; Scott isn't big enough to have his number. They called a third party, the thirty party calls Shug, Shug calls the gunman. The gunman then has to go get a gun and a car. If he doesn't live close by, then it could take anything up to an hour. Around the half-hour mark is maybe more likely. It feels like the half-hour has passed. He's not wearing a watch, never does on a job. Nothing that could identify you. Scott's giving his mate dirty looks, but Clueless isn't picking up on it. His nerves are all over the place. He's not picking up on anything.

'You're gonna get shot, old man,' Clueless is saying now, leaning in close enough to smell his breath. Frank's turning to the side, but he's not saying anything. Don't make this fun for them. The boy wants to provoke a reaction, preferably a scared one. Frank will give them no joy. 'How you feel about that, old man? Thought you were supposed to be some big shot, huh? Thought you took down a shitload of people. Couldn't take us down, could ya? Huh?'

'Knock it off,' Scott's saying. Saying it quietly, trying to calm his friend down. Trying to calm them both down.

'Come on, man, we got the bastard. We beat him.' Clueless is pleading for the chance to have fun, to act the way he thinks a tough guy would. He has it all wrong; it's not how real tough guys act at all. Scott, in his silence, is closer.

'Our man will be here soon. He won't knock hard on the door, and he won't want to have to knock a second time. Let's keep it quiet.'

Thinking well when the heat's on. Staying smart and aware, and cooling his friend down at the same time. Frank respects that. Maybe this kid isn't some hopeless little pisspot peddler who got out of hand, after all. Shame Jamieson didn't spot his talent before it got this far. Not Jamieson. Young. Shame Young didn't spot his talent, because that's his job. Scott will ditch his dim-witted friend eventually. Scott will realize that the only chance he has to get ahead is to leave people like Clueless behind. Ambition will snap the bond of friendship. Can't let a deadweight hold you back. Many best friends fall out of the picture. Clueless doesn't realize it, and will probably never understand. That'll be his punishment. Left where he belongs, at the bottom of the heap. This is his pinnacle. It's only Scott's beginning.

Now there's a knock on the door. Two knocks. Light – nothing that might alert the neighbours. That's the gunman. Here comes the end of the world. Frank's surprised at how calm he is about it. He doesn't feel he deserves it, but this is how a lot of gunmen take their leave from the business. He keeps thinking back to that first job he did, and wishing he could think of something better. He was a tough kid. Benson was a big fat bastard, slippery and full of words that meant nothing at all. He knew the business, though. Sent Frank after some bookie who was keeping money to himself. Frank can't remember the bookie's name for the life of him, although people in the business apparently knew him well. Caught up with him in a street near his house, dragged him into an alleyway and kicked him senseless. Frank was just a thug back then. Now he's getting a thug's ending. Maybe he does deserve it after all.

Scott's moving towards the door, the gun still in his hand. He's looking more nervous now, obviously keen to make a good impression. The gunman's more important to Shug than he is. Scott needs the respect of the people who matter, to reach the top. The little prick Clueless is grinning now, looking down at Frank and smiling, mocking. Scott's stepping over Frank's outstretched legs. He's at the door, glancing back. A quick look through the peephole, just a glance. Then looking back at Frank. He's smart enough to know that he shouldn't turn his back for long. Doesn't matter if the old man's on the floor. Frank has a reputation for being dangerous, one you need to respect. He doesn't stop being dangerous just because he's sitting down. Opening the door, trying to look between Frank and the new arrival.

'Come in,' Scott's saying, 'he's right here.' You rarely get to choose your last words.

A figure in black walking into the room, pushing the door shut behind him. Frank notices that he already has his gloves on. A pro then, leave nothing to the last moment. A glance at the face. Recognition. His first feeling is not of relief, it's of betrayal. Calum must be working for Shug. Typical really, you should never trust anyone in this business. Such a quiet boy. Says little because he doesn't want to give anything away. Those are the ones you can never trust. He's feeling a sense of personal failure too. Frank recommended Calum to Jamieson. Now Calum's putting his hand in his coat pocket. Scott and Clueless are still looking down at Frank – they haven't seen what's about to happen. Now the relief's washing over Frank. He's worked it out. Frank's looking at Clueless, and now he's smiling back.

Calum's quick. As soon as he's closed the door behind him he's reaching into his pocket for the gun. Not waiting for a moment to present itself, just going for it. Up against the clock. Shug's gunman can't be far away. Raising the gun and pointing it at Scott. Scott's turning, looking at Calum, but he doesn't have time to look surprised before Calum pulls the trigger. It sounds so loud in the cramped corridor. It always shocks, the bang of a gun; doesn't matter how used to it you are. There's a red explosion from Scott, specks of blood hitting the walls on either side, much more to the left than the right, hitting Calum and Frank. Not much, but enough. They'll have to destroy everything they're wearing. Scott's falling backwards; Frank can hear the thump of his head hitting the floor, a dead weight. His gun's fallen beside him.

Calum isn't stopping. There isn't time for hesitation. You hesitate and someone else might not. That's the end of you. Clueless has backed away, towards the kitchen door. There's a puzzled look on his face.

'No,' he's saying quietly, 'it's him, not us.' He's saying it with a bemused sort of smile on his face, like this should be obvious to the gunman. He can't work out what's happening to him. Not under all this pressure. Clueless to the last. Calum's walking right up beside him – Clueless just standing there and watching. Letting the gunman do what he wants, because that's all you can do with a gunman. Clueless looks like he's about to start crying. Calum's pressing the gun against the side of the boy's head, funny sort of angle. Clueless is closing his eyes as tight as he can. He understands now.

Frank's slowly getting back to his feet. He's a little unsteady; too long sitting in the same position. He's trying hard not to look feeble. Not that it matters, Calum's not even looking at him; he's still wrapped up in finishing his job. He's a good pro, this one. Walking over to Scott and reaching down with the gun. He's wrapping Scott's left hand around the gun, getting prints on it. Now the right, trying to make it hold the weapon in a natural position. Pressing the fingers down all over the gun, making it look like he handled it regularly. Now over to Clueless. Taking his time, pressing both hands against the gun again. Not so often this time. People are more likely to believe it was Scott's gun than his dippy mate's. Scott's prints should be more prevalent. Now trying to get a partial print onto the trigger. Holding the gun in Clueless's right hand, lifting the hand slightly off the ground. Then letting it drop. The gun's hitting the floor, falling out of his hand, just beside Clueless. It looks natural.

Now Calum's looking at Frank. Two men and two dead men, in a narrow corridor. Unpleasantly cramped, and not likely to get any more pleasant. Many people let go of their bowels when they're shot. Most gunmen prefer not to hang around long enough to catch a whiff.

'Take your gun with you,' Calum's saying to him, all matter-of-fact about it. 'Have you got your balaclava with you?'

'Yes,' Frank sighs as he straightens from picking up his

gun from beside Scott. He's pulling the balaclava from his pocket and looking at the two bodies. 'You think that'll fool them?' he's asking. He's never been much of a fan of clever set-ups; the police tend to see through it eventually. Making it look like a murder-suicide is fine, but will it hold?

Calum's shrugging. 'It'll slow them down a little. Buy us time to get rid of anything that needs getting rid of. Come on, Shug's man will be here any minute.'

That's a bloody shock. Frank had been trying to work out how this all came about. He thought Calum was double-crossing Shug on Jamieson's behalf. Now it turns out Shug does have another man, and he's on his way. Which means this was a rescue mission. That's a shock, too. All this risk to rescue him; he can't help but be embarrassed. It could still turn into an enormous disaster. As they're stepping out of the flat, all in black and wearing their balaclavas, Frank's feeling more annoyed with Calum. Why waste all that time with the prints? It's the one criticism of him. He takes things way too slow, always has. Someone in the building must have heard the gunshots. Two separate shots to hear: harder to dismiss as a random bang. They should be out by now. Someone must have called the police. Surely. Maybe not the person at the other end of the corridor, but there are three flats occupied on the floor below. One right underneath.

Pressing the button on the lift. The doors opening,

nobody there. Inside and down to the ground floor, both standing in silence. The doors open to an empty foyer. Out into the cold night, walking briskly to the car Frank borrowed for the night. Relief, again.

17

Frank's driving. Calum's sitting in the passenger seat of the car, watching the block of flats get smaller behind them. There are no more lights on now than when he arrived. That's something to be positive about. No great commotion in the building after the shooting. A glance at the clock in the car: fourteen minutes past two.

They're both silent. Some people chatter, some say nothing. They both fall into the nothing category. Most professionals do. Chatter is a comfort blanket for nervous amateurs. There's little for either of them to say. Plenty of talking to come for both of them, they know it, but not with each other. For now, it's nice to have a little quiet. Frank hasn't even said where they're going. Going to switch back to his normal car, of course, but that could be anywhere. Calum trusts him to get them there.

They're onto an industrial estate now. There are vehicles all around them – these are working companies. Seems an odd place to switch cars; likely to be security cameras around. It's not a place Calum would have used.

'Jamieson owns a couple of these units,' Frank's saying, guessing Calum's thoughts. 'He handles security round here.

It's a safe place to use. That's why I used it,' he goes on, without feeling the need to add that this is his first job back. Easy job, every best precaution. Breaking him back in gently. Every precaution, every benefit, and it ends like this. He's pulling up beside his own nondescript Vauxhall Astra. They're both out of the work car, getting into Frank's. This feels like a moment of safety, shedding the skin they escaped in.

'Where to?' Frank's asking.

'The club. My car's there.'

'Huh,' Frank's saying, but saying no more. You don't leave your car outside your employer's place of work when you're going on a job. It's sloppy and amateurish. He would say something, but he knows why Calum had to do it. It was all to save him. Every mistake any other person made on this night is his responsibility. They were all compensating for him, and they'll all be talking about it from now on. Some fuck-ups cast a shadow you can never shake off. Good men. Talented people. One mistake and they're forever tainted. Everybody treats you differently, because you forced them to make mistakes. They don't forgive that, no matter what they say. He's driving carefully, his instincts guiding him well. You never lose those.

The adrenalin's wearing off for Calum; he's starting to feel his hand now. The gloves are uncomfortable, too. Frank's taken his off; they're in his car now, after all. Calum's keeping his on. He doesn't remember ever being in Frank's car before now; his prints shouldn't be here. If you can avoid putting your prints in the car of another gunman, then you avoid it. If you can avoid putting them anywhere near a crime or a criminal, then you do. The silence is starting to grate. It feels like there's something they need to discuss. They're coming up towards the club now; it's along the street on their right. Frank's pulling up along from the entrance. He knows he's just out of view of the security cameras. Instinct.

'Listen, Calum,' he's saying. 'You did a great job tonight, did me a real turn. I owe you. If I can ever repay the favour, I will.'

Calum's smiling, trying to take the awkwardness out of it. This is embarrassing for both of them. 'I hope you never have to.'

Frank's nodding now. 'So do I. Still, this business, you never know. Thanks.' Hard words to say. So hard it almost sounds like he doesn't mean it.

'Forget about it,' Calum's saying, and he's opening the door to get out. As he steps onto the pavement after closing the door, Frank pulls away. Calum's walking along to his car, and he knows things have changed. It's a horrible thing, very sudden, but a reality. This night has changed everything for a number of people, him included.

He'll never look at Frank the same way again. He was always the gnarled old veteran, the man who had seen and done it all. Done it all to a better standard than anyone else.

The man who had killed more people in the city, and got away with it, than anyone else. A master of the trade. He's still that person. He's also now the person who was slumped in a corridor with two lousy peddlers standing over him. They said Scott was one to watch, a talent who was rising fast, but he let Calum in without even checking his ID. He can't have been that sharp. The other one was just a good old-fashioned moron. And they still got the better of Frank. Once you've looked down on a guy like that, it's hard to look up to him again. It's not as if Calum and Frank were ever especially close. They were never master and apprentice. Still, Calum liked and respected him more than any other gunman he'd ever met. He still likes him, but a good deal of the respect has been left behind in Tommy Scott's corridor.

He's dropping into his own car now, and pulling the gloves off with relief. Trying to clench his left hand, knowing that the discomfort will pass. How much longer is it going to be like this? Now he's looking in the mirror, checking for specks of other people's blood on his face. He can't see any. He's starting the car. There won't be anyone in the club now. Jamieson and Young will have left soon after Calum and Kenny. They wouldn't want to be there any longer than necessary. He's pulling away and driving back home, thinking about his clothes. Thinking about Emma and his clothes. She's back in his world, now that he's done the job. There's bound to be specks of blood on them. He's going to have to get rid of his coat and his trousers, his shoes too. He'll do it tomorrow, when she's gone to lectures. In the meantime he's going to have to treat them like he would normal clothes. Breaking habits, just to keep her around.

He's parking in what's becoming his usual spot, just a little way along from the front door. It's nice to start forming habits in your new home. He's making his way up to his flat. Still not entirely safe. Could be a bunch of cops waiting for him at the top of the stairs. They could be in the flat, talking to Emma right now. He'd left his keys in the car while he was doing the job; now he's taking his door key out of his pocket and putting it in the lock. There's always a moment of nerves returning from a job. Who could be in there? There are worse people than the police. People like to get their revenge quickly, no matter what the common serving suggestion may be. It's worse now. No matter who else might be in there, Emma definitely will be. He has to face her. Remember the lie, try to make it sound convincing, don't push it too far. The door's open, the flat's in darkness. He's switching on a light. Nothing lurking. A little relief.

There's one more thing he needs to do before he goes back to bed. Another break with common sense. Jamieson asked, so he has to do it. If the boss asks you to do it, then you do, regardless of how stupid it is. He left his mobile on the kitchen table when he went out. Hopefully Emma didn't get up and see it. Not likely, she's a sound sleeper. He's picking it up, looking for Jamieson's number. He wanted a yes or no answer to the question: Has Frank been rescued? Calum's texting the word 'yes' and nothing else into the message. It's a stupid breach of standards. A cop could easily find out that he texted Peter Jamieson at twenty to three in the morning. How would he explain that one?

Too many breaches of etiquette throughout this job. Too many ways for it all to go wrong. It's hard to believe that Jamieson would have sent him in there to save anyone else. Probably only Frank has earned the right to be rescued. God knows, they wouldn't have sent Frank in for him. The more he thinks about it, the more he thinks they should have left Frank to his fate. He's sent the text message. He's taking off his coat, hanging it in the hall with the others. He's pulling the coat next to it across a little. Shoes off, pushing them halfway under the radiator, out of sight, for the same reason. Normally he'd strip off and put all the clothes in a bag. Not tonight. Not with Emma there. She complicates everything.

He's walking into the bedroom, silent in his socks. He's pulled his trousers and top off, and now he's pulling his socks off, sitting on the side of the bed.

'How's your brother?' a slightly muffled-sounding voice is asking from the other side of the bed. She's facing the other way, half-asleep.

'Drunk and apologetic,' Calum's saying, throwing his socks onto a chair and getting in under the duvet. Say as little as you can get away with. Loading it with detail only makes it sound less convincing, more rehearsed.

'He didn't give you any bother?'

'Bother? No, course not.'

'Huh.' And that's all she's saying. Enough to tell him that she knows he wasn't picking up his brother. Calum's not going to sleep tonight.

18

Shaun Hutton's pulling up outside the tower block. What an ugly-looking building it is. Ugly-looking area. It says two twenty on the clock in the car he's using. Almost exactly an hour since Shug called him. Not so long that he can't justify the time taken; long enough to keep his word to John Young. Timing's important to any gunman.

No activity around the building, which is a good thing. If Young got a man to the scene first, he might be in there now. If he's been and gone, then the police might not be far away. Don't get caught at the scene with a gun in your pocket. Whatever else happens, don't get caught at the scene by the police. He's moving fast, into the building and along to the lifts. If Young's man hasn't been yet, then he might be here soon. Could be a nasty encounter. Get this done quick. No sign of anyone yet. Going up, not sure what he's going to find ahead of him. Uncertainty is always an enemy. The lift's opening and he's stepping out into an empty corridor.

There's no sign from the corridor of anything having happened. No doors open, nobody gathering round a doorway to gawp at a bloody body. He's standing at the door to Scott's flat, listening. No sounds coming from within. If he could hear Jamieson's man in there, then he'd happily leave him to it. Shug's not paying quite enough for him to barge in and take on someone else's man. No sound from inside. He's knocking on the door. Waiting; still no response. Knocking again, louder this time. Don't wake the neighbours. He's starting to get impatient. He's starting to realize he's probably not the first, or even second, armed man to turn up at this flat tonight. He's had his gloves on since he picked up the car, so he has no qualms about handling the letter box. He's lifting it up, peeking inside.

Jamieson's man left the dim light on in the corridor when he made his escape. The two bodies are easy to see. Hutton doesn't know which is which – just two nondescript young men. One of them is close to the door, slumped sideways against the wall. There's blood visible on the wall beside him, although Hutton can't see how high up it goes. There could be a lot more, he knows, if the boy was standing when the gunman shot him. The other body's further away, lying on his back by the door at the other end of the corridor. He can't see the wound from here, but he can see a gun lying by the body's right hand. The gunman left a weapon behind. Interesting. Playing games with the police. Dangerous game to play. He doesn't know which body belongs to which person, but he knows neither of them belongs to Frank MacLeod. Both look much too young for that.

He's walking back to the lift. Moving more quickly now.

There have been at least two gunshots, a real chance the police are close. Hutton can't help but smile to himself. They actually sent someone to rescue old Frank. Or maybe Frank found his own way out. That would be impressive, would prove the old boy still has sparkle. Either way, Shug's going to be pissed, and Hutton's going to have to handle this the right way. First priority is to get some distance between him and the building. He's in the lift and making his way down. Right now there's only the rumble of the old lift, then the ping and the sliding doors. As soon as they've shut behind him, it's silence. No sirens, no cars pulling up outside the building. He's out and across to the car. There isn't a person stirring in the world around him.

Hutton's long clear of the building now; he's been driving for more than ten minutes. The cops aren't going to surround him any more; he can relax. Time to play a part. He's thinking about Shug, what his reaction's going to be. You never know with an inexperienced boss. They'll often look for someone to blame. Anyone other than themselves. They like others to see them lash out, to punish people they think have let them down. There are two dead guys lying in a grotty flat, whom Hutton will make sure take more than their fair share of the blame. He's driving back to his own car, climbing into it and getting back to his house. Shug must think the job's been done by now. Nice and simple. Kill an old man, weaken Peter Jamieson. This isn't going to be the phone call he's expecting.

'Hi, Shug, it's me. I wake you?'

'No, go on.' He sounds guarded already. His gunman shouldn't be calling him straight after doing a job. It was Hutton who told him so.

'Look, I don't know what the hell's going on, but you have two dead bodies and no old man. I got there; there was no answer at the door. I looked in the letter box. Two dead guys in the corridor. Young guys. I'm guessing your guys. They ain't Frank MacLeod anyway. He was nowhere. Must've got out. You got a problem.'

There's silence on the other end. Shug's nice and smiley, but he can be tough when he wants to be. Wouldn't be here otherwise. 'So they're both dead?'

'Looks a hell of a lot like it.'

Shug hasn't said much, he's thinking it all through. Hutton's waiting, not going to press him.

'What's your opinion?' Shug's asking him. His tone is cold. It's as if he's telling him that he's not beyond suspicion himself. Nobody should be. Fair enough.

'I don't know,' Hutton's saying with a sigh. 'There was a gun still in there. Maybe Frank got the better of them. Unlikely, but not impossible. Not like your boys were the best in the business. Maybe he got a message out. Could have been a set-up from the start, but I doubt it, too much risk. My best guess? One of your men made a call or two to brag about their capture. Word got out. Peter Jamieson or one of his men found out and went straight round there. They did it in a hurry, left a gun behind. Wouldn't be a surprise if the police find something interesting there. You do a job in a hurry, you make mistakes.'

More silence. Hutton can almost hear the wheels turning. 'That would sound most likely,' Shug's saying now.

Hutton needs to go on the offensive, time it right. 'Listen to me, Shug. You need to sort out who you have working for you. I went round there, put myself in the middle of it. I must have just missed the shooting. I mean, seriously, by a couple of fucking minutes. I get there after a shooting and the bloody cops could be there. I was lucky I didn't walk into the middle of a dozen fucking detectives. Think about that. I turn up in that shit-storm with a gun in my pocket and I'm looking at twenty years, minimum. Seriously, I need to know you have reliable people working for you. I need to know that when I go to a job, you have good people there. I don't know these kids, but they fucked up bad. Could've taken me down with them. Could've ended up taking you down too.'

'I understand that,' Shug's saying. There's sharpness in that voice. Sounds a little bitter, defensive. 'You're right; you shouldn't have been put in that position. I'll speak to you soon.'

Shug hangs up first. Hutton's standing in his living room, in the darkness. He's done his work for the night. Shug's new, but he's a smart one. People come into the business all the time, thinking they can get rich quick. People like Shug. They have legitimate money behind them, or they have some connection to the business that they think gives them a chance. Most don't last. Some only do it because they're in trouble. Get rich quick and get out. Doesn't work that way. Most will lose more than they make.

Shug might be different. He's not desperate, for a start. He seems to understand the business. He took on Peter Jamieson, and he hasn't lost yet. That makes him dangerous. It takes a dangerous man to survive a battle with Jamieson this long. He may not win in the end, but he can cause a lot of damage before he departs. Damage to the people he thinks are against him. Hutton's thinking about that as he undresses for bed.

19

'I said to the other guy a wee minute ago. I heard them last night, thumping about. Not the first time. He's not a bad lad, but sometimes they make a bit of a racket, so they do. Woke me up last night, so it did. It stopped, though, so I left it. Came up this morning to have a word. Not the worst kid, that boy. You can talk to him – not like some of them. Some of them treat you like crap. Real bastards. It's the parents. Having them too young. So I come up. I knock on the door. Nothing. I think, uh-huh, what's going on here? So I looked in the letter box. Wouldn't normally, you understand. I was concerned. That's when I saw them. Then I called your lot.'

Your lot. Michael Fisher's been a cop for twenty-three years; he loathes the dismissive description of the police. He'll never get used to it now. So many people who can't accept that the police are on their side. He's long since decided to get on with helping people, whether they like it or not.

He got the call less than half an hour ago. In his house, all alone, getting ready for work. Possible murder-suicide, possible double murder. Two young men, found in the flat belonging to one of them. He's there now because one of them has possible links to organized crime. Thomas Scott was once reported for dealing, but was only charged with possession. Even that charge went nowhere; he got away with a few hours' community service that he probably never carried out. The other dead man, Andrew McClure, doesn't seem to have any record. Only known as a friend of Scott's. If they were friends, then McClure was almost certainly involved in the same life as Scott.

Fisher came straight here from home. He found a few cops here ahead of him, some plods and a couple of detectives. The scene wasn't under control yet – people wandering around the corridor and using the lifts. That changed drastically two minutes after his angry arrival.

After a glance at the bodies, he had sought out the man living downstairs. He's the one who reported it, the closest thing they have to a witness. The only one who seems to have anything to say for himself.

'This noise they were making, can you describe it?' Fisher's asking him now.

'Describe it? It was noise. Thumping about. Could have been music or anything, I don't know – the things that pass for music. It was noise, so it was. I heard it, I was going to say something, but it stopped. I came up this morning to have a word. That's it.'

It's obvious to Fisher what's happened. The man in the flat below heard the gunshots. He would have known they were gunshots. He thought about doing something, but didn't want to get involved. Not yet, anyway. Wait until the danger has passed. Next morning he comes up to nosy about, sees the bodies. He calls the police and swears that he heard nothing sinister, just noise. He's trying to keep himself out of it.

Fisher's scowling at him now. Hard to respect someone who stands in the way of an investigation just because being a witness is inconvenient. Two men are dead.

'So this noise. It was loud enough for you to notice. How long did it last?'

The man's puffing out his cheeks. Colin Thomson, he introduced himself as, pointing out the lack of a p in his surname. Seems to matter to him. He liked being the centre of attention, until the questions got tough.

'I don't know,' Thomson's saying now. 'Could've been for a short while. Maybe not. I noticed it once or twice, that's all. Woke me up, you see, so it might have been going on a while before it woke me up, I don't know. Bothered me, is all. Inconsiderate. I went up this morning to tell him so. I'm not young any more, and my health hasn't been good, you see.' He's pausing for a few seconds, waiting for an expression of sympathy that isn't coming. 'They're saying his wee mate killed him and then himself. Is that right?'

Fisher's extricated himself from the pointless interview and gone back upstairs. Just standing in the doorway, looking at the two bodies, trying to take it all in. Work out the movements of a killer. If it was the boy with the gun beside him, then work out his movements. The first plods there reported it as a probable murder followed by suicide. It looked like two mates turned on each other. An argument over some stupid thing. There's a gun in the flat. McClure pulls it out, waves it around. Scott says something provocative and McClure fires. Seeing that he's killed his friend, and knowing he's not capable of getting off with it, he turns the gun on himself. That's the story the scene tells. The story it's supposed to tell. It could be telling the truth. He'll wait on the toxicology reports, to see if drugs were involved. If they were, then he might believe it. Otherwise, he'll retain a healthy scepticism. When someone in that business dies, there are always other suspects worth looking at.

Fisher wants to get into the flat, have a good rummage around, but the forensic team is still on its way. Let them do their work, then have a free run at it. He's seeing a plod he recognizes coming along the corridor. Higgins, a good young cop, lot of potential. In his mid-twenties now, been in the force a few years. He's good enough to make progress, Fisher's decided. Might push to get him out of uniform soon, make better use of him.

'Any news?' Fisher's asking the younger man.

'We've woken most of the building – anyone who's likely to have heard or seen anything.' Higgins is shrugging. 'Not many of them. Most of these flats are empty now. Fellow down the corridor says he didn't hear anything. Neither did anyone else, apparently. Not sure how much I believe them; I think they just want to avoid bother. Just the guy downstairs who'll admit to hearing anything. Have you spoken to him?'

'Yeah,' Fisher's nodding, 'I had a word.'

Everyone goes deaf. Two gunshots at least. If the weapon on the floor is the killer, then it's a standard handgun, no silencer. It's not as if the walls in this damp-ridden dump are terribly thick. They must have heard it. That bastard downstairs knew exactly what it was. He didn't report it until morning to make sure all danger had passed before he got involved. Other people get to pretend they heard nothing at all. It's not just a fear of giving evidence against a killer. People fear being mixed up in organized crime, they fear that they'll be forced to shut up. Fair enough. There have been plenty of cases where criminals have targeted witnesses; Fisher doesn't blame them for their fear. Others just aren't willing to get involved in any court case. Not just with organized crime, but with any case. They won't suffer inconvenience for the sake of justice.

'I want to find out everything there is to know about this pair,' Fisher's saying to Higgins. 'I want to know who they were working with, if anyone. We know Scott was selling on the street. He has to have been getting his supply from some-where. Let's try to find out if there was a puppet-master behind these idiots. Find out who else was in their circle of friends, see if there's anyone with more than a dozen brain cells. Find out about their families, any interesting connections.'

'Yes, sir,' Higgins is saying, and wandering off. He's a good cop, but he's not likely to find out much by himself.

Where the hell is that forensics team? Fisher wants in there and he can't get past the body until forensics have worked their magic. A crappy little flat in a grotty tower block is a horrible place to have to do his job anyway.

20

In normal circumstances you wouldn't contact the person who hired you for a job for days, maybe weeks, afterwards. It's common sense to keep your distance. Those first few days are the days when the police are most likely to be watching you and your employer. These, evidently, aren't normal circumstances. John Young called him up about twenty minutes ago, asked to meet him in a cafe halfway across the city. Awkward location. A long way from anyone who might be interested in them. Calum doesn't go to the west end often – a little out of his price range. Thankfully, Emma had left before Young called. He's now packing last night's clothing into a carrier bag, and he'll dump it in a random bin on his way. It's the sort of thing he might have done last night, but Emma prevented that.

He's in the car, trying to find somewhere to park that's even remotely close to the cafe. He managed to dump the bag in a big green industrial bin that was lurking on a pavement, waiting for a bin man. Now his thoughts are with Young. Another dip in standards. They ought to be keeping their distance, at least for another week. A double killing and he wants to hang out and get a coffee. Obviously he wants a debrief, but he should be more patient. He should be more careful. This isn't like Young. Jamieson's hand is pulling the strings here. Young would wait, Calum's sure. He's not one for emotion. No matter how important Frank might be to him, he would take the time to do things properly.

He has to walk two streets to find the cafe. Have a cup of coffee with a man you don't much like. There's something about Peter Jamieson that makes him almost likeable. His admirable bullishness, maybe. The who-gives-a-shit nature that he lets you see. Most of it's bluff, but it makes him approachable. Young's not. He's a schemer. Calum's wondered for a while about the night he killed Glen Davidson. How much did Young know beforehand? Calum told Frank that Davidson was sniffing around. He's sure Frank told Young. He hasn't asked, because you don't ask questions, but he's sure. Young knew Shug was lining Calum up for a hit, and did nothing. He left him exposed when he could have moved him. The little schemer. Calum can see him sitting at a small table in a corner at the back of the cafe as he's opening the door. Young's glancing towards him and then looking away.

It smells lovely, this cosy little place full of real wood and broadsheet newspapers. There are a lot of people wearing expensive glasses, sipping coffee that's more expensive than Calum finds acceptable. Young's nodding to him to sit down. They're only just out of range of the nearest drinkers. The waitress is hovering. Calum's ordering something unpro-nounceable.

'I like coming here,' Young's saying, once she disappears, 'no chance of running into other people in the business.' He's pausing. 'Their little blow-up dolls flutter in and out now and again, thinking it makes them classy.' He's saying it with a knowing smile, like he knows Calum has a girlfriend now. He almost certainly does know. Knows who she is. Knows she's not the usual hanger-on. Calum's saying nothing. Young's happy knowing what he knows; Calum's not going to add to it.

The waitress has put a suspiciously small cup in front of Calum and moved on to another table. He's frowning at it. It's obvious he doesn't eat out much. He's not the kind of person who finds comfort in the company of other people. Young's smiling, but he's here for business, and he needs to do it quickly.

'You did one hell of a job last night,' he's saying, almost in a whisper. 'Tell me what I need to know.'

Calum's puffing out his cheeks. 'I got there, knocked on the door. It was Scott who answered. Let me in. He obviously didn't know who to expect. Did it quick. Him, then his mate. His mate I did side-on, make it look like suicide. Left the gun there. We left. That's about it.'

Young's not reacting. Takes years of practice to learn not

to react. Young's never killed anyone. Better to have people like Calum, so cold and detached, who can do that for you. They seem to have no problem with emotional baggage, with nerves. Lucky for them.

'And how was Frank?'

Calum's shrugging. 'He was on the floor. Wasn't much he could do. Scott had his gun.'

'Was he calm?'

'Yeah,' Calum's saying, 'I would say so.'

It's taken a few seconds for Calum to realize what a big conversation this is. This isn't just catching up on the interesting events of last night. This is Jamieson and Young trying to work out if they can trust Frank with a job again. This is his future. They want to know if Frank bottled it. They want to know if his health caused the botch. And that's putting Calum under pressure. What he says will have a big impact. It'll impact on Frank's future, of course, but on his own as well. If Frank's gone, then that's a lot more work for Calum. He becomes Jamieson's only gunman. Even if Jamieson brings in someone else, which he eventually will, Calum will now be senior man. The first option on every job. So it serves him to help Frank along here, to try to keep him in the game. He doesn't want Frank's share of the work. He doesn't even want his own.

'How did it happen?' Young's asking him. 'I haven't spoken to Frank.' Letting Calum know that his side of the story comes first. His doesn't have to tally with Frank's; Frank's has to tally with his.

'Seems like he turned up and they were waiting for him. They must have found out he was after them.'

'A leak?' Young's asking. There's real concern in that voice now. If it was down to a leak, then Frank would be in the clear and someone else would be clinging to his life by a thread. Anyone who leaked that sort of information from the organization would be a dead man.

'Don't know. How many people knew about the hit? Could've been a leak, but if you played it close to your chest, then I doubt it. Could've been that someone spotted Frank watching them, when he was prepping the job.'

It had to be said. It's by far the most likely reason they got the jump on Frank. It puts all the pressure back onto Frank, though. It's his responsibility to scout a target without the target finding out.

'Once they knew he was after them, he walked into a set-up. It happens, I suppose. Hell of a place to do a job anyway, a block of flats like that. Hate them. They knocked him down, but they didn't have it in them to kill him. When I got there, he was still where they'd dragged him, just inside the door. He was handling it well, I thought. He was cool about it. Kept it quiet. Let me get on with what I had to do. We got down to the car fine. We switched back to his car and he dropped me off at the club.'

Young's nodding along, but there's no expression. Not enough detail in the face for Calum to know what he's thinking. That'll be deliberate too. Well practised.

They've fallen silent. When they're not talking work, they're not talking anything. There's no real relationship there. Something else that'll change if Frank's not around any more. It'll have to. Jamieson will try to pull him closer. There are so many reasons to talk Frank up right now. One good reason not to. Frank botched the job. He shouldn't have given them any chance to spot him. If he's making sloppy mistakes, then he's a danger not just to himself, but to all of them. Calum will look like a liar if he talks Frank up now.

'You think Frank told them anything?' Young's asking.

'About the business? Nah,' Calum's saying, with honest confidence. 'He wasn't bawling or anything, he was calm. He won't have told them a thing. Even if he did, they're not going to tell anyone now. But I'm sure he didn't.'

He's left Young in the cafe, ordering another coffee. Calum's back at his car now, heading home. He should never have left. Lie low after a job. Keep to a normal routine. Do nothing that stands out. Driving halfway across the city for a ten-minute coffee with John Young stands out. Anyone watching him now knows that he's up to something unusual. If he was ambitious, then he could have destroyed Frank today. Ended his career. If he liked Frank less, then he could at least have damaged him. Instead, he's trying to prop up someone who blundered. Dress it up how you like, Frank can't be trusted with a job. There's no escaping that.

He's pulling up beside his flat. It's all in Jamieson's hands now. Calum will have nothing more to do with this.

21

Young didn't drink that second coffee. It's not like he comes here for the coffee anyway. It's for the escape. He waited for Calum to leave and then made his own way out. Back to the club. Back to Jamieson. Sitting behind his desk, looking miserable. He's been in the office all morning. Not in the mood to see anyone. Not in the mood to talk to people. He's been waiting for Young to come back with news. It's a horrible thing, being the top man and not being able to do things for yourself because of it. The more successful he is, the less it's safe for him to be seen doing. He's giving Young a grim look as he walks across to his usual place on the couch.

'You speak to the boy?' The boy. Calum's twenty-nine, nearly thirty. They've become so used to thinking of gunmen as being Frank. Old men, gnarled veterans of many a battle.

'I spoke to him,' Young's nodding.

He's gone through the conversation, telling Jamieson everything Calum had to say. Almost word for word. He might as well have recorded it. There wasn't much to remember. Jamieson's listened intently, hasn't said a single word throughout. Not even a nod of approval. Listening, building up a picture of events. Trying to picture everything that happened last night.

'He was a long time in that flat with that pair,' he's saying, now that Young's finished.

'He was.'

'The boy did well.'

'He did,' Young's agreeing.

Jamieson's tone is miserable. Casting doubt on Frank. Complimenting Calum. It sounds like he's trying to persuade himself that Frank's time has passed.

Jamieson's taken a bottle of whiskey from the cabinet behind his desk. He hasn't switched on the two TVs on top of the cabinet today. That's unlike him, but this requires his full attention. He's pouring out a glass. Kenny can drive him home. He doesn't offer one to Young; he wouldn't accept it anyway. Not much of a drinker. Not in the daytime anyway.

'I wish we knew for certain what went wrong,' he's saying, sitting back at the desk. 'If there was a leak . . .'

'Highly unlikely,' Young's saying. 'Only you, me and Frank knew. We kept it close, nobody could have guessed. I didn't tell anyone. I assume you didn't. Frank's a pro; he wouldn't have breathed a word. He was spotted.'

'Aye. I guess he was.' A gunman who gets spotted prepping a job isn't much of a gunman. It's a fundamental part of the job. You get in and out without raising any alarms. The killing is supposed to be the easy part.

'Your opinion,' Jamieson's saying. 'Honest-to-God opinion.' He's saying it with trepidation. He has a good idea where this conversation is going to go now. He needs to hear the words.

'I . . .' Young starts, but now he's stopping. He's trying to think of the right way to put it. He can usually be as blunt as he wants with Jamieson. They're normally talking about people who don't matter much to either of them. Frank's different. Frank's earned the right to respect. 'I think maybe we still see Frank as he was when we first started working with him. He's not that guy any more. He's out for months, getting a hip replaced. Now, first job back, and this happens. I trust Frank. With my life. I'm just not sure we can rely on him for a job any more. I know he gives his best, but now maybe that's not enough. Whatever you do with Frank, last night proved that Calum's the best gunman we've got.'

'Fuck's sake!' Jamieson's whispering. He's annoyed because he agrees. Three months ago and Frank was the best gunman in the city. He had been convinced of that. Had been since the day he hired him. Now he can't trust him to do a simple job. This has to be down to the hip replacement. He's convinced it was the recovery time. Frank resting up, out of the business altogether. Not able to come and hang around the club, keep in touch. Sitting with his feet up instead. Then he sent him out to Spain for a couple of weeks' holiday in his little villa. Frank switched off. Now he can't switch back on.

Tempting to give him another job. Get him back in the saddle. It might give him a chance to redeem himself, get back to being the Frank MacLeod he was. It also might just get him killed. He's too much of a friend to take a risk like that.

Jamieson's thumping the table with a flat palm. Decision made, stick to it, get on with life. That's how he works. Decisive. Determined. Committed to his judgement.

'I'm going to have to speak to Frank,' he's saying. 'Maybe give it a few days first. I'll see if there's something else he can do. I won't just throw all that experience overboard.'

'There's nothing else he'll want to do,' Young's saying. Warning: you could only offend a man like Frank with the offer of a lesser role. He's a gunman. Nothing else. If he accepts, it'll only be because he, in turn, is scared of offending Jamieson.

'I'll talk to him, see what he says. You,' he's saying to Young, 'need to keep your ear to the ground. The boy still isn't properly committed to us. He's good, but I don't trust him yet. I won't have him as our only option. Find another one. A good one. A trustworthy one. Someone young would be preferable. Someone from within would be ideal.'

He always does this. He always gives Young an unobtainable target and sends him out to find it. If they had someone in the organization who met all those criteria, Young would have identified him by now. To be fair to him, he doesn't bitch if Young falls short. Jamieson knows he asks a lot, and is generally satisfied with how close to the mark Young gets. There are plenty of ambitious young men around. Never a shortage there. How many of them have the talent to back it up? A tiny minority. You have to find the one person who has what it takes. Sometimes that person belongs to someone else. You have to try to persuade them to cross over. It's possible. A lot of people are attracted to working for Jamieson. It's a well-run organization. An organization that rewards talent. People like that. They trust you more than they would a family business. Nobody wants to work for a firm where you have to be a family member to have a real chance of climbing the ladder.

Young's out of the office, into the city. He always has people to meet. Make sure the business is ticking along nicely. Meet contacts, get information. Keep your ear to the ground – that's what Jamieson said. But he's going to tell Frank within the week. Which means they'll be relying on Calum alone from then on. A good guy to rely on. Keeps doing well under pressure. Young has never worked with a gunman who's had two absolute stinkers in succession and handled them so well. He's a boy with talent. Jamieson's right, though. Calum's still not committed to them. Young told George to get closer to him. He did. He told George to get Calum settled down. He did. Got him a girlfriend, which was going too far. Still hasn't settled him – not the way they want.

He's still reluctant to be a part of what they're doing. He's still a man who could walk away and leave them exposed.

Jamieson isn't thinking about Calum. He's not thinking about Young, either. He's tapping the top of the desk with his forefinger. Telling himself he's being stupid. He's had to ditch people he liked before. It happens a lot in this business. You keep the ones you need, not the ones you like. It's not as if Frank's a father figure. He's overreacting. He's getting emotional about the job. That's just damned unprofessional. You don't need to like the people who work for you. You need to be able to trust them. That's about it. Trust, maybe a little respect. Anything else is a bonus.

He got used to having Frank there. Likeable, trustworthy and utterly professional Frank. Too used to it. Complacent. Maybe it's because Frank was a gunman. Such an important job. A job that requires so much trust. You get someone you trust and you cling to them. He didn't even want to think about replacing Frank. You can replace an importer, or a dealer, even someone good at counterfeits. Replacing a gunman is hard and dangerous. He needs a pro. The only one he's met and liked was Frank.

22

Calum has his laptop out. Sitting at the kitchen table, mindlessly browsing a few sites before he goes to the one he really wants. Local newspaper website. Looking for any mention of last night's work. People must know by now. He uses the *Evening Times* website every day; there'll be nothing unusual about it being in his browser history. It's the third story on the main page. Just a headline with a link to the story. Two men found dead in flat, police not looking for anyone else. He'd love to click on the article, see what detail they go into. He won't, though. He's clicking on the sports tab instead. His browser history will tell them nothing. The headline says enough. People know, they're not looking for anyone else. So they believe it. Looks like they bought the little trick he played. But you don't take it for granted. The police play tricks, too.

They want him to be complacent. They'll be desperate for him to do something stupid because of that headline. Not that they know it's him. The killer. They want the killer to do something stupid, whoever he may be. Break routine. Come out into the open. Make their job easy for them. They want him to help them avoid a long and difficult investigation.

It's a paranoid instinct. Has to be. You have to believe that they're all out to get you, because they are. Be paranoid about everything and everyone. See a story in the papers that says the police aren't looking for anyone. Assume it's a lie. Assume that the story was written with you in mind. Takes a little bit of egomania to believe that you're the centrepiece of other people's thoughts. How else to avoid detection? Paranoia works.

A quiet afternoon, lounging around. Nothing to do, no one to talk to. It's comfortable. It's the life he's used to, the one he created for himself, and which recent changes washed away. Ten years of building an isolated life, and then it's gone. Working full-time for Jamieson. More work than before, tied to one organization. That alone is enough change. No longer in control of your own path. Throw in Emma, and a life of simplicity has been replaced by more complications than any gunman should carry. It's not just having her there. It's having to create an entire back-story to lie to her with. The life story of a life he didn't lead. When she asks about meeting his friends, what does he say? He doesn't have any. He's spent ten years hiding from the world for the sake of work. There is no circle of friends, just a few acquaintances through work. He has no intention of introducing her to them. It's embarrassing, and it's hard to explain. It's also the reason he slipped up and let her into his life. The loneliness of the gunman.

There's a knock on his door at about half two. Calum's reading a book, *Red Harvest* by Dashiell Hammett, if you care. He's taking his bookmark – one he got free at Waterstones with a book about ten years ago – and he's marking his place to the line. Calm and quiet, but questioning. The day after a job, and there's a knock on your door. A knock you don't expect. That's worth being worried about. When you build a life with nobody else in it, you don't get unexpected knocks at the door. He's walking across to look out through the peep-hole. A recognizable face staring back at him. George Daly. The closest thing he has to a friend. That doesn't mean he trusts him. George is a nice guy, but people who tempt you to let your guard down are the ones you must be most careful with. The day after a job and George turns up on his doorstep. This is odd.

Calum's slowly opening the front door, looking out at George. No visible weapons, but then there wouldn't be. George is no gunman. He's spent years avoiding that end of the business. Chances are he'd be good at it, if he was willing, but he's not. He's never come straight out and said it, but he's not willing to cross the line. He'll beat people, intimidate them into paying their debts to Jamieson, but no more. He's the best muscle Jamieson has, although he's not particularly muscular. He's shorter than Calum, not much broader. That's really not the point. Good muscle is someone who knows how to fight, how much punishment to dish out, how to treat each job. You don't just wade in. Each person has to get only what they deserve. They must know that there's worse to come if they defy Jamieson again. Good muscle is someone who always understands where to draw the line in the sand, and never be tempted beyond it.

'Hey, man, what's up?' George is smiling, waiting for an invite to come inside.

'Uh, not a lot. Yourself?'

'Bugger all. I was bored out of my skull. Thought we might fire up your PS3, kill a few hours, and you can tell me how terrible it is being in a meaningful relationship.'

Calum's smiling despite himself. No meaningful relationship has ever caught up with George. It might not be such a bad idea. Why wouldn't a friend come and visit? Makes it look like normality, which is what you strive for in the wake of a job. Let any witness see the things they would consider unremarkable.

'Come in,' he's saying, holding the door open.

George is on the couch now, wrestling with a controller. He's done his usual routine, complained that there's no beer in, complained about Calum's lack of first-person shooters for the PS3, and then complained that he's having to complain about these things yet again. Calum's watching him lean left and right as he tries to steer a car round corners. He doesn't look like he's come to deliver a warning. The suspicion that Jamieson had sent a friendly face round to deliver some message has fallen away now. Too much time has passed. George wouldn't hang around. He's made no mention of last night. Maybe he really doesn't know. Maybe he came round of his own accord, and would have stayed at home if he'd realized. Either Young sent him to check up on Calum, or Young will be furious with him for going round. It's beginning to look like the latter.

George is gossiping about people in the business. Not the sort of thing Calum's interested in, but you do need to know what's going on. A good gunman listens, and learns all he can about potential future targets. Apparently Jamie Stamford owes the Allen brothers, who are actually cousins (if that matters to you), eighty grand in gambling debts. He's refusing to pay because he reckons they cheated him. Which is bullshit; he just doesn't have the cash. It's a big enough debt to cause friction between the Allens and Stamford's boss, Alex MacArthur. MacArthur's a big player; the Allens are no small fry themselves, so that could lead to trouble. Apparently, one supplier who worked with both has already abandoned the Allens. Profitable trouble, for people like Jamieson.

Also, there's a story that one of Shug Francis's best dealers got himself shot dead by his own best mate last night, which is a stroke of luck. Apparently, the mate shot himself as well, so double your pleasure. Tommy Scott, his name was. George thinks he remembers running into him once, when Scott was working for someone else, but he's not sure. And some idiots smashed up Bobby Peterson's printing shop. He's blaming Marty Jones because they fell out over some deal or other, but Marty denies it. He denies it even more since he found out that Jamieson owns a share of Peterson's business.

And so it goes on. The usual tales – just change some of the names around every week or so. Other people's problems, except for Tommy Scott. George obviously doesn't know. He too believes that McClure shot Scott. Seems like that little story has traction, which is ideal. It gets to a point where people won't even consider an alternative truth.

'Any word from our dear friends in the plod yet?' George is asking. He knows that Glen Davidson called Calum before the stabbing. The police must have found that in Davidson's phone records, hard to believe that they didn't even check. Yet there's been nothing.

'Haven't heard anything from them,' Calum's shrugging, 'but I must be on their radar.' It's a horrible thought. Years spent avoiding any detection. Once they spot you, that's it. They could be watching him, waiting for him to do another job. Like last night's.

It's nearly five when George's phone rings. He's glancing at the screen. 'Nuts, it's Young. Hold on.' He's moving to the kitchen, almost out of earshot. Calum can hear snatches of a conversation. Young's doing most of the talking; George seems to be voicing occasional, if unenthusiastic, agreement.

It takes about thirty seconds. George is walking back in, stuffing his phone into his pocket. 'Well,' he's saying, 'seems like someone finally had the good sense to stick a knife in Neil Fraser. Did a piss-poor job of it, though – nothing much wrong with him. He's in the Western General, not talking to anyone. He's so dumb he couldn't even come up with a lie. I got to go down there and find out who did it. Young's worried it might have been one of Shug's boys.'

Calum's puffing out his cheeks. 'You think so?'

'Nah, not their style. There's better targets than that moron. Probably some trouble he started for himself. Anyway, I better go. I'll see you around.'

Fraser is more traditional muscle working for Jamieson. Muscular, for a start. Intimidating to look at, but as bright as a black hole. Looks like George is going to be under a little pressure himself, having to work out what's happened. That's of no interest to Calum.

Afternoon's disappearing into evening. George has gone, off to tidy up someone else's mess. How often does he have to do that? Every week, probably. It's a once-in-a-lifetime thing for a gunman. Calum will probably never have to do it again. Thank God for that. It's not pleasant work. You can only react to what other people have done. That's no way to do a clean job. Sort of job where you're bound to be caught out eventually. Hard not to worry for George. He's smart, but that might not be enough. If they keep putting him in tough spots, then no amount of smart will save him. He's the best muscle they have, so they're bound to keep putting him in these positions. Calum's suddenly smiling. Things must be changing; he's worried about a friend.

23

Two days now since it happened. Nothing. Not a word. After any other job, he would have thought that was a good thing. Usually you only get contact if something's gone wrong after the event. Something went very wrong during this event. He's been expecting a call from Young. Friendly chat, invite him along to the club. Young would make it sound so casual, no big deal. That's his style. Frank would go along, have a chat with Jamieson and discuss what happened. Talk about the future. What future? They should have called by now. It's only polite. Okay, not professional, but they must know that he's waiting for them. After what happened, Peter must know that Frank's sitting in his house, waiting for that phone to ring.

He's not naive. Been around too long for that. Seen too many good people fall by the wayside to think it couldn't happen to him. They'll have been talking about him. All day yesterday he would have been the subject on their lips. How would you do it? How would Frank investigate a botched hit? Find out all the detail before you talk to the man at the centre of it. That's the smart way. Peter Jamieson, whatever else he is, is a smart man. So they'll have spoken to Calum. A hard boy to second-guess. Another smart one. He doesn't want to work for Jamieson. That plays well for Frank. Calum won't want to be the lone gunman in the organization. Frank's thinking that he should have made more effort to make friends with Calum. He saw the boy's potential a long time ago. It was Frank who recommended him to Jamieson. Told him he was the best young gunman in the city. Told him he was the best freelancer of any age. Get him on board. Frank likes Calum, respects him enough to give him his space. The boy wanted to be left alone, so he left him alone. Now he doesn't feel like he can pick up the phone to him.

It's into the afternoon. Still no call. It's wet out there, but he's bored and he has to stick to normal behaviour. Walk to the pub, have a pint on your own, then stop off at the corner shop for a bag of groceries on your way back. It's a way to kill an hour or two. Long, boring days where nothing happens. If you don't like daytime TV, and you really shouldn't, then boredom will begin to rankle. Seems to be easier for the kids. They have their computers and whatnot. Harder if you grew up in a different era. Harder to stay professional. Frank grew up in an era where you went to the pub. That's what you did. If you wanted to blend in, seem like you were just another average guy, then you went to the pub.

He has his jacket on. He was almost tempted to buy a flat cap the other day, but he drew the line. He's never felt his age. He's always felt as though he was in his thirties or forties. His life, and his lifestyle, hasn't changed much in the last twenty years. Made him feel like he'd hardly aged. It was an easy fallacy to believe in. Much harder now. Twenty years have raced past in two days. He's an old man with a plastic hip and a short future. He can feel it. One last glance at the phone. Nope. They're not going to call this afternoon. Out the door and into the rain. Exercise the hip. Stop yourself from seizing up; don't let the muscles get lazy. The sort of thing that only an old man needs to think about.

Walking to the pub, he passes three young men. Doesn't look at them, doesn't make eye contact. Three kids in tracksuits who've never run round a track in their lives. One of them has a dog on a lead. Not the usual vicious-looking creature that kids have these days; a wet and sad-looking collie. Still, Frank knows their type. Kids who think they're big men. They'd see an old man like him and think he was an easy target. Soft touch. It would never occur to them that he's killed so many. They'd never imagine how dangerous he could be. He doesn't blame them. There was a day when he was the same. He started as muscle. Thought he was a big tough guy. You start to believe yourself. You believe that the little old men you pass in the street are weak and you are strong. Then he met Dennis Dunbar.

A skinny little guy in his fifties. Bald on top, thin little moustache. He looked like a joke figure. Used to wear coats that were too big for him. Frank had seen him around a couple of times, didn't think anything of him. Knew he was in the business. Thought he was probably a bookie or a counterfeiter, or something of the sort. Then someone told him Dunbar wanted to meet him. He went round to his house, nice middle-class area in the days when there were very few of those about. This little guy invited him in. Told Frank he had a job for him. He wanted him to shoot a man dead. Don't worry, though; Dunbar would be going with him. Dunbar taught him many things he needed to know. The little routines. The ability to disappear. How to get rid of a gun. The more he found out about Dunbar, the more remarkable he seemed. Dunbar had killed a couple of dozen, which seemed unbelievable. Now Frank's killed more than that in the forty years since.

He's past the kids. They didn't glance at him twice. Learn to hide away. Don't limp along like some old man and let them see you're weak. Don't stand bolt upright and look defiant. Hide in the middle ground. Into the pub, asking for a pint. Don't take it at the bar; the barman might want to talk to him, and Frank doesn't want conversation. It's a grubby place, plenty of grubby people around. The kind of people who always have something to say for themselves. Take the pint to a little table in the corner, sit facing away from the rest of them. Be the tragic old man who comes in for a pint and says nothing. If the barman even knows his name, then he's heard it second-hand. Frank's across at his table, sitting with his back to the few people who are in at that hour. There's always a few, who ought to be somewhere better. They'll think he's an old man, drinking his pension. He never thought he looked his age. He always thought other people would see him as he saw himself. That's changing, too. Been changing for a while. That'll be a good thing, he learned that from Dunbar. Let people see you the way they want, don't force your own self-image on them. Let them see you through their eyes, not yours.

People come and go behind him; he doesn't turn to look. He could do this at home. He could sit there with a bottle or can of beer and drink in private. He would prefer it, these days. It's just not what people expect of a man of his generation. His job forces him to do what other people expect of him. It kills time. Enough dead time for today. He's losing the will to bother with these things. Losing the discipline. That's a bad thing. Getting up and walking out of the bar, not making eye contact with anyone on the way. There's always that temptation to turn round and tell them what you really are. It might be best for his job, but it's infuriating to have the world think of you as pathetic. An old man living on his own. Never married. No kids. Few friends to speak of. They might be right.

Walking into the corner shop. Only a few things to get. Shopping for one. No need for a basket. He's always lived simply. One of the difficulties everyone in the business has, how to account for your money. The dumb ones just throw cash around and expect the world not to care. They think people won't wonder and then start digging around. If you can't justify the money you spend, then you can't spend. So you need a fake job. Frank's always got that from his employers, one of the perks of working for big organizations. Jamieson's got him down as a security adviser to his club and a couple of pubs that he owns. Security adviser doesn't mean anything. Nobody can prove that you haven't given advice. Can't prove the advice wasn't worth the thirty-four grand a year that the accounts say Jamieson's paying him. There's as much as another twenty to thirty grand being paid in bonuses, depending on how much work he does in the year. That's legitimized through Jamieson's various accounts too. People can ask, but they won't find anything interesting.

He's paying for the bag of groceries. Doesn't come to much. Living frugally. He's always done that. Even with the cover story, he worries about it. Money's a trap. It's the thing people in the business tend to trip over. Things like women and pride are dangerous, but neither is universal. Money is. Some people hanker after every pretty girl they see and it gets them into bother. Some are obsessed with their own self-importance, can't keep the ego under control. All need money. You need it to survive. You try to hide money, but eventually you need to spend it. Someone finds it. Money is the cop's best friend. Frank's always worried about it. Seen too many good men fall over piles of cash. Cops couldn't get them from real evidence, but the criminal couldn't explain where he got the money. So he's always lived well within his means. Now he has plenty of money in the bank, and nothing to spend it on.

Back in the house now, putting away the little shopping he bought. He's checked the phone – nobody called while he was out. If they were looking for him they would have called his mobile after the house. He wouldn't have answered it in the pub, but he'd have come straight home. They're not looking for him. He's sitting in the living room now. The TV's off, but he's staring at it anyway. Wondering if he should switch it on. Wondering what the point would be. Switch it on. Flick through the channels. Switch it off. Ten more minutes of his life thrown away. Every minute is a waste. Just accept what you already know. They're going to push him into retirement. They can't keep him on after this. Maybe, just maybe, Peter Jamieson will be sympathetic; he'll give him one last chance. Nah, no second chances. Nobody gets a second chance. Jamieson would be stupid to give him one. Everyone gets one chance, and that's all. His chance has lasted a hell of a lot longer than most.

Most gunmen say goodbye to the world with a bang. Frank's still here. He's lasted longer than he should have. Retirement, old age, they aren't things men in his line of work usually have to deal with. It's okay for the likes of Young and Jamieson; they expect to live to a ripe old age. There are plenty of men at the top who have waddled into the sunset in their seventies or eighties. Not a lot of gunmen. Most peak in their thirties or forties. Most are gone by the time sixty gets here. There are so few pros anyway. Sometimes a handful, sometimes a dozen or so. Sometimes there's a spike, and there'll be more than usual in the city. That happens when there's trouble. Sometimes it happens organically, and someone has to make way. Right now, there are maybe a dozen pros working for seven or eight organizations. There might be another seven or eight freelancers who choose to work more rarely, but have pro standards. A few months ago Frank thought he was better than any of them. Now, he feels beaten.

24

Peter Jamieson. Shug Francis. John Young. Glen Davidson. Calum MacLean. Okay, put the first three aside because they're obvious. It's the last two. The last one in particular. Fisher's been thinking about all of them for so long. Trying to get a meaningful investigation off the ground. Get funding, some people to help him. Nothing. All he has is a vague link to the death of Lewis Winter. A death that most people stopped caring about right after it happened. Trying to put these people together. Trying to get information that will clear the fog. Nobody talking.

A few things make sense now. Things that he didn't know before. Shug's decided to get into the drug trade, that's certain. Clears up a few things. Dumb move. He's trying to get in by taking Peter Jamieson's patch. Dangerous move. Anything thereafter, Fisher knows little about.

Lewis Winter may have been working for either Peter Jamieson or Shug Francis. It seems more likely to Fisher now – sitting at his desk, months after Winter's death – that he worked for Shug. He has nothing solid to prove it. It's guesswork. Jamieson wouldn't need a guy like Winter. A desperate case. Shug needed him, because Winter was willing to take risks on Shug's behalf. Which would mean Jamieson most likely had Winter killed. The likely candidate would have been Glen Davidson, but phone records changed all that. That scumbag Greig comes to him and tells him that Davidson's disappeared. He makes it look like maybe Davidson murdered Winter and did a runner. Fisher hasn't seen much of PC Paul Greig lately. Keeping his head down. Fisher sees him round the station now and again, but his name isn't coming up as often as it used to. He's making an effort to be low-key. Wise move. Fisher longs for the moment that Greig slips up.

When he thinks about a bent copper like Greig, he gets angry. Then he loses his train of thought. Davidson. Phone records. They showed that Davidson called Calum MacLean the day before Greig reported Davidson missing. Think about MacLean. An odd case. A man pushing thirty who doesn't appear to have had a job in his life. Living on the sick, apparently. Turns up for an annual medical, lies through his teeth, gets away with it. Some people are good at that. Fake mental illness. A bad back. Some muscular problem that no doctor can get to the bottom of. The real smart ones send someone else to take their medicals for them. The doctors don't have pictures. As long as the person's the right age. As long as they have the right, identifiable illness. As long as the same wrong person has been doing the medicals from the start, you can get away with it. Some genuinely ill people make good money on the side. Helping criminals hide amongst the unemploy-able.

MacLean has to be involved in the industry, although none of Fisher's contacts seem to know him. Questioning those close to him now only alerts MacLean that he's on the police radar. Far more likely to slip up if he thinks he's unknown. That's all he is for now, on the radar. There's little to nothing against him. Besides, Calum MacLean's confus-ing, but there are more pressing concerns.

Toxicology reports on Scott and McClure were a little sur-prising. Some trace of drugs in McClure, but days old. Alcohol in both, but again, traces of drinks consumed at least sixteen hours before death. Neither had drunk anything or taken any drugs in the day before death. Which would suggest that McClure killed his best friend, and then himself, whilst sober and clean. Fisher's not sure. Not sure that McClure would do it drunk, less sure still that he would do it sober. It doesn't give him evidence. It doesn't give him something that he can meaningfully use, but it builds a picture. These two were clean and sober. Best friends who turned into murderous enemies in the course of a few hours. Nope, not buying that.

Shitty day. Rain pouring down, dark-grey sky. Another investigation going nowhere. Too many of those lately. A cop can get a reputation: a man who doesn't know how to close a case. Even good cops can get tainted with that. Bad luck plays a part. You get lumbered with a few cases in succession that nobody can crack, and you take the blame. There are a number of bad cops who've managed to stumble their way to a reputation as closers. Guys who get the job done. Nothing the bosses love more than that. Cops who don't deserve their reputations. Fisher's shaking his head. There are many people round here who wouldn't even be cops, if he had his way. He would do it differently. Too many people just looking to climb. Looking for a reputation. That's when he tumbles back into the cliché of the grouchy cop with high standards and a decent heart. That makes him shake his head again.

They've spent the day chasing contacts, looking for info. Christ, even DC Davies has managed to look busy. Still nothing. You just keep building that picture. One thing's become quickly obvious. Scott had a rapid ascent, followed by a quick ending. He was working for Shug, but it hadn't been for long. A month, maybe less. Scott worked hard and fast. He built a small network quickly, used all the contacts he had, pushed people hard. He took weeks to go from nothing to leaning on Jamieson's established men. That was obviously the patch he was aiming for. Get rid of people working for Peter Jamieson. Correction, probably working for Peter Jamieson. Hard to prove. That's the word from his contacts, and Fisher believes it. The problem is evidence. None of these peddlers has ever met Jamieson; a lot of them probably don't even know that they're working for him. He's too good for that. Interesting, though. Lewis Winter tries to muscle in on Jamieson and he's soon dead. Scott takes the same journey. Building a picture.

Everything done in a hurry. That was the secret to Scott's success. People didn't know how to stop something moving that fast. Also the most likely reason for his failure. Everything in a hurry. Mistakes made. The hurry included the gun. Fisher's convinced of it. Scott wouldn't have had a gun when he was peddling round the estates or running in a gang. He would have had blades, obviously, but probably not a gun. This clean handgun suddenly turns up lying next to McClure's body. Maybe, just maybe, he went and got one when he started working for Shug. Scott seems to have been smart. Smart enough to understand that he was going places. Still, it's likely that the gun had been in his possession for a few weeks at the most. Days more likely.

Pulling on a jacket, out of the building, into his car. He's checked with almost all the useful contacts he has, drawn a blank. Everyone on the investigation team has. Not surprising. Most of their contacts still thought Scott was working solo. The ned on the bike, most of them called him. They knew who he was, though, which shows he had more talent than most.

Meeting another contact. This one an awkward one. There are some you get, and you string them along as a contact because they're not worth arresting. The kind of criminal his boss can replace within an hour of you taking them off the street. Better to have them out there as a contact than just have to start from scratch. Then you get contacts like Mark Garvey. Fisher only got close to him so that he could arrest him. A gunrunner. Buying and selling, putting weapons into the hands of killers. A smart gunrunner. Fisher got close, but Garvey knew why. Brilliant at covering tracks, excellent manipulator. Always happy to give the information you want. Always happy to keep your eye on someone else's business.

Took the best part of the day to set up the meeting. A car park outside a supermarket. Pick him up, drive around and talk, drop him back there. The bigger they are, the more precautions they take. Garvey's big enough. Should have arrested him by now. No chance has come along. No chance has come along and, if we're being honest here, Fisher hasn't chased one. Too good a contact. You shouldn't settle for having him as a contact when you should be locking him up.

Pulling into the car park, parking by the big recycling bins, as agreed. Sitting in the car with the radio on for four minutes, when the passenger door opens and a figure drops in. Early fifties, but youthful. Probably dyes his hair, silly sod. Should know better at his age. His wife's in her thirties, apparently. Bit of a smooth operator, likes the sound of his own voice. Smart, though; says a lot of words and none of them meaningful. A useful skill.

Driving out of the car park, haven't said anything to each other yet. They won't pretend that they're friends. Some try –

the dumber contacts. They seem to believe that they can create a friendship, and that will somehow protect them. Garvey's smarter than that.

'You'll have heard about Tommy Scott,' Fisher's saying to him, eyes on the road. It's a statement of fact, not a question. If Garvey hasn't heard, then he should have.

'I heard. Him and his wee buddy – terrible shame. Happens, though. You know better than me. What percentage of killings are carried out by people you already know?'

It's a bullshit question. 'I want to track the gun that was used. I want to know when they got it.'

'Well, I'm sure I wouldn't know anything about the buying and selling of prohibited weapons, Detective,' Garvey's saying. Keep up the pretence. Deniability. Don't admit in private what you later may have to deny in public.

Fisher doesn't have the patience to play at these sorts of games. Might be why he doesn't have as many good contacts as he thinks he ought to. Most are scared away from an aggressive cop.

'I can tell you a wee rumour I heard about that pair, if you want, though. Don't know how reliable, but there you go.' Garvey's shrugging.

'Go on.'

'Word is, the day before they popped it, they were out looking for a piece. Went to more than one person, couldn't find anyone who would help them. That's what I heard. See, kids like that, they have no reputation. People don't want to risk selling to them. I heard that they came away empty-handed. I guess that events show that wasn't quite true.'

Fisher's driving, watching the road. They went looking for a gun and came away with nothing. Not impossible. Still most likely that the gun was their own, but not impossible that someone else brought it into the flat on the night. Someone comes in, kills them and then sets up the murder-suicide angle. Nobody moved them post-mortem. The blood patterns on the walls show they died where the neighbour found them. But maybe not with their own gun. Again, not usable evidence, but building a picture.

'Anything else you might want to share with me now?' Fisher's saying. Share it now, because if I find out you held back on me, you're in trouble. That's the implication.

'That's all I know about Scott and his mate. Scott was the brains of it, in case you haven't worked that out. I guess you worked out that the guy called Clueless wasn't the brains of the business. That one was just a hanger-on. Came as a surprise to me that Scott had a brain. I guess now he doesn't,' Garvey's saying with a chuckle.

Dropping him back at the supermarket. An unpleasant little man. One day Fisher's going to have to do something about him. There are worse runners in the city, but that's not the point. Driving back to the station. He needs a target. He doesn't have a trail of evidence to follow, so he needs something to aim for. Jamieson would be nice. The big fish. Bigger, at least. Bigger than Shug Francis anyway. Won't be long now until Jamieson makes a move against one of the three big sharks in the local water. The three organizations that dominate. Jamieson has the talent to take one of them down, become a dominant force himself. But there isn't enough evidence for Fisher to chase him. Lewis Winter and now Tommy Scott. Jamieson benefits from their deaths. Usually a good indicator. Maybe Shug, though. He's the better option, thanks to that one phone call. His employees screw him over because he's new; he hits back. The connection with Davidson would make some sense of that. Finding out who MacLean is would help more. Damn it! All going round in circles again. Happening too often. Only there's one more possible contact now.

25

One of the best things about being a driver is that you don't have a heavy schedule. Kenny maybe works four days a week. The days he works might be long hours, but it's long hours doing nothing. Waiting to pick people up, mostly. Boring stuff, you have to have a lot of patience. The most important thing, he realized early on, was never complain. Most people think you're lucky to be a driver. You're getting decent money to do something anyone could do. You're taking fewer risks than most of the people around you. If you complain, they think you're an idiot. Be happy to do the job, and remember that most other people will needlessly complain. It's the single reason he's driving Jamieson now.

He's not bad at what he does. He knows the city, knows his way around. He checks his routes regularly, driving around for the sake of driving. You can't be a driver who gets lost. Still, even that's boring. People don't understand. He's making twenty-two thousand a year to be bored whilst helping criminals. It's that last bit that gets him. The money is fine – more than he'd get doing anything else. He knows he's not smart enough to get rich. He's thirty-seven now; he hasn't really done anything else in his life. He has a steady girlfriend, but no kids. He's not entirely faithful to her, but she isn't to him, either. They both know it, and they can live with it. It's a good coupling that neither of them wants to abandon. She's made a few hints about him finding another job. She's worried that he's going to end up in court. Probably more worried that she's going to end up there beside him. When someone pesters you enough, you start to worry.

He's been thinking about it for a while. More than a year, truth be told. Almost did it once and backed out at the last minute. Too intimidating. The consequences were too big. Consequences are still the same size, he's just more worried. A few things have tipped him. It would have been nice to have a little more praise. A little recognition. He's not needy; it just feels like everyone else is a part of a team, and he's their only spectator. It's the Shug thing, too. It's dragging on. People are talking. He takes most of what he hears with a pinch of salt, but there's some truth in what they say. It shouldn't take this long for Peter Jamieson to deal with a guy like Shug. He should have ended this weeks ago, yet it's still rumbling on. Jamieson has to do more jobs to try to get the better of Shug. The more jobs he does, the more risk of failure. Everyone in Jamieson's organization is entitled to be concerned.

It's been keeping Kenny awake at night. Making him think of trying again, one last time. He made the phone call, set up the meeting. Now he has to decide whether to keep it. Didn't last time, but that was last time. Jamieson seemed strong then. He seemed like the man who was going to take over the city. Now he looks weaker. Looks a little bit run-of-the-mill. This time Kenny can't persuade himself that he's overreacting, that he's just being a sissy. This time it feels like he needs to do this. Why shouldn't he protect himself if he can? Chances are lots of other guys are doing it. Lots of guys in the business. They wouldn't admit it – more than their lives are worth – but people take precautions. He can't be the only one. Doesn't make it okay. Doesn't lessen the nerves.

He's sitting in the car, outside the place they're supposed to meet. He could drive away. If someone sees him – Jesus, it doesn't bear thinking about! It looks like a normal house to him. Terraced street, kind of old-fashioned. The door will be unlocked, just come straight in. Three steps and he's in. There's nobody around, not on the street anyway. There might be someone peeking out from behind the curtains. How many times has he heard people complain about nosy neighbours? This one small step is tearing his guts apart. How do they do this? How do people go out on a regular basis and do dangerous jobs? They have something inside them that he doesn't. Or maybe it's the other way round. He's opening the car door and stepping out. Closing the door, pressing the keyring to lock it. Three long steps and he's at the door, pushing it open.

It's gloomy inside, which seems about right. He's in a narrow corridor. Go through to the kitchen, he'll be waiting there. No mention, when they spoke, of the previous aborted effort. Nothing that might rock the boat. They both want this to work for them. If it's possible. That's what Kenny's thinking as he's walking towards the kitchen door. Too late to back out, anyway. You're in. What if it can't work out for both of them? Surely they can't both want exactly the same thing. He's pushing the door open. The man's sitting at the kitchen table, a cup in his hand. Tea or coffee. Kenny only just about recognizes him. It is the right guy, and he is alone. That's a start. He's nodding a hello. They always tell you to stay away from people like him. Don't think you can handle them, because they're always working against you. They'll do you no favours. Can't stop the fear, though. The fear that they're going to catch you anyway. Might as well try to take some control of it. Might as well go and meet a detective.

Fisher's looking up at him, waiting for the driver to sit down. Been a long day of meeting scumbags. This one's not so bad. Not so many moral questions about having a man like Kenny McBride as a contact. He's just a driver. Close enough to hear things that matter, easily replaceable. Arresting him makes no difference to a man like Jamieson, so you leave him where he is and use him. It puts the contact at risk, but Kenny knows that already. He must know that Peter Jamieson would kill him if he ever found out he was meeting cops. Something's made him come to this meeting, though. The same reason he had a year ago when he backed out, more exaggerated now. Treat it carefully, cautiously. Some contacts are unstable, have nothing of value to offer and think they can hide behind you. They can be troublesome, but there are worse. Some are a set-up. Sent by their employer to feed you false information. Those ones can cost you a career.

Kenny's sitting down opposite him at the kitchen table. Dingy little place, but safe. Fisher won't offer him a cup of tea; he doesn't want this to go on for long. A short meeting. An introduction. Leave the driver knowing that he hasn't done enough to gain any favours from you yet.

'Do you understand how this is going to work, Kenny?' he's asking him.

'I guess,' Kenny's saying. 'I give you information, help you out.'

'And what do you expect to get in return?' This one always stumps them. They never want to say that they expect you to keep them out of jail. They can't pretend they're doing it out of a respect for the law. Most of them don't have an answer. They worry that the wrong answer could spoil their chance at protection. It won't.

'I know that what I do is illegal, but all I do is drive. I figure I'm not important. It would be tough for you to prove that I've done much illegal, other than keep information to myself. Still, if I end up in court, things go wrong; I want this to be remembered. I want this to play in my favour. I want something to play in my favour.'

172

Not too dumb for a driver. Knows the limits of what he can expect. That's good. Maybe too good. Sent in by an employer to tell the cop what he wants to hear. If it wasn't for that call a year ago, he would be a lot more sceptical.

'Seems fair,' Fisher's saying. Kenny's sitting right across the table from him, trying to look calm. He's aiming for aloof, but his nerves are in his eyes. Looking round too much, blinking more than a well-sighted man should. Looking to Fisher to guide the conversation. 'I appreciate that you're taking a risk,' Fisher's saying, 'but that doesn't change the fact that I need you to give me something. I need to know that you're serious about this.'

Blinking even more heavily now. 'I'm serious. I don't know what exactly you want, though.'

Here's the bit where you have to tread carefully. Don't scare them away. Ask for too much in the first meeting and you might never get a second. Then again, you always have this meeting to hold over him. You have to ask for something useful. Stay present. Don't delve into major cases of the past – they can come later. Try to get something immediately useful.

'I know that Peter Jamieson is in conflict with Shug Francis,' Fisher's saying. 'You can confirm that.' A basic test of honesty to start.

'For a few months now,' Kenny's agreeing. This is a nice easy one. 'Shug's been trying to set up a network, take Peter's business. To be honest, he's making a piss-poor job of it. Still, he keeps causing bother. A lot of people are surprised that Peter hasn't stopped him yet.'

Ah, here we go. A lot of people are surprised. Some people are rather worried. Some people think that Peter Jamieson might be losing the golden touch, so they've come running for cover.

Move it along a little. 'You heard about Tommy Scott?'

There's a pause. Nervous eyes moving too fast to read. 'I heard he got killed by his mate. He worked for Shug, I'm pretty sure.'

Talking faster now. His thick Glasgow accent a little harder to understand. Nervous, but for what reason? 'Did you ever meet Scott?'

'Nah, never,' he's saying, a little too quickly this time. 'I heard of him. Heard people complaining that Scott was taking clients. He was a nuisance, is what I heard. I don't know that he was a big deal, though.' Kenny came here prepared to talk about any job he had played no part in. He drove Calum to the flats to kill Scott. He didn't know he was doing that at the time, but he does now.

Fisher's nodding along. Kenny could be telling the truth; he might just be nervous at the meeting. Hard to trust. Take another approach, one last roll of the dice. Better not to throw too much at him right now. Save the rest for a later date.

'Do you know a guy called Calum MacLean?' he's asking. Might draw a blank, or might open the curtains on a dark room.

Kenny's shaking his head slowly. 'No, don't think so.' He drove him to the flats to kill Scott. Now the police are looking at Calum. Accessory to murder. That's a damn sight more than driving people around. 'Doesn't ring any bells. Should it?'

Fisher's shrugging. 'I don't know. Thought he might have done a job for Jamieson.'

'I'll be honest with you; I don't know everyone who does jobs for Jamieson.' A little more confident now. 'I only get to see the ones he doesn't mind me seeing.'

'Fair enough.'

He's let him go. No point in holding a nervous driver when he has little to tell you. It seems above board. Seems like Kenny wants a little shelter and is willing to give info to get it. You do have to wonder how much use he's going to be. Fisher himself isn't certain. Kenny could turn out to be a diamond, might come up with something terrific. Or he could be a driver who isn't told anything useful to begin with. In which case, he's useless. If he's useless, he gets no shelter.

Fisher's giving him a head start before he leaves the house. Washing the cup in the sink – no hot water. Took a while for Kenny to start his car before he left. Fisher was listening for it. Might have been phoning Jamieson to tell him that the cop had bitten their hook. More likely he was looking around for any sign of someone following him. He's right to be paranoid. The risks are all his, the rewards mostly Fisher's. Might just be a driver, but it's his own life he's playing with now.

26

It's ringing. Finally, it's ringing. Three days he's been waiting. It feels longer. Nobody else has called him in that time. Nobody's been round to see him. His life without his job is empty, and that's starting to worry Frank. If they kick him out, this is what it's going to be like. Every day until the end of his life. You see people his age who just go off a cliff. They stop working, stop socializing, and their health falls apart. He's been thinking about that for hours. What will his life be like without his work? Empty is the first answer. Dangerous is the second. He's moving to the phone, looking at the display. It's the number of the club. It'll be Young, inviting him to come round. He's their security adviser, so there's nothing suspicious for the neutral observer in the call. He's nervous as he answers. He hates himself for that. Nervous about a bloody phone call.

'Hi, Frank? It's John here, from the club. How've you been keeping?' Blandly asked, he's not looking for an answer.

'I'm okay. Everything okay with you?' Equally blandly put. Going through formalities for the sake of someone who probably isn't listening. Always nurture your old friend, paranoia.

'Yeah, we're all good. Listen, there's one or two things we

wanted to talk about – work stuff. Why don't you come round to the club this afternoon, we'll chat. Be good to see you.' Trying to sound friendly. You never know with Young. This would be easier to judge if it was Jamieson. You could tell if he was in a depressed mood or not, but Young's different. He's always cold, never shows a lot of emotion.

'Sure, I can be round this afternoon. Say two-ish?'

'That'll be great, see you then, Frank.'

Young didn't sound angry, but then he wouldn't after three days. They've had enough time to find out everything they're ever going to find out. They'll know what Calum had to say. They'll know what the police are saying about the case. They'll know, but they might not tell him. Put himself in their shoes. That's what he's been doing for three days now. If he were Peter Jamieson, he would cut Frank loose. As soon as you lose trust in the ability of a gunman, you get rid. It has to be that way. That's what Jamieson has to do. Frank's hoping for a reprieve that he would never think of giving himself, if he was the man in power. He would actually think less of Jamieson if he proves soft enough to brush this under the carpet. They have to get rid of him, and that's where the big problem starts.

He becomes the man on the outside. He knows where the bodies are buried, literally and figuratively. He becomes a danger to the security of the people he used to help. Obviously he would be in as much trouble as them, if the truth ever came out. That ought to reassure them, but it won't. He knows how these things work, how people's minds move. They push you out. They want rid of you, to make themselves feel safer. As soon as you're out, they find another reason to be afraid of you. They convince themselves that your incompetence was a danger, so they get rid. Then they convince themselves that your previous competence was equally problematic. You did work for them. You know things that nobody else outside the organization knows. Somehow, the fact that you're outside the organization matters more than all your previous displays of trustworthiness combined.

Frank's been thinking about a man called Bernie something-or-other for the last hour. Bernie was in the business, in a roundabout sort of way. Had a small haulage company and moved a lot of counterfeit gear around. Not involved in drugs, which he seemed to think made it okay. Eventually he got chatty, people started to realize what he was up to. This was back in the days before Frank worked for Jamieson. Must have been late Eighties, although he couldn't put an exact date on it. He was working for Barney McGovern back then. Barney wasn't one of the big players, but he was reliable. He took a heart attack in the early Nineties; no one was surprised, given the size of the man. He died and his whole operation fell apart. Anyway, Barney stopped working with Bernie, but it still wasn't enough. Barney convinced himself that Bernie knew far too much. A man on the outside with that much information was too dangerous for his tastes. He called Frank.

Bernie went on a fishing trip by himself to the Highlands. Frank followed him. Killed him beside a quiet loch. Beautiful and tranquil, warm as well. That's what happens to people with dangerous knowledge. Where will they follow him, if they have to kill him? There's nowhere to go. He sure as hell isn't taking up fishing. They'll have to send someone round to the house. Maybe they'll call him to a secure location. Yeah, that would make more sense. Set it up that way, because you know the person. You can lure them somewhere safe and do it there. They'd have to use Calum. There isn't anyone else. Or is there? He's been out of the loop for three months now. Things move quickly. He hasn't been around to hear the hints and rumours. No, it would be Calum. You use the best you have, and that has to be Calum.

He's grabbing his car keys. Fed up of thinking the worst, plotting out all the likely death scenarios. It's idiotic; there are other ways this could happen. Just get there and talk. If you go in with all these thoughts in your head, then you're likely to say something you really shouldn't. You have to play this carefully. Talking to a man who's about to push you over- board is a delicate business. Frank will have to pick every word carefully. Say nothing that might give Jamieson reason not to trust him. Try to present himself as calm and confi- dent. A little apologetic for what happened, not making excuses, not living in the past either. Ready to move on to the next job, not likely to make the same mistake again. Listen to every word and the tone. Even if he kicks you over, make sure he ends the conversation believing he can trust you. Nothing matters more than that.

It's good to be in the car again. That was one of the things he missed most when he was recovering. The freedom to go where he wants to go – nothing beats that. Pulling away from the house, heading for the club. He'll be there in twenty minutes, earlier than agreed. No harm in being early. It strikes him, when it's too late to matter, that he could be walking into a trap right now. He's pulling up outside the club, a little along the street. It's so unlikely that he shouldn't pay the thought any attention, but still, it's natural to worry. They would never kill him in the club. They would never use the club in any job. That would be an unpardonable risk on their part, putting everyone around them in danger. No, don't even think about it. Just go in.

In the front door. Technically he's an employee, on the books, no need to sneak around. The place is silent. Nobody in the club downstairs; that's always a little unnerving. You expect to see bar staff and cleaners around. Nobody. Just a very large silence. There'll be the usual afternoon drinkers at the bar upstairs. The unemployable, mostly. It's not the sort of bar where the retired often choose to drink. Not with a club downstairs.

Up the stairs then. The one thing he still has any trouble with after the hip replacement. It just feels stiff stepping upwards. He kicks against a step. Damn it all! These stairs are a death-trap. Jamieson's been talking about having them fixed since he bought the club, but it's never happened. Too much disruption. Besides, it's become an institution, laughing at people falling up them. Don't give them a reason to laugh at you. Ridicule's even worse than pity.

Top of the stairs, double doors on your right. He can hear people beyond them. Someone talking loudly – some drunk at the bar with an opinion that he's proud of. All the snooker tables laid out in front of them. Two in use, both by people he doesn't recognize. Both playing by themselves, which seems pointless. Looking for a familiar face. Kenny the driver is there. Frank's never been close to Kenny. He always seems a little nervous.

'Afternoon, Kenneth.' Frank's smiling to him. 'How have you been keeping?'

'Me?' Kenny's asking. More nervous than usual. Nervous about talking to the guy who botched a job. Understandable. You don't want people thinking you support the guy who isn't trusted to do his job properly. Especially if you are replaceable, too. 'I'm okay,' Kenny's saying. 'You want me to go tell Peter you're here?'

'Yeah,' Frank's saying, 'you do that.' An excuse to get away.

27

He's never rehearsed a meeting before. Never run through in his head what he planned to say to someone. Never been in a meeting where that seemed like a good idea. Most conversations need to be spontaneous to get the best out of them. Even business conversations. Sure, Jamieson's had meetings where he knew pretty much what he was going to say. Meetings where there was little to say. This is different. This means something to him. More than money. It's not that he's scared of retiring Frank. He's more scared of losing his friendship. Only Frank and John Young matter that much in his life. Only they would be worth a rehearsal. Never thought the day would come when he would have to have this conversation with either of them. Frank's made the most difficult part of this business so easy for so long. Can anyone replace that?

There's a knock at the door.

'Come.'

Kenny's sticking his head in the door, nodding to both Young and Jamieson. 'Thought you might want to know that Frank's here.'

Jamieson's looking at his watch. He's early. It's the first sign that this isn't going to be easy. Turning up early feels almost confrontational. 'Okay,' Jamieson's saying, 'ask him to come through.'

Never delay. Handle him gently. Whatever happens, make sure this meeting ends on good terms. There's a danger that goes way beyond losing a friend. There's a danger that Frank might cross over to another employer, take all his dangerous knowledge with him. One of the big operators in the city would be happy to have him. Might never use him as a gunman, but they'll want what he knows, along with his reputation.

A knock on the door, and it's opening without waiting for a response. Frank's walking in, smiling and looking relaxed. He looks like his usual self. Well turned-out as always, not a hint of a limp in the way he walks across the room towards the desk. He looks the picture of health, which is probably the point. Jamieson doesn't notice, too concerned with other thoughts, but Young can recognize that the swagger is forced. Frank's trying to present himself as at the very height of his vigour and he's overdoing it. He doesn't usually walk with that stride, Young knows. Young's sitting off to the side on his couch, watching and saying nothing. He'll be the impartial observer. He needs to play that role now more than ever. Jamieson won't be able to judge Frank's tone, his reactions. He likes Frank too much to spot anything they ought to be concerned about. As much as he respects Frank, Young won't allow the blindness of friendship to strike.

Jamieson's sticking out a hand, Frank's shaking it. There are smiles, as though they're not about to have an awkward conversation. Trying to convince themselves that it's just business as usual, Young can see. Both these men are struggling with their emotions.

'How are you, Frank?' Jamieson's asking with the usual bounce in his voice.

'Feeling better than I have for a few years,' Frank is saying, but his tone tells another story. Jamieson asked him that question almost a week ago; Frank had the same answer then, but more confidence that he meant it. Frank isn't saying anything else; leave it for Jamieson to bring up the Scott incident. Jamieson isn't saying anything right now, tapping the table lightly with his forefinger. Trying to think of a way to bring it up that sounds friendly. There's no chummy-sounding way of telling someone they've blown it.

'We both know what we need to talk about,' Jamieson's saying, ignoring the fact that there's a third man in the room. This is what they always do. Young sits off to the side and stays silent, observing. Encourage the guest to forget that he's there, and see if he gives something away. A worthwhile strategy, even with a friend.

'We do.' Frank's nodding.

Jamieson taps the desk again. 'Tell me what happened,' he's saying. It's a way into the conversation that doesn't sound like an accusation.

Start at the beginning, Frank knows. Jamieson will want detail. 'After you gave me the job, I scouted the boy. Checked the flat, checked his movements and worked out who was likely to be with him. I knew his mate would probably be there. Siamese twins, those two. I found out who else was in the building, what other flats were occupied. I was as careful scouting them as I ever was on any other job. Must have been a fluke. Either someone saw me, or someone leaked that this was happening.'

He's left that hanging in the air for a few moments of silence. Giving Jamieson the chance to dispel any notion of a leak. A leak would turn everyone's ire towards another target; give Frank a better chance of escaping his failures. It's what Frank hopes happened, but he knows it's unlikely. Most likely, someone saw him.

'We don't think there was a leak,' Jamieson's saying quietly.

'Then someone must have spotted me. I took every precaution, as I always do. Some bastard must have lucked out, saw me, reported it to Scott. Anyway, I assumed I was clear when I went into the building on the night. Left it until late. Saw his mate McClure leave about eleven-ish, which should have raised an alarm. He stayed over with Scott a lot. Had the previous night as well. Lives with his parents, though, so not a huge shock to see him leave. Must have gone out the front and round the back. Makes me look stupid now, I know, but

I couldn't watch front and back at the same time. If I had seen him go back in, I would have known something was up. Would have called the job off. I went in thinking it was just Scott in there.'

He went in thinking wrong. Nobody will say it – you don't embarrass a man like Frank – but all three men in the room are thinking it. Frank was sloppy. He saw McClure leave and didn't bother following him to see where he went. You don't have to follow him all the way home; just for a couple of minutes to make sure he's going for good. One of the skills of the job, knowing who to follow and when.

'I went up, found the flat. There was nobody else about. Quiet building, a lot of empty flats. I was standing at the door, making sure I had a grip on my piece. I gave the door a knock. Couple of knocks. Not too quiet, make it seem like someone with nothing to hide. I was waiting for him to answer. Give him twenty seconds, and then kick the door in. I didn't want to have to do that. I wanted him to open it, make it less of a drama. I suppose he or his mate must have been in the flat opposite. I don't know, but it must be how they did it.'

And Frank didn't hear it. Didn't hear the door open behind him, didn't hear McClure creep up on him. Didn't even think it could happen. Another black mark against him. They're beginning to stack up. Jamieson knows what it's like to be in a nervous situation. Sometimes all you can hear is your own blood pump. People like Frank need to be above that. Need to hear and see everything. No excuses. It hasn't yet occurred to any of them that Scott and McClure handled the situation very well up to this point. This isn't a meeting about the successes of others. This is a meeting about Frank's failures.

'I got a whack on the back of the head,' Frank's saying with a miserable smile. 'Next thing I come to on the floor in Scott's flat. They didn't know what to do with me. Not a clue. They wanted me dead, that was obvious, but Scott was looking for excuses not to have to do it himself. So he called someone up.'

Ask this next question with care. Make it a friendly enquiry, not an accusation. 'Did they say anything when you were in there?' Jamieson's asking. 'Anything interesting? Ask you anything?'

Now they're getting to it. He doesn't want to know if they asked Frank anything; he wants to know if Frank told them anything interesting in return. 'They were a couple of kids,' Frank's shrugging. 'All they said was nervous nonsense. Bull-shit. McClure did most of the talking. Making fun of me, trying to provoke a reaction. Showing off. He was hyper, but Scott was keeping it together. He was telling the other one to shut up. I think he had it about him, I really do. He could have been very useful, the boy Scott. Shame he didn't work for us.' The tone isn't sharp, but the words are. Scott could have worked for them; Young didn't spot the talent. A subtle barb.

'They didn't say anything that might be useful,' Frank's going on. 'When Scott made the call, he took it into the other room. Spoke quiet. They should've killed me themselves,' he's saying, nodding as he does. That was their failure – not killing him straight away. 'They didn't have the bottle for it. They called up their contact with Shug, asked for a gunman to be sent round.' Frank sees a flicker of reaction from Jamieson. He's stopping, looking across at him.

'I'm just thinking,' Jamieson says. 'They made a phone call to someone connected with Shug. Just interesting, is all. They ain't learning lessons. Go on.'

Frank's nodding. 'I was sitting there, I don't know, half an hour, three-quarters maybe. They wouldn't let me move, so I just sat there and kept my mouth shut. Would have been suicide to go for the gun. Two of them, one of me. The other one, McClure, he was nearly climbing the walls by the time there was a knock on the door. Scott was nervous, but he was keeping it in check. Telling the other one to quieten it down. The knock comes: gentle, like it's their gunman arrived for his work. Scott opens the door, lets him in. I saw it was Calum, saw right away. Jesus, that was a shock.'

Frank and Jamieson are both smiling. Both laughing. It's the kind of industry where you have to be shockproof. People do things that logic simply can't explain. You shouldn't be shocked any more, certainly not at Frank's age and after the career he's had. They're both smiling at the idea of Calum managing to shock him.

'I'll be honest: when I saw him, I thought he was there for Shug. I thought he was there to do the job. Good job I didn't say anything, call him a traitor or anything. As soon as the door shut, he pulled out the gun and shot Scott in the head. Even then, I was thinking he was double-crossing Shug. Triple-crossing, whatever. He got rid of the other boy straight away, didn't dawdle. I always think of Calum as someone who takes too much time with things. It was only when they were dead that he started wasting time.'

'Wasting time?'

'Yeah, setting the whole thing to look like murder-suicide. Pointless, I think,' Frank's saying, and he's looking to Jamieson for agreement that isn't going to come.

Maybe it's a generational thing. Jamieson can't escape the feeling that he's suddenly talking to an old man, complaining about the new generation. Yes, Calum took a little extra time, but it was worth it. These days you need to take every chance that comes your way. In the old days, sure, you could gun and run. Not now. In a world of forensics and blood patterns and CCTV, you need to grab every little advantage. God knows, there aren't many. Harder and harder to get rid of a person cleanly – Frank should know that. He should know that anything that diverts police attention is a good thing. Anything that delays them is good. Even if it's just for a short while.

Delays mean something else comes along and steals their attention. It means the case loses officers before they start investigating what matters. It gives you a chance. In the old days, you didn't need it. This isn't the old days.

'He shot the boy McClure in the side of the head to make it look like suicide, so I guess he had to follow up on that,' Frank's saying. Making a concession, grudgingly. 'He put both their prints on the gun, more of Scott's than McClure's. He put the gun in McClure's hand, then let the hand drop to the floor. Then he announces that Shug has a fellow coming round to kill me. I wasn't too happy with that news. Wasn't expecting anyone else to come along. We got down unseen, into the car. I drove him on to my car, then back to the club. I went home; lay low, acted as normal. The usual.'

Jamieson's nodding along to all this, taking it all in. Frank standing in the flat, itching to leave, wanting Calum to hurry up. Calum carrying out a textbook job in nightmare circumstances, again. Before he sent Calum, Jamieson knew that he wouldn't send Frank to rescue the boy. Now he believes that Frank wouldn't have been capable, even if he'd tried. It's crushing.

28

He doesn't know that he's on Jamieson's mind; Frank's too. Calum has other things to concern himself with. Emma's at the flat. She lives with two other girls from the university, and she's fleeing them now. Something about them causing a racket when she's trying to study. She came to him for peace. He's made her a cup of tea, and he's leaving her alone in the kitchen. This ought to be pleasant. This should be Calum and his girlfriend, spending a little quiet time together. Like normal couples do. Instead, he's sitting in the living room, worrying.

He never worried before. Never had anything to lose before. There were times when he was concerned for his brother and his mother. His brother more so, because he's used him in jobs. Only minor use – borrowing cars from the garage William works at – but still, worth worrying about. People could use it as an excuse to go after William. Target his family to make him suffer. But there was never any possibility of William stopping being his brother.

Emma seems to have got bored, he can hear her moving around. Looking for distractions, probably. He's standing in the kitchen door now, watching her wash her cup in the sink.

She's turned round and she's smiling at him. Not a loving smile, more an understanding one.

'Sit down,' she's saying, 'let's chat.' She can be a little bossy, he's learning, but it's a flaw that she carries with charm. Not everyone does.

He's sitting opposite her at the kitchen table. Small kitchen, a little cramped. He may not have a lot of experience with relationships, but he knows this is ominous. This is one of those relationship chats. Most people dread the 'Where are we going?' conversation. He's dreading the 'What have you been doing?' one.

'What's up?' he's asking. Smiling; play it casual, make it seem as though he's not concerned. She's too smart to buy that. He's trying so hard to convince himself he's not concerned. He's not even fooling himself. Calum ought to be starting this conversation. He should be pushing her towards the exits, for both their sakes. Can't bring himself to. It's weak and it's unforgivable.

'I'd like to talk about us.' Just as he expected. 'Don't worry, it's not one of those conversations,' she's saying with her smile. They both know she's not being entirely honest. It's always one of those conversations. 'I just want to talk about work.'

There it is. That's the word that scares him. She must see the reaction; she must see that she's made him nervous. If there's one thing that's going to scupper their relationship, it's talk of work. Maybe it's a good thing; surely this will compel him to push her away.

Yet so many other guys in the business must have these conversations at some point. There are a lot of married men, or men in long-term relationships. A minority of gunmen, admittedly. Still, some of them manage to make relationships work, and yet the very thought terrifies him. This job does not go well with a relationship. It has to be one or the other.

'I just think that your injuries seem healed – enough to work anyway,' she's saying. She's giving him a curious look. This is her attempt to coax the truth from him. It won't work. You don't spend more than a decade guarding a secret like that and then blurt it out just because someone asks sweetly. Even if that someone is a cute girl you're sleeping with.

'I suppose they are,' Calum's saying. 'You accusing me of skiving off?' Asked with a smile, and with the hope of diverting the conversation.

'No, just wondering if you have work to go back to, that's all.'

Or what kind of work I have to go back to, Calum's thinking. 'I don't know. Maybe, maybe not,' he's saying. This is something he hadn't planned for. The relationship wasn't supposed to last this long. She's not supposed to be here.

'Don't you think you should find out?' she's saying, putting a little pressure into her voice.

'Okay, I will.' She's obviously annoyed with his flippancy.

'I'm okay for money, so it's not like there's a huge rush,' he's saying.

'That's not the point. Don't you want to work?'

Boy, there's a question and a half. If she had any inkling how much that question meant to him, she would have given him more time to answer. Instead, he's sitting dumbly, while she picks up the conversation again. He's watching her, seeing her get exasperated. Perhaps this is the way out. Let her think he's lazy and pathetic, unwilling to work. That might drive her away.

She's lecturing him on the responsibility his employers have, given that he was injured at work. 'You were injured working, weren't you?'

Now she starts digging, looking for details that he can't provide. She's trying to trip him up in this conversation. Trying to lure out a confession. He resents that. It's hard, in any circumstances, to forgive someone for trying to trip you up. If she has any understanding of what he does, then she must understand this is not the way to find out about it. She needs to come straight out and ask. People rarely come straight out and ask. Be blunt and straightforward. No games.

'Yeah,' he's saying, 'I was injured working.'

'At a printer's.'

'Yes, at a printer's. Is there something else you want to ask?' The tone is sharp enough to hurt. Emma's looking down at the table. She's thinking about whether she wants

195

to answer that question or not. He's wishing he hadn't asked it.

She starts with a sigh. Preparing herself before she says something uncomfortable. Letting him know that something unpleasant for both of them is on its way. 'I've been talking with Anna. You remember Anna; she was there the night we met. I think she hooked up with your friend George, the chatty one. She was talking about him. He never called her back, by the way, and she's not too impressed with that. She wanted him to call her, so that she could turn him down. She was telling me that she's sure your friend George is involved in some illegal stuff. She doesn't know what exactly, but she's convinced it's not proper. That he's some kind of gangster. I laughed at first, but she wasn't joking. She also thinks you're involved in the same sorts of things.'

He's waiting, considering. She doesn't know anything, she's just guessing. Stabbing in the dark. Something he's familiar with. 'What sorts of things does she think I'm involved in?'

'I don't know exactly, but not good things. She thought maybe drugs, something like that. She thought George was the sort of guy who could be involved in anything. I don't think of you that way. Am I wrong?'

How far do you take the truth? He has to give her something, Calum knows that. A little act of honesty, because outright lying isn't an option any more. It might be an option if he wanted to get rid of her, really wanted to. He tells himself he does, but when push comes to shove, he can't push or shove.

'I'm not involved in drugs,' he's saying to her. It's half-true. He's never sold drugs. Never used them. He's killed people for being involved in the drug trade, though. By any sensible measurement, that constitutes involvement. 'I can't guarantee that people I know aren't involved in them in some way, though,' he's saying. 'I know people I probably shouldn't. I've done things that I guess you would frown upon. I don't know how that changes things.'

She's looking at him and nodding. 'I don't know, either.'

It's Emma who doesn't want to talk about it any more. She seems to think they need to stop and contemplate everything they've discussed so far. She's packing books into her bag. She reaches up and kisses him.

Okay, she kissed quickly and left without saying anything else, but she still kissed. That has to mean something. Calum didn't want to stop, but he can't have a conversation by himself. He wants to resolve this – never leave things hanging. That comes from his work. You never leave loose ends flapping in the wind. If you need to deal with something, then deal with it now; leaving it will only cause trouble later on. Loose ends tend to entangle themselves in other things. He's sitting at the kitchen table. Sitting in silence. It feels as though that was such an important conversation, yet he has no idea of the outcome. You never really know which conversations are vital. You're not always a part of the ones that matter most to you.

29

Frank's told him everything he can. Told it straight. Now he's sitting in front of the desk, waiting for a reaction. Waiting for Jamieson to make the judgement that will shape the rest of his life. Jamieson's tapping the desk with his forefinger; he does that whenever he's thinking. Presumably does it when he's nervous too, although he usually makes a point of keeping his nerves to himself. He's looking at Frank, then sideways at Young.

'John, could you leave us for a few minutes.'

Young doesn't say anything, but Frank can see out of the corner of his eye that he's already halfway to his feet. Young would have expected this. Jamieson doesn't want anyone else around when he makes the difficult speech about how much they've appreciated everything Frank's done for them. How much they'll miss having him around. If there's anything they can do for him, he need only ask. All the usual shit people tell you as they push you off a cliff.

The door closes quietly behind Young. Jamieson's looking over Frank's shoulder, making sure nobody can possibly hear them. Now he's leaning back in his chair and sighing loudly.

'What a fucking situation,' he's saying with a weary smile.

'Sort of situation that's only supposed to happen to other people.'

'I seem to be getting a few of those lately.' He's looking at Frank. There's no way out of this. He knew from the start it was going to have to be this way. He's going to soften it as much as possible, but it'll still feel hard to Frank. 'I think we both know what has to happen now.' Jamieson's looking to Frank for a reaction. Please make this easy for me.

What happens now is you throw me overboard, Frank is thinking. He won't come out and say it, but he's not going to roll over, either. He hasn't worked this long, done all that he's done, just to walk away with a whimper. He deserves better, and he knows he's still capable of better. No matter what other people might think.

'I think I can guess where this is going to go,' he's saying. Frank doesn't realize, but Jamieson can see the hard look in his eyes. The look of a man about to fight. The last look he wanted to see. 'I know that I can still do this job. I can still do it better than ninety nine per cent of the other guys in this business. Maybe, a few years ago, I could do it better than a hundred per cent of the rest. That doesn't make me useless. That doesn't make me some old cripple who needs resting. I can still do this job, and I don't want you, or anyone else, thinking otherwise. I made a mistake. I'm not stupid enough to think I earned the right to make a mistake. Nobody earns that right – we both know that. Mistakes are usually the end of it for people like me. But I earned the right to prove it was only once. That's what I reckon.'

Jamieson's nodding along politely. Heard it all before, old man. This salvo, uncharacteristically effusive from Frank, and sounding off-the-cuff, is so familiar. You hear it every time someone lets you down. The chance to prove it was all a one-off. Ignoring the fact that once is once too many.

You can sweeten a conversation like this all you want; a man like Frank will still see the truth of it. Jamieson understands that.

'I'm not going to retire you,' Jamieson's saying, knowing that's exactly what he's about to do. 'But I think we need to take a look at things. What happened with Scott,' he's saying, and pausing, 'can't happen again. Calum got you out once, but I won't send him a second time. That wouldn't be right.'

Frank's nodding, he gets it. Jamieson's admitting that he shouldn't have sent him the first time. He should have left Frank to die.

'We need to make sure you don't get into those circumstances again,' Jamieson's saying. He's talking slowly, and aware of it. Picking every word, sounding unlike himself. 'I'm not saying that I won't give you another job, but maybe we need to look at other things you can do. Just for now.'

Frank isn't reacting. Isn't saying anything, isn't nodding along. Frank's thinking: he's throwing me overboard, but he's tying a rope to me, so that I won't drift far. Neither out nor in.

No-man's-land. Dangerous, but useless. They don't want him wandering off into the darkness where they can't see him, but they don't want him doing any more jobs he might botch.

'What sort of other things did you have in mind?' he's asking, after a ten-second pause that felt longer.

Jamieson's shrugging a little. 'There has to be plenty that a man with your talent and experience can bring. Advice, for one. Helping organize things, I guess. There's plenty. If I take you off gun jobs, that leaves me with Calum. I don't know how committed he is yet. You could play a part in helping me with that. I'll also want someone else on board for cover. I'll need to find someone worth recruiting. You can definitely help with that.'

Frank still hasn't reacted. This is all beneath him, and they both know it. He doesn't want to do the kind of work Jamieson's suggesting. The kind of work other people can do. Might as well ask him to make cups of tea and wash his fucking car for him.

'Listen, Frank,' Jamieson's saying, leaning across the desk. There's a pleading tone to his voice. 'I know things like recruiting are bullshit to you. John can do all that. But I will need you around. I got to stamp on Shug Francis; all this crap with him has gone on a lot longer than it should have. I should have wiped him out inside a month, instead it's four months and growing. People are talking. I stamp him, and then I make a move. A big move. I need to show people that I still have strength. I need to step it up. I'll need good people around for that. Hell of a lot of work. I'll need experience around to help me through that. Key roles, no bullshit.'

He said more than he intended. Telling Frank his plans for the future wasn't supposed to happen, but it's out of the bag now. So Frank has to offer some sort of reaction. Jamieson's said everything he can. It's now either Frank or silence.

'Smart move,' Frank's saying. 'Good time to step it up, pick a fight with a bigger organization. Need to pick the right one. I'm sure you'll have that worked out already, though.' Agreeing with Jamieson, but not committing to helping him. His tone wasn't just wary, it was almost dismissive. A tone that suggests he doesn't want to be involved. Frank didn't notice that he was giving that much away, but Jamieson did.

'So what do you think?' Jamieson's asking anyway. 'You think you might have a big role to play in that?'

Frank's looking him in the eye for just about the first time in the conversation. 'I suppose I could. The best work I could do would be the work I've always done. If that's not available, then I'll do the best I can.'

There were a few minutes of chit-chat – nothing either man will remember. Now Frank's leaving the room. Jamieson's watching the door close behind him, knowing that John Young will be opening it within the minute. He'll want to know where they stand. Jamieson's not in the mood.

Young will be cold and analytical. He'll want detail, he'll want precision. Jamieson wants a whiskey. He's opening his drawer, taking out a bottle and a glass. The door's opening without a knock and Young's walking across to his couch, noting the bottle and glass. Noting the glass filling three-quarters of the way up.

'Went that badly, huh,' he's saying, after a respectful pause to let Jamieson drink.

'Yep.'

'So what now?'

He wants those details that he loves so much. Jamieson's tapping the top of his desk. It's not details that he has, it's a sense. A horrible sense that things are going to change, and that he's not going to like it.

30

It feels like a busy time. Yet, there's nothing much to do. Young knows everything that needs to be done, and has it all in hand. Other people run around carrying out the orders he gives them. He sits back and waits to hear the results. Always safe. Never directly involved. There are so many people between Young and the person who carries out the order. Usually they have no idea who they're working for. Young is the last in a long line of gatekeepers before you reach Jamieson. He's never felt this bored by the job before.

In the old days, it was different. Old days. That's a laugh. Young's only forty-three, Jamieson a couple of years older. Nonetheless, they've been at this for nearly twenty-five years. They've always been good at it. Young's strategic brain, Jamieson's guts and personality. In the beginning Young thought his brain was their best asset. He learned different soon enough. Jamieson mattered most. People wanted to work for him. They wanted to be a part of the things he was doing. It's still that way. No jealousy, though. Just a little disappointment that he doesn't have a more exciting role to play right now.

It's a curious time. This Shug thing is a drain. An annoyance. They need to deal with it, sure, but it isn't exciting. It's street stuff out of proportion. It's just a matter of when they crush him, not if. If it wasn't for the Frank issue, it would be done by now. Jamieson knows how to deal with it, but he needs a second gunman he can trust. Calum plus one. Then on to something bigger. That's what Young's looking forward to. It's what he's always lived for. The great leap forward. One after another. They're due another one. They've been flatlining for a while. Working out of the club because it's still the biggest business they have. Biggest legit business, anyway. That'll change when they take another leap. They'll find an opponent and go to war. They'll take them down. It'll be a constant struggle. Day after day. Always something happening. Always something that you need to do. News to react to. Waking every morning knowing something's going to come out of the blue. Thinking on your feet. Young can't wait. They just need to resolve this irritating Frank issue first, and then stamp on Shug.

He needs two gunmen. There are two people Young would like for the job. Trouble with both. The best candidate would be George Daly. He's smart and tough, certainly not squeamish. He's been loyal to them for years now. Started out as a teenager doing the crappiest of jobs. Never baulked. That was nine years ago. Now he's the best muscle they have. Best by a considerable distance, it's worth adding.

A little bit of a playboy at times, but he knows where to draw the line. Throw in the fact that he's about the only friend Calum has, and he's perfect. Except he won't do it. Not willing to take the responsibility. Not willing to accept the sacrifices. A great candidate who doesn't want the job. That leaves one other person in Young's mind. A good gunman. An awkward situation. Awkward timing, anyway. That's for another day.

There's something else to ponder. It's Jamieson and his gut instincts. Still refuses to accept that Calum can be trusted. He's convinced Calum's going to do a runner or turn his back in some way. Young's told him umpteen times that you have to be patient. It takes time to build trust in a business like this. Jamieson hasn't known Calum long. So the boy doesn't look happy. So what? Miserable sod never did. Not even when he was freelance. Okay, there's a commitment issue there, but Young can work on that. In fact, that's a little job to pass the time with, until something better comes along. He needs to put a little pressure on Calum. Not too much. Carrot and stick. They got him into the Davidson mess. Well, Young did. They cleaned it up, though. Looked after him, and looked after him well. Found him a new place to live. Did all they could to provide comfort. Let him take all the time he needed. First job back, he proves what a good investment that was. So now Young's checking up, making sure there's nothing else they can do for him.

Ringing his flat. Why shouldn't he? They're acquaintances, of sorts. The one worry is that the police might check the phone records of the club. That might lead them back to Calum. They're going to find him eventually. If they haven't already. Just a question of what they're able to do with him when they do. Young will need to talk to Calum again about Frank. Let him know that Frank's taking a backward step. That Frank might not like it. Gunmen are a tight group. They all know each other, or know of each other. Mostly all loners. Most don't like people poking about in their business. Don't like giving away detail. Frank won't want anyone knowing that he's being pushed aside. Not even the guy taking his place. It's not a question of honour. Never is in this business. It's a question of mentality. Someone's going to have to keep an eye on Frank.

The phone's ringing. Young's waiting, expecting to hear the now almost familiar voice. Young but flat. Never betraying emotion. Always disinterested. But that's not the voice that says hello. The voice that says hello is young, perky and female. The girlfriend. It could only be.

'Hello, is Calum there, please?' He's being polite, not looking for general conversation. How much has Calum told her? Almost certainly nothing. He'll be playing her along, giving nothing away. He'll be safe when it comes to work. A smart gunman is always secretive. So she knows nothing. At least, very little. She won't know who Young is.

'No, he just went out. Can I take a message?'

Engage with her or not? It's worth finding out how involved she is with Calum. Women were never an issue with Frank. By the time he came to work for them, Frank had resigned himself to isolation.

That's what Calum should be doing now. This is the price of youthful talent, Young's realizing. They're still working out how they're going to live the life. Still learning from their mistakes.

'I'm sorry, who am I talking to?' Young's asking. Drag it out a little. Let's hear how smart she is. She's a student, he knows that. Doesn't tell him anything. He's seen some students being indescribably stupid in his time. There's quite a difference between being well educated and being intelligent.

'I'm Emma; I'm Calum's . . . friend.'

Okay, so they're not yet at the point where they're declaring a relationship to all and sundry. That's good. But the fact that she's alone in his flat suggests they're getting there.

'Ah, Emma,' he's saying, as though he's heard of her. Which he has, of course, but Calum doesn't know that. 'Just tell him John called. It's not important. I'll catch up with him in the next few days.'

He's waiting for her to say okay and hang up. That would be the decent thing to do. She's not, though. She has something she wants to ask.

'Are you a friend of Calum's?'

That's a little forward. Well, of course he's going to say yes. 'That's right.'

'George's too?' she's asking.

Now she's interesting. She's trying to plant him in the same circle as those two. So she knows something. Not everything, or she wouldn't be fishing for info now.

'I know George.'

'Uh-huh,' she's saying, and she's trying to sound knowing.

You know nothing, girl, he's thinking. If you sound disapproving now, you wouldn't be there at all if you knew the truth. That's positive. She doesn't know anything dangerous yet. Yet. 'It was nice to talk to you,' he's saying. Just enough sarcasm to be noticeable, not so much that it provokes a response. 'You'll let Calum know I called.'

'I will.'

He's hung up the phone and he's sitting back in the chair in his living room, smiling. This is something to do. Something that needs doing. Part of his responsibilities involves stopping problems before they appear. This girl Emma could be a problem. They have one gunman, and one young woman looking to lead him astray. A little game to play while passing the time. How to break up the happy couple. She must come to no harm, that's obvious. The last thing he wants is this little project drawing police attention. Break them up without her feeling any need to make a noise. Probably won't be able to do it on his own. Calum can never find out. There's also the worry that a break-up will make the boy even more miserable and difficult to handle. It's starting to sound less fun now. Still necessary, though.

31

He's been retired. It doesn't matter how Jamieson dressed it up; fact is, he's been retired. The old man on the outside. Frank knows what that makes him. Dangerous. That's why Jamieson was talking about advisory roles. Complete bullshit. He doesn't need advising. Not even when he's going up against a big organization. Jamieson's got this far precisely because he doesn't need anyone's advice. He knows what he's doing. Instinct and intelligence. If you have those two, you don't need much advising. The idea that he'd have Frank run around doing errands during a war is absurd. When the police know there's a war on, you keep your big guns off the radar. The police know Frank. Can't arrest him, he's never left them evidence, but they know him. In a war, Jamieson would use him, but carefully. Only occasional contact. Give him a target and let him get on with it. A war is the most isolating time for a gunman, but also the most thrilling. You know there'll be work. Challenges to overcome. It tests you. A good gunman thrives on it. Frank won't even be involved.

He's sitting in his kitchen, holding a cup of tea with both hands. Old hands, he's thinking. Old hands that have done it all before, and done it well. He can tell himself that all he likes

– it doesn't matter. It's not the hands that are at fault. It's the hip. Actually there's nothing wrong with the hip now. It feels much better than it did in the six months before he had it replaced. Yet, in those six months, Jamieson thought Frank was the bee's knees. He respected and admired him. Trusted him. If Frank had botched a job in those six months, which he didn't, when his hip actually did trouble him, he would have got a second chance. There's no doubt in his mind. Jamieson would have been pissed off, sure. More so than he is now, in fact. Now he's just sad. Anger would be better. But he would have let him go back to work. Instead, he thinks of Frank as an old man. Tired, decrepit and dangerously incompetent. All because of the hip. All because he got it fixed. If only he had just struggled on in pain.

Too late for that now. He has a sprightly new hip that nobody wants to play with. No more work. No more work that matters, anyway. Not with Jamieson. There could be work with someone else. That sends a shiver. Working with someone else means making an enemy of Jamieson. A good friend. A deadly enemy. Frank knows what would happen. He wouldn't even do one job for a new employer before Jamieson found out he'd crossed. He wouldn't get the chance to do one job. Jamieson isn't stupid. He won't let emotion conquer him. If he considers Frank a threat, he'll remove the threat.

Taking a sip of tea. Considering his options. No longer on

the inside. Doesn't matter what Jamieson says – Frank's not an insider now. Some guy who's supposed to offer advice when he's asked, which will be rarely. That's not inside. That's way out.

The thought of being an outsider. He's been here before. He's lived with the danger of it, and come through. Been a long time, though. Different circumstances. He worked for Donnie Maskell. How long ago was that? Jesus! Thirty years. Worked for him for seven years. Things started to fall apart for Maskell. Frank knew what was going on. Maskell had lost control; his business picked apart by supposed friends and definite enemies. Maskell put on a good face, but Frank knew he had to get out. He moved to the outside. Went off the radar. Did a couple of jobs freelance, but stayed low-key. Maskell wanted him dead. Dangerous times, you're right, but by the time Frank resurfaced, Maskell didn't have the ability to get rid of anyone. That was the last time Frank was on the outside.

Peter Jamieson is no Donnie Maskell. He's in a much stronger position. He's smarter. He has people around him who could easily make it happen. A late-night visit from Calum MacLean is a visit to avoid. Could Frank go up against Calum? He's smiling. Never happened to him before. No gunman has ever gone after him. Partly because he's been good at not making enemies. Partly because none would want to. He had too much respect. Admired as the best in the business. Nobody wanted to take him on. It's not arrogance that makes him think that. It's a fact. Most gunmen are smart enough to take on only a target they know they'll beat. That'll change now. An old man on the outside. Easy prey for a good gunman. There was a day when he wouldn't have feared Calum. Wouldn't have relished it, either, mind you. You never relish being the hunted. Now he would fear it. Calum's good. Cold and smart. A good planner, who knows how to improvise. He's what Frank used to be. What he thought he still was.

Nearly finished that cup now. So hard to be decisive. That might be the big failure in Frank's career. He's never made the difficult decisions. Okay, he's had to decide who to work for. A couple of tough decisions about walking away from employers. But that's it. He's always been an organization man. Always letting other people make the tough decisions. You put yourself in an organization; you put yourself at their mercy. Their choices. You just follow orders. It's reassuring, while it lasts. You don't have to think about anything. You get a call. You go and find out who your target is. You do the job. If you're good at the job, then the whole thing is simple. You rarely have to engage your brain. Go through the routine and everything's fine. Comfortable and comforting. Now, suddenly, he has to think for himself. He has to make a difficult decision. The quicker, the better.

Standing over the sink now, rinsing out the cup. There are

people he could go work for. Good people. Strong people. People he worked against in the past. There isn't a major organization in the city that he hasn't struck against at some point. Some of it's ancient history. It would still be an issue. People have long memories. They might hire him, but they wouldn't forget. They would never let a man like Frank hold responsibility. They would keep him at arm's length. Maybe use him now and again. Give him basic protection in exchange for the information he has on Jamieson. Always at arm's length. The only organization he could go into without baggage would be a new one. There are none local. There are people poking their noses in from outside. Organizations from other cities, looking for a cut. They work with free-lancers, or bring in their own. Outsiders are especially hated by those in the business. The last meaningful organization to grow in this city was Jamieson's. Freelance isn't an option. No protection. Nothing to gain for a man in his position. It would have to be an established organization. He can't think of any that would trust him. Can't think of any he doesn't actively dislike.

There is one more option. One more thing he might do. It repulses him to think of it. The indoctrination begins on day one. Taught that nothing could be worse. That nobody does it. Anyone who does must be punished with death. Enemy number one to everyone in the business. That's all bullshit, of course. The concept of honour among thieves is moronic.

These people make their living from lies and deceit. Far more people inside the business speak to the police than are ever caught. Okay, hands up, Frank doesn't know that for sure. He's guessing here. There are people out there who should be in jail. That's obvious. People against whom the police have enough evidence to convict. People who are still on the outside. They have a form of protection that even an organization can't guarantee. There's plenty of them if you take a good look around. None on Frank's level, though. The police can't turn a blind eye to everything he's done. Can they?

32

A busy day. The good kind of busy. Lots of things he wants to do, people he wants to meet. All of them meetings of his creation. This is how the job should be, Young's thinking. The first meeting is with that dick Kirk. He's been getting them phone info for a couple of years. He's usually dealt with by someone further down the chain. This time was more important than usual. Kirk went to his handler and told him he had a request for info from Shug Francis. The handler, knowing his place, passed it up the line. Maybe Shug is learning from his mistakes after all.

Young's taking this meeting himself. Don't even let the handler get a whiff of what happened with Frank and Scott. Nobody needs to know about that. Kirk won't get it. He couldn't put the pieces together with a picture guide and a tube of glue. Bless him. Just the kind of useful idiot everyone wants a piece of. Unfortunately, the kind of useful idiot who's liable to panic under pressure. Young's put him under a little. Now he needs to go and pat him on his empty head and tell him everything's going to be okay.

It was supposed to happen tomorrow. If the boy had any sense he would wait, but he doesn't. Panics. He called his handler a couple of times, wanted to meet today. Demanding that he see Young again. He doesn't know who Young is, doesn't know how important he is. He knows he's more important than his usual contact, though. All he wants is reassurance. He'll want his money too, of course. Mostly he just wants to know that he's not going to get in any trouble. He can play the big man. The tough gangster, stealing and tampering with vital info. Truth is, he'll be terrified right now. Caught in the middle of something he doesn't understand. Suddenly aware that he can't live with real gangsters. He has no means of protecting himself. First rule of playing with the big boys: get a defence. Second rule: never look weak. Little Kirk has broken both.

Meeting in a greasy-spoon place on the south side. Not ideal, too public, but it's where Kirk meets his handler. No point spooking him by meeting somewhere else. No point showing him one of the better private meeting places Young typically uses. Kirk isn't important enough for that. He also has a big mouth, might spill some beans. Eventually he's going to calm down, and then his mouth might open up again. He might find out how important Young is and brag about them meeting. Boast that he helped Young out. It happens. Hard to believe people can be that stupid and useful at the same time, but it's true. Young's walking into the place now. Grotty little dump. He'll order a cup of tea and a bacon roll for appearances, but he won't touch them.

It seems the sort of place where hygiene is less of a concern than it should be.

Kirk's in the corner. He's playing with a packet of sugar. For a man living the dangerous life he craves, he looks miserable. Young's sitting opposite him now, not saying a word. Kirk's looking at him, waiting. He doesn't want to speak first. It seems respectful to wait for Young to say something. That's what they do in the movies. They show respect to their superiors.

'You wanted to see me, Kirk?' Young's asking.

'Yeah. Yeah, I did. I wanted to see you.' There's a slight slur in his speech. Not much, but enough for Young to notice. Seems like Kirk's been trying to drown his nerves in booze. Works for some, not for others. Not for someone like Kirk. Young's guessing that it's made him more nervous. More emotional. That'll make him harder to handle.

'You tell me what you need, Kirk,' Young's saying. Use his name, it shows you remember. Friendly tone. False, but friendly. 'I'm at your command.' Oh, he'll like that. He's just stupid and drunk enough to think it might be true.

'I did the job,' Kirk's saying, getting the feel of it now. 'It was darker than usual, you see. They switch off some of the lights at night. Just a skeleton crew working the phones. They call it a twenty-four-hour service, but if you don't call during working hours – tough titties, you got to wait. So I'm working on the computer, getting into the database. Then this bird I work with comes over. Big fat thing. Think she has her eye on me. So she starts talking, I keep working like nothing's up. I'm thinking: If she spots this, I'm fucked. But I keep going.'

And he keeps on going now. Talking and talking, loving the sound of his voice. Let him talk. His nerves are still running from his efforts last night and this morning. He wants to tell someone, and that means Young has to listen. Kirk has a big mouth and only one person he can safely open it to.

It's a small price to pay. Kirk works for a phone company. Works on technical support at a call centre. He can get access to phone records. He can fiddle around with the records he finds. If the police go sniffing, they won't find anything of interest. No calls made by Jamieson, Young or Calum, according to the official records. It's not the sort of precaution you want to rely on. Better to make no calls at all. Wasn't possible with the Frank situation. Calls had to be made, and then they had to be removed. That was Kirk's job. He did that, and then got another call. One from Shug's right-hand man, David 'Fizzy' Waters. Kirk had just enough sense to keep his work for Young a secret from them. They wanted to see phone records. Calls made by Scott, McClure and Shaun Hutton on the night of the killings. Kirk told his handler, who told Young, who saw an opportunity. Protect Hutton. One good turn deserves another, they say. Hutton should be very useful in the near future. Protect him, remove the call.

According to the official records, Hutton made only one outgoing call that night, to Shug himself. That should leave Shug as baffled as ever. He'll believe Frank got a message out, no doubt. Another nice little victory.

'And you did a good job,' Young's telling Kirk. 'What can I do for you?'

He's nodding, the boy. Trying to look thoughtful. Like he's working it all out in his head. Like he's capable.

'I need . . . assurance,' he's saying. Had to stop and think of the right word. Did well. 'I need to know that this isn't gonna come back on me. There's big risks, you know.'

He needs a little pat on the head. 'Listen to me, Kirk. We all know the risks you've taken. We know they're big. We appreciate it, we respect it, and you have our full protection. We see you as integral,' Young's saying. 'You're vital to us. We protect those who are vital to us. You have my word, Kirk. I can't possibly offer you more than that.' The honour of a man's word. As though it has any value. Kirk doesn't know that, lost in a world of wannabe gangster life. He'll accept it, Young knows.

'Okay,' Kirk's saying, nodding his head. 'Okay.' He's getting up to leave. Young's waiting. Now Kirk's turning back, as expected. 'Seeing as we're both here,' he's saying. Young's taking an envelope out of his pocket. Looking around. Nobody watching. Sliding it across the table. Kirk picking it up in full view, stuffing it quickly into his pocket. The kind of quickly that draws attention. Young's grimacing, but Kirk's already heading for the door.

Second meeting. George Daly. Good lad, no doubt. Useful employee. Very useful. Reluctant, though. Lack of ambition. Not lack of bottle, Young's ruled that out. He's always willing to do difficult jobs, so long as they don't cross a line. He simply won't do anything that might progress his own career. He's reached a place he's happy with and will go no further. That's annoying. It's a waste of talent. Particularly frustrating for Young. It's his job to find the talent and promote it. George has talent. He should be promoted. It's tempting to force him. Put him in a position where he can't say no. Then you have an unhappy camper. You have someone who'll want a route out. You lose him altogether. Keep what you've got, and look for alternatives. You still ask, though. Just to let him know you're always keen. Just to let him know the opportunity is there, if he ever changes his mind. He won't. But it should at least make him feel wanted.

They're meeting in the back room of a bookie's. Jamieson owns half, has done for years. Safe little place. Young collects money from here now and again, mostly for the sake of making an appearance. George has tagged along a few times. They had to change the manager about a year ago. Terribly messy. He was the nephew of the other co-owner. Feckless halfwit too. Got the job because of the family connection. The other owner claimed the lad had business experience. He had a degree in something or other. Jamieson shrugged and let him have the gig. Little work to it. All he had to do was not steal anything. He stole something. About four grand, in the end. George helped with the punishment. By the time light-fingered nephew was out of hospital, there was a new manager. Grumpy, reliable old fellow with lots of experience. Jamieson's appointment, this time. For the sake of four grand the co-owner was pushed to the periphery. Jamieson can now handle the business as he likes. Good conclusion to a bad situation.

George is there ahead of him. Doesn't have anything else to do with his time. Not exactly a hard worker. The majority of people who do his job have other things going on. Little deals and connections that make them other money. Keeps them busy. Distracts them sometimes. Not George. He's never done any other work. Lazy bastard, Young thinks. It's convenient – means George doesn't have the distractions that a lot of others have. A lot of muscle get themselves involved in all sorts of nonsense. Dealing, mostly. Thinking they can use their muscle to make a bit of money at street level. Some go into loan-sharking. That's a brutal business, though, as bad as drugs. Most muscle steer clear. Few of them make any money worth talking about. Don't have the brains. Most get into trouble they shouldn't. Most need rescuing. George has never needed that. Too smart to get into trouble. Another mark in the pro column.

He's sitting at a table, watching a little TV up on a bracket in the corner.

'I don't get it,' he's saying to Young, as Young's closing the door.

'Don't get what?'

'Horse racing. I don't get it.'

As a sport, Young doesn't get it, either. As a business, he does. 'Money,' Young's saying. 'Punters think they can get rich from it. You need that catch in a sport as pointless as that. You hook them with the promise of winnings.'

'It's got to be rigged, though, hasn't it?' George is asking. Making conversation. He's not terribly interested. He's already decided that it has to exist just for people like Jamieson to make money from it.

Young's smiling. Maybe it's a knowing smile. Maybe it isn't. He's sitting down without offering an answer.

He needs to handle this carefully. George is smarter than the average. Don't think you can push him around. You can't. Might be lazy, but he has guts. Offer him something he'll turn down. Put it to him. Let him let you down. Then offer another one that he ought to turn down. Something he won't like. He can't say no twice. Well, he can. George is one of the few who might. But he probably won't. He knows the consequences of letting the boss down. He's smart enough to understand how vulnerable that could make him. You can only say no so often. He'll say yes to the second offer.

'How've you been, George?' Young's asking him. Being polite. Getting it out of the way. Easy with George. You can relax. He won't make life difficult. The pleasantries are out of the way. Business. 'You hear about Frank?'

'Frank? No. He okay?'

George really doesn't know. That's good. The story is staying locked up for now. 'He's taking a step back,' Young's saying. 'Not retiring exactly, slowing down. His hip. Hasn't recovered well enough. Not so quick on his feet. He can still do some work, just not everything he used to.' It's a little disingenuous, but it has to be. You can't blurt out the truth. George should be able to read between the lines.

'Shame for him,' George is saying. There's caution in his voice already. 'Hard to imagine Frank's life without his work. You'll be bringing someone else in.'

'I know who I would like to step up and replace him,' Young's saying. 'Someone from within. Someone young. Someone who knows the business in the city. Someone who knows our organization. I'd like you to do it, George.'

George is already frowning. He doesn't need time to consider. 'I'm not a gunman,' he's saying. 'I never will be, either. It's not what I want.'

Young's nodding. Looking disappointed. Not looking surprised. Can't fault George, he's honest at least. Most people would never admit it. They would blunder through. Pretend that they were willing, and bottle it later. Strange thing about

George. He'll ride shotgun on a hit. Done it a couple of times. He's willing to be there. Just won't pull the trigger. Nothing that jeopardizes his lowly status. He's a strange boy. Anyway, time to play the game.

'You sure?' Young's asking. 'We could make allowances. Give you a light schedule.' It's half-hearted, a little bit of pressure for the sake of it.

'No. It's not something I could do. I'm not a gunman.'

Those same words. I'm not a gunman. Young's starting to see the problem. George knows what it takes. He's seen the sacrifices proper gunmen make. The lives they have to lead. It doesn't appeal to him. It's not squeamishness at pulling the trigger. It's a fear of isolation. A fear of the lifestyle.

'I won't pretend that I'm not disappointed,' Young's saying. Still playing. 'I think you'd be brilliant at it. Still, if you say no.'

'I do,' George is saying. A rare moment of insistence. Young doesn't encounter that much in his job. It's nice to see that it still exists. Defiance. Strength. Shows what a good candidate he would be for the job.

'I thought you might say that. I was hoping otherwise, but there you go. I have another job I need you to do. No killing. No violence. Nothing much. Should be simple.'

'Go on,' George is saying. Smart enough to know that 'should be simple' is what often trips you up. It's a term to be wary of.

'You know Calum has a girlfriend. Emma, her name is. Seems like a nice girl. Seems smart too. She worries me. She's too close to him.' He leaves it hanging there. George should be able to work out the job from that.

'You want me to . . . what, break them up?' George is asking. A little incredulous, but not a lot. This is exactly why he doesn't want to be a gunman. Everyone thinks they have a right to stick their nose into your business.

There was a little tone of disgust in his voice. Young's watching him. George needs to be a little careful here. Honest is fine, but don't push your bloody luck. Young's always thought George knew where to draw the line. Time to find out.

'I want you to be subtle about it,' Young's saying. 'Careful. I don't want any blundering into Calum's business. This is for his own good. His own protection. Sometimes you have to do these things. Protect people from themselves. It's the way of this life, you know that. Calum's making a mistake here. He ought to see it himself. I'm surprised he doesn't. Maybe he does. Maybe he just needs a push. We need to solve the problem for him. You're going to do that. I know you can be subtle about this. Work out a way to end the relationship. Without acrimony. I don't want him moping around. He should have been smart enough to do this for himself, you know. You're doing him a favour.'

'Uh-huh,' George is saying. He has that reluctant look on

his face again. 'And if he finds out? And he decides it wasn't a favour?' It's a silly argument. Calum wouldn't do anything. He's far too smart to turn nasty over something like this.

'You can handle it,' Young's saying, and getting up.

This conversation isn't going to go anywhere positive from here. Something else Young has learned. When to bail out of a difficult conversation. George knows he has to do the job. Sticking around is only going to lead to an argument. Get out. It was the conversation Young expected.

He's in his car now. Wishing George would be a gunman. Wishing he had the ambition that so many, much more stupid people have. Then George wouldn't have to do jobs like this. Wouldn't have to lower himself to meddling in relationships. His choice. He'll live with it. Do the job. Break them up. Keep it quiet. He won't like it. Another lesson for him. You do jobs you don't like. You do them and you move on with life. People have done worse. Much worse. Young could tell a few stories. The people he's met. The things he's ordered. The sacrifices people have made. He could tell. He never will, of course. That's the other thing George is smart enough to know. You never talk. Not even to a loved one. Not even to complain.

33

It's cold and dark now. Gloomy, that might be a better word. That's certainly how Kenny feels. Parking two streets along from the house this time. Walking the rest of the way. Going to meet a copper. Looking around him with every third step. He could do little more to look guilty. Along the street and up to the front door. A last look around. There's nobody following him. One of the first skills a good driver learns is spotting a tail. In through the front door, closing it quickly behind him. A new set of worries. There's a light on in the kitchen, but who's in there? Should just be the detective. Kenny's shaking his head in the darkness. This whole experience is far more work than his job. Can it be worth this, just to have a safety net? Stupid bloody question. Of course it is. He needs that safety net, and this is the only place to get one. He's forcing himself into the kitchen.

Fisher's there, by himself. Sitting at the table, cupping a mug of something hot in both hands. Glancing up at Kenny, nodding hello, looking away. Not offering a cup of whatever homely brew he's enjoying. Fine, be that way. Kenny's sitting down opposite him. Waiting for the cop to say something. Can't say something wrong if you only answer the questions you're asked. Fisher's taking another gulp from the cup. Bit of a slurp. Now he's looking at Kenny. Not the friendly look of a cop to a valuable contact. Looks like he's judging him. Looks like he's not happy with something.

'I need something from you, Kenny.'

'What?'

'Anything useful,' Fisher's saying. 'I'm beginning to question how much use you'll be. Whether I need you or not. Maybe I could get better info elsewhere. I'm not going to throw you to the wolves, not yet. But you have to give me something, Kenny. Something to make me think you're worth the effort.'

It's laying it on a bit thick, but he's desperate. Investigation going nowhere. Cops being moved to other cases. Murder-suicide now widely accepted. Another failed case for Detective Inspector Michael Fisher. This is all about Shug and Jamieson. He has no contact close to Shug. He now has one close to Jamieson. Time to use it. Something. Anything. A thread to pull at that could lead to something big. It's how these things often happen. You don't rush directly to them, you stumble across them. Some bigmouth drops a hint that leads all the way to court.

Kenny's stammering in front of him. Puffing out his cheeks. Obviously trying to think of something. Something that doesn't incriminate himself or a friend. Information that could have come from someone else, so that he doesn't expose himself. Give him time. Let him reach a conclusion he's happy with. Whatever Fisher's just said about him not being a good contact, he's still the only one close to Jamieson. Push him around, but don't push him out.

Thinking. Thinking some more. Anything that doesn't implicate himself. Anything. It's bad enough to have spoken to a cop. To speak and get no protection in return is unthinkable. A risk that could destroy him. There has to be something. There is.

'There's a rumour that's been going round the club. Last couple of days. Just a rumour, but . . .'

'Go on,' Fisher's saying. Most rumours are bullshit. Some rumours are gold.

'People are saying that Frank MacLeod's being put out to pasture. I don't know how true that is.' He's pausing. 'Came from one of the girls who work the bar. I think she's close to Jamieson. Apparently Jamieson's a bit upset about it. He got all drunk and chatty. I don't think he named Frank, but she knew who he was talking about. Didn't want to have to retire him, because he likes him so much. They don't think he's physically able to work any more. He had his hip done, you see . . .' Kenny's trailed off. He's said about as much as he's comfortable saying.

A jolt when he heard the name. He's tried to hide it. Kenny's so busy inventing barmaids he hasn't noticed Fisher's reaction. Frank MacLeod. Frank-bloody-MacLeod.

And bloody is a very good word to use. A sly old bastard, if ever there was one. A gunman. Jamieson's gunman, no less. A gunman going back many years before Jamieson came on the scene. How many people has he killed? Never once charged. Never once convicted. A man who should have spent the last thirty years in jail. The next thirty as well, if there's any justice. They've watched him before. Tailed him for months. Never gave anything away. Even managed to convince a couple of senior officers that he wasn't involved in crime. On the periphery, maybe, but not directly involved. A victim of vicious gossip. Poor little Frank. Now he's been retired. That's the strangest part of all. A guy like Frank being retired. Rare, and very dangerous.

People like Frank don't retire. They work until they drop. Being retired makes them targets with no protection. He'll be feeling awfully vulnerable right about now. There are issues with this rumour, though. The source, for one. Doesn't matter how drunk and emotional Jamieson was – no way he would spill his guts to a barmaid. No matter how sexy and available she was. Kenny's spinning a yarn on the source. Probably found out by eavesdropping. Or from someone he doesn't want to admit knowing. So he's lying about the source, big deal. As long as the source is good, it doesn't matter. Fisher also doesn't like the way Kenny refers to Jamieson. Always by his surname. Maybe he's just falling into the pattern that Fisher himself created. He calls Jamieson by his surname because he doesn't know the man. Kenny should know him better than that. He's his driver, for Christ's sake. He works with him practically every day. Surely he should be calling him Peter by now. Using the surname feels like he's talking about someone he barely knows. How close is Kenny to Jamieson exactly?

'So you're saying he was pushed out?' Put a little pressure on, but not much. Time to back off. This is good info. Be gentle with the questions and tell him he's done well.

'I guess,' Kenny's saying. Nervous again. 'I doubt he wanted to go. He's a good guy. Well, not a good guy. He's a criminal, so he's a bad guy. But he's a nice man. Well . . .'

'Okay, Kenny,' Fisher's saying. He doesn't have the patience to sit and listen to yet another criminal pretend he isn't one. Or pretend that he's the only nice guy in his industry. They all say it. Some of them even believe it. 'This is better. I'm thinking you and I could work together after all. I won't forget that you helped us with this. There is one other thing. If Frank's been pushed out, they must have someone ready to step in and replace him. Do you know who that is?' Not mentioning what job they'll be stepping into. Not mentioning that Frank was a hitman, because that would mean Kenny admitting that he knew Frank was a murderer. He won't admit that. Fisher won't make him.

Kenny's blinking more than he should. He forgot that they don't know about Calum. They really should know. He's not going to tell them. Not yet, anyway. Keep that one back for later use. Maybe never. Kenny never took Frank on a job. Not once. Old Frank was always nice and polite, but he never needed him. Calum did. Just that once, but still. He was an accessory. He drove Calum to the flats. Two men died in those flats. They call it murder-suicide, but Kenny knows better. That was Calum's work. Had to be. Double murder. And he literally drove him to it.

'I don't know,' Kenny's saying. 'Maybe they do, but I haven't heard. It wouldn't be Jamieson anyway. It would be Young. He seems to handle that sort of thing. Hiring and firing.'

'Even to replace someone as important as Frank Mac-Leod?'

Kenny's shrugging. 'I guess. I don't know. He handles that sort of thing is all I know. Jamieson has the final say, obviously, but it's usually Young that does all the donkeywork. That's all I know.'

Oh no, it isn't, Fisher's thinking. That's all you're willing to say now, but you know plenty more. Kenny will be holding things back. You can't know about someone as important as Frank without knowing a lot more about the rest of them. If he's smart, he'll be holding back the best information he has. Dribble it out over the course of years. He'll hold back anything that incriminates himself. Anything that embarrasses him. Anything that might jeopardize either his place within the Jamieson organization or this safety net he's trying to create. That's enough for now. Frank MacLeod. Fisher's sitting back in his chair, thinking about that man. How best to use this information. Kenny's still there. Still looking cold and nervous. Waiting to be told that this meeting is over.

'This is the sort of thing I need to know,' Fisher's telling him. 'You get anything more like this and you contact me. You still have the number I gave you?'

'I have it.'

'Okay. Thanks for coming,' Fisher's saying. 'You go first.'

He left with a last grumpy look at the hot cup of tea. Fisher's still clasping it. Considering. The best scenario would be to arrest Frank MacLeod. Can't do that. Nothing to arrest him for. He's a killer, but a good one. Good enough not to leave proof lying around. What will Frank do? Pushed out of one organization, he might run to another. There'll be a few that he's made enemies of over the years. Can't last as long as Frank without making enemies. There will be someone, though. Someone will hire him. Someone looking for a credible name to have around them. Get an elder statesman on board. Another young gun with ambition. The kind of person Jamieson was when he hired Frank. He'll go to them for safety. Frank needs protection. If he's being forced out, then something must have happened. Something unforgivable. You don't retire Frank MacLeod because you think he might be slowing down. He must have botched something.

Or screwed someone over. More likely botched. He was too safe where he was to rock the boat. Frank's essentially been sacked for incompetence.

Washing the cup at the kitchen sink. Fisher's going straight home from here. He has a nice little house, but he finds it boring. Everything's boring except work. There's nothing wrong with loving your work to the exclusion of other things. Not in Fisher's mind. That doesn't make you some sad-sack cliché, does it? What else could compare to this? Frank MacLeod, out on his arse. Vulnerable and unprotected. Looking around for some sort of shield. He must know that he's just become everyone's number-one target. Everyone with a reason to hate him now has a chance to kill him. They'll try too, when they find out Jamieson's ditched him. That's why Frank will move fast. One person already knows that he's vulnerable. Jamieson knows. Jamieson's tough, ruthless. Charming, so they say, but ruthless. He'll be front of the queue to get rid of Frank. Would be a mug if he wasn't. Frank knows more about Jamieson's manoeuvres than almost anyone else. Jamieson will need to keep Frank's mouth shut. Which is why Fisher knows he has to move fast, too.

34

A phone call. Not from Young, but Jamieson himself. That's unusual. He doesn't sound like himself. He always tries to be cheery. Always tries to seem like he's your pal. Not this time.

'Calum, it's Peter. I want you to come round to the club. Come straight up to my office.'

'Okay,' Calum's saying. Doesn't need to say anything more than that. Sounds like another job. A late call usually is. Sounds like something unusual. For a job, Young would call. It's organized to make sure that it's always Young. Consistency is important.

'Come round right away,' Jamieson's saying. The line's dead. It's been part of the Jamieson ploy to sound as chummy as possible towards Calum. Always light and breezy. Always complimentary. The tone this time was formal. Businesslike. It didn't sound like him.

Calum's put the phone down. He's pacing around the flat, getting a coat from the wardrobe, making sure he has nothing identifying on him. This seems like something to be worried about. He might have to go straight to a job. Car keys, and out the door. Driving to the club. Pointless to speculate. Don't even think about what this might be. You get there and you find out. Why bother yourself with speculation? He doesn't like driving in the dark. Occupy yourself with the effort of the journey. Young's not involved. Why not? Maybe he is. Maybe he'll be there; he just didn't make the call. Why did Jamieson sound so down? It has to be Frank. It can only be about Frank. Bad news about Frank means bad news for Calum. Stop speculating, for God's sake. Just find somewhere to park. That's work enough round here. Up and down the street twice, eventually finding somewhere that'll serve. A short walk in the cold to the club.

It is cold, too. Not that you'd know it, looking at some of the people outside the club this evening. Young women – some too young – in short skirts, some too short. Summer wear, it seems to Calum. They're laughing and chatting among themselves, waiting to go in. There's something resembling a line outside the club. Young men and young women, trying to impress each other. Never used to be this way. Used to be struggling, this club. Jamieson turned it around. Made it fashionable, which in turn made it profitable.

It's not a great place to have your office, Calum's reflecting, as he walks past the twenty or so people on the pavement. Jamieson's big enough to use somewhere quieter, somewhere innocuous. It's sentiment, as much as anything else. The club was the first big legit business he got his hands on. It made sense to use it as his office then. He made a success of the club too, proved that he could be a legit businessman. That always means a lot to guys in the industry. They like to show that they can cut it in the legit world, too. Now he's building an empire, and it's surely past time to leave the club behind. But he doesn't. It's his comfort zone.

A few people are looking at Calum now. He has his head down, trying to be ignored. He's walked past the crowd and turned towards the door. Some people think he's cutting the line. The bouncers are looking at him, probably ready to turn him away. One of them recognizes him. Puts a hand out to stop his mate from saying anything. They step aside, let him through. No words spoken. They have their instructions. They know who's here to party and who's here to see the boss.

Inside. Into the thumping music and body heat. People call this fun, you know. Squeezing up against random strangers, half-deaf and mostly drunk. The club to his right, the stairs in front of him. Four people sitting on the stairs. A young woman crying, being comforted by a friend. A young couple a few steps further up, halfway down each other's throats and slurping. Calum's stepping past them. Careful not to bump into anyone. Careful not to draw attention. Careful not to trip up on these treacherous steps. None of the four on the stairs pay him any notice, and he's pushing open the door to the snooker room now.

Quieter up here. Fewer people about. Three tables in use,

half a dozen old sots propping up the bar. A few looking at him as he walks past them, none taking a long look. People up here know better. Jamieson's never open about what he does; he never brags about it, but people aren't stupid. They know people going back along the corridor to the owner's office might be people it's safer not to stare at.

He's knocking on the office door. You stand out in the corridor and you wait for Jamieson to call you in. Not a question of good manners, more a question of not walking in on anything you shouldn't see. Unlikely with Jamieson, he's much more careful than that. Still, you never know. There's a muffled call from within. Calum's opening the door, stepping inside, closing the door quickly behind him. Jamieson's alone, sitting behind his desk as usual. The couch to the right is empty. No Young. It's a little unsettling. Calum's trying to remember if he's been alone with Jamieson before.

'Come in, sit down,' Jamieson's saying, gesturing to the chair in front of the desk.

Calum's sitting in front of him, trying to read his expression. He looks tired, for one thing. Looks annoyed, too. Calum's not saying anything, not going to. It's up to Jamieson to lead this conversation. Whatever the issue is, it belongs to him.

'We need to have a talk,' Jamieson's saying. 'Maybe not an easy one.'

It's never the first thing you want to hear. Calum's

sitting, expressionless. Determinedly expressionless. Don't let Jamieson see that you're concerned. Don't let him think that you're easily spooked. Looking calm, listening to what the boss has to say.

'We need to talk about Frank,' Jamieson's saying. His tone says he doesn't want to. It says he'd rather talk about anything else. 'You saw what happened,' he's saying, throwing up a despairing hand. 'He botched it. Badly. I'm going to be honest with you here, Calum – I shouldn't have sent you. You didn't deserve to be risked that way. A guy like Frank, he knows the risks. He knows if he gets stuck, then he gets left behind. I sent you in there, and I shouldn't have. I'm sorry for that. You handled it brilliantly, but still, I'm sorry.' Showing weakness, letting Calum see that he can admit his mistakes. In this business, most people think that's weakness. Very few apologies offered. Almost none from the boss. It's a moment to raise an eyebrow.

Calum's nodding. Accepting the apology, trying to make it seem like no big concern. He's worried, though. He doesn't want to hear this contrition. He knows what it's leading to.

'The whole thing with Frank,' Jamieson's saying now. 'That whole job was a mistake. I should have seen that he wasn't fit for it. His hip, and all that. I wanted to believe that he could just come back and be himself again. Like nothing had changed. It made my life easier if he could. I need two gunmen. You and him. Even if the roles changed, I wanted it to be you two. Maybe you became the lead and him the reserve, but still you two. People with talent that I can trust. Those are hard to come by. You have no idea,' he's saying with a grim smile.

All this honesty is creating a heavy atmosphere. Jamieson can sense it. Time to get to the point.

'Frank's been retired. I'm trying to keep him on the books. Trying to get him to take an advisory role, but I doubt he'll go for it. Not in the long run. He's not the advisory sort. He might still be around now and again, but you have to think of him as retired.'

There's a warning in there. From now on, you tell Frank nothing. You don't go to him for help or advice. You don't tell him about any job that's being done within the organization. Frank's become an outsider.

'That's . . .' Calum's pausing as he looks for the right word. 'Sad.' Seems like the right word to go with. True, but non-committal.

'It is,' Jamieson's saying, and nodding his head like he means it. Calum's never seen him sad before. Jamieson has a style that he uses all the time. Doesn't matter what his under-lying feeling is, he can hide behind the bluff. This is a rare moment when he's not even trying. He's deliberately letting Calum see how much this means to him. It's an offer of trust. It's not an offer Calum is eager to receive. 'Sad, but it has to be,' Jamieson's saying. 'He made a mistake that we can't allow a repeat of. Shit, he should be dead already. If I had done the right thing that night, he would be.' There's an unspoken message there. Frank should have been left to die. Keeping him alive has only created problems. It's obviously not an easy thing for Jamieson to say about a friend, but he's right. Death, in retrospect, would have been better for the organization.

This is a promotion. This miserable, excruciating exchange is what constitutes career progress round here. There's only one thing Jamieson can say next.

'You understand what this means for you. Frank's basically gone. As a gunman, he's finished. You will become our senior gunman.' There's a pause. 'I don't want you to think that you're getting that position by default. You would probably be getting it anyway, even if Frank was still going. You're shit-hot; the last couple of jobs have proven that. It's your time.'

Calum's nodding along. Polite acceptance. This isn't the time for enthusiasm. Calum isn't the person for it. Not now, and not even at the best of times.

'This isn't some sort of bullshit ceremony,' Jamieson's saying with a smile. He's sounding like his usual self now. Full of bluster and swear words. 'Some kind of handing-over of the torch. All that fucking rubbish is . . . well, fucking rubbish. Usually I wouldn't even mention it, you know. I figure you'd work it out for yourself anyway. It's just that these ain't the usual circumstances. Not after what happened.' He's back to sounding quieter again. Morose.

There doesn't seem to be anything left to say. Calum clears his throat. Trying to come up with something polite. A throwaway line. Something that doesn't sound like an outright lie. Thank you would be conventional, but a lie. He's not thankful.

'Well, it's good of you to let me know,' he's saying. 'About Frank, I mean. I wouldn't have known how to handle him if I'd bumped into him.' That's not true, he'd have known. He'd have played it cautious, as always.

Jamieson's smiling. 'You'd have worked it out on your own. Listen, Calum, I know you haven't been with us long. And I know we're the first organization you've worked for. Properly worked for anyway, not freelance. This might not feel like a big deal to you. Maybe you don't even like it. I get that you're probably not comfortable with us yet. I do, I get it. You're used to having more freedom than you get in an organization. I want you to know that I get that. You're not going to be the only gunman we use. I'm not going to overuse you. I'll keep your schedule as close to what's comfortable for you as possible. Obviously, sometimes, it can be out of my hands. But I'll try. I'll also make sure you enjoy the best protection and backup that anyone in this city could ever get.'

These are the professional promises. Reasonable, generous and predictable. Some of them are promises that will be kept, some are less certain. Jamieson can't guarantee the best protection and backup, he can only strive for it. It feels like it's time to go. They've said everything that needs to be said. Well, Jamieson has. Calum's remained mostly silent.

'I appreciate that,' Calum's saying now. Form the right sentences to round off the conversation. 'I think I'm starting to get used to it. Just that the injuries slowed things down,' he's saying, raising his hands. Still scarred. Still ugly. Jamieson's nodding in response. Hopefully the kind of nod that ends this. Calum's no conversationalist, but Jamieson knows that already.

'There is one more thing,' Jamieson's saying. Looking down at the table, back to miserable face. The atmosphere suddenly heavy again. It seems this is the real reason Calum's here. 'With Frank being retired now,' Jamieson's saying, and pausing. 'With him not being part of the inner circle, I don't know how he'll react. It's a big change for him. First time in forty-odd years he hasn't been doing this job. Well, I guess he had breaks, but, anyway . . .' He's trailing off. He's going to ask Calum to do something unpleasant. It almost doesn't need to be said. 'Thing is, I trust Frank. Normally, I trust him with my life. I don't think he would do anything he shouldn't. I don't think. I can't be one hundred per cent sure. I don't want you to do any harm to him; I just want you to watch him. Carefully, of course. You don't want to piss off Frank

MacLeod, retired or not. Just watch and see what happens. I'm sure nothing will, but still. I'd like to know.'

Calum's nodding along again. Silently, again. This is not a job he wants to do. Not on any level. But he has to nod along. And he knows he's going to end up doing the job. Of course Jamieson would have Frank followed. It's just a surprise that he would have him followed by a gunman.

'Okay.'

'I know you don't like it,' Jamieson's saying, holding up a hand and smiling knowingly. 'You're a gunman. This is probably a bit beneath you. I agree. Thing is, this has to be done by someone I trust. Someone I know is good at the job. Right now, you're damn good at your job. I also think,' he's sounding a little more thoughtful, 'it would benefit from having your eye. You know what Frank should be doing at this point. You can spot things other people wouldn't. Things will stand out to you. You think like him,' he's saying with a smile. 'You might not realize it, but you do.'

35

He's left it as long as he reasonably can. Hoping that Young would call him and tell him not to bother. No such luck. No such call. So now George has to make one of his own. Do it with subtlety, Young said. Yeah, because muscle is famous for its subtlety. It's a stupid thing to have to do. Stupid and treacherous. Muscle trying to be subtle, pissing off a gunman. What could possibly go wrong? Calum's stable, that's one thing. Not the sort of guy to go over the top with his reaction. Doesn't change the fact that he's a guy who knows how to punish people.

He should probably have made this call last night. Get it out of the way. That's how George has always done his work. People think it's because he's decisive. Enthusiastic, even. It's just common sense. You get a job and you go do it. Don't sit on it. Don't let it fester. Most muscle jobs are simple enough, so there's no need to agonize over them. Go and do your work.

This would be easier if he knew Emma. Call her up, sit her down and chat about it. Go through it. Make her understand. Don't tell her anything incriminating, but enough so that she works it out for herself. Give her the chance to do the sensible thing and walk away. No heartbreak, just common sense. But no, it's never that simple. He doesn't know her. Met her once, hardly remembers what she looks like. He remembers her friend Anna Milton. She was George's date for the night. Pretty little blonde thing. He liked her, for the first ten minutes or so. Then she started to grate. Really grate. Annoying laugh. Clingy. Loud. By then he was getting drunk enough not to notice. In the morning, when he woke up, he noticed. He said he would call her. And here he is, more than a month later, calling her.

There's a slightly puzzled tone to her voice as she says hello. She doesn't recognize the number.

'Hi, Anna, it's George. You remember me? George?'

There's a pause on the other end. 'Oh, I remember you,' she's saying. The polite phone voice that said hello is gone. It's been trampled underfoot by the loud and angry voice that she so prefers. 'I remember giving you my number. You said you would call me.'

'And I am,' he's saying, going for the cheeky-chappie tone. 'You wouldn't believe the trouble I've had getting your number. It took me weeks to get my phone back. I only got it back yesterday,' he's saying, winging it. 'I bet you're real pissed off with me, aren't you?'

'Got your phone back from where?' she's asking. Not angry, puzzled. He knows he's got her.

'I don't blame you,' he's saying. Determined to avoid that

previous question. 'Listen, how about lunch? My treat. To say sorry.'

'Today?'

'Sure, if you're available.'

'Yeah . . . I guess so.'

Do the job. Get it out of the way. One lunch date, and then never call her again. Work the conversation round to Calum. Give her enough ammo to go to Emma with. Then go through life pretending that you didn't stab your friend in the back.

He's getting dressed. He'll pick her up. They'll go somewhere nice. Easier to control a conversation in generous surroundings. No need to book ahead for lunch, just make an effort not to stand out when you get there. He can't cause a scene. There are so many ways this could get back to Calum. It may well get from Anna to Emma to Calum. George's name could be passed along the line. More so if Anna's unhappy with him, again. Nice shirt, plain trousers. Tidy hair. That'll do. Out the door and into the car. He remembers where she lives. Nice enough area for a student. Probably paid for by the bank of mum and dad. He doesn't begrudge her wealthy parents. He'd have scrounged from his parents too, if there was anything to take.

It's not her he's thinking about as he drives. It's Calum. His friend. Does Calum think of him as a friend? Surely. Not like he has that many of them. He must consider George a friend. After that night, surely. George was the one he called.

The one he trusted. Calum needed someone to help him. To rescue him, if we're being honest. He'd killed Davidson, but Davidson had stabbed him in the hands. He was useless. Still mentally strong, but he could do nothing for himself. He needed someone he could trust. George went round there. Middle of the night. A strained phone call asking him to come round. He didn't know what he was walking into. Calum toughed it out. Ordered him around. They got the job done, and done well. Removed the body. It helped enhance both their reputations with Jamieson. George was the first guy Calum called. The guy he trusted most when the odds were against him. This is how George repays him.

She's waiting outside her flat. Looking into the car as he pulls up. She is pretty, he'll give her that. She would never get away with that personality if she wasn't.

'Good to see you,' he's saying with his happiest smile. 'It should never have taken this long, but we can make up for that.'

She's smiling back. 'I'm sure we can,' she's saying suggestively. What was it Young said about subtlety? Probably shouldn't be using Anna then. 'Are we going somewhere nice?' she's asking.

'The best I can afford. You'll like it. It has class.'

'I didn't think I was going to hear from you again, you naughty boy,' she's saying. Grating already. She doesn't waste time. Suffer her. It'll make you feel better about the betrayal if you're suffering too.

They're in the restaurant. It's quiet, which is a blessing. They've ordered now. She's waiting for George. She's going to ask about the phone. He's going to change the subject. Keep the lies as simple as possible. Give yourself little to remember. Work the conversation round to Calum. Food's arrived. They're both eating, which shuts her up. She hasn't mentioned the phone yet. Maybe she won't. Maybe she doesn't want to push her luck. Maybe she'd rather accept the vague lie.

'So how're your studies coming along?' he's asking her. A polite way of working the conversation round to Emma.

'Okay, I suppose. Sometimes it's not, you know, involved enough. I can't wait to be finished and get working. There's so much I want to do.'

He's nodding along between mouthfuls. Keeping it polite. Doing his damnedest to seem interested.

'Let me ask you something,' she's saying. Putting her fork down. Reaching a hand across the table. Going for something intense, it seems. 'What do you do for a living? I think I know, but I want you to tell me.'

It's a question he doesn't want to have to answer; it's the subject they're here to talk about. It's not just her. He won't answer that question to anyone. A loudmouth least of all, obviously. It's not impossible that this is a set-up. She's annoying, but she's not stupid. He doesn't underestimate her ability to screw him royally. She could even be wired. Pity the poor bastard that has to listen to her recordings.

'What do you think I do?' he's asking. Going for the cheeky smile.

'No, I asked you first. What do you do?' Her voice is low. Conspiratorial.

It's going to be another vague one. 'I do all sorts of things. Odd jobs, I suppose you could say. This and that.'

She's frowning now. 'If you're not going to be honest with me, then this isn't going to work.'

He's not going to be honest with her, and this isn't going to work. Still, he needs to make this relationship last to the end of this conversation. Beyond that, it can be happily consigned to oblivion.

'Okay, I'll be honest with you. I'm involved in all sorts of things. Not all of them are – how can I put this? – on the books. I play around in some slightly iffy things, I'll be honest. Nothing too hot,' he's saying. He's raised a hand as though in defence of his honour. Trying to sound earnest. 'I know that some of the things I do I shouldn't be proud of. Still, I've never crossed the line.' Time to pull the conversation round to a direction that suits his purpose. 'I know a few people who have, I admit. There are times when I've run with a rough crowd. Been friends with people who are way over the line. Involved in some things I don't like at all. I've just been trying to make a living. Keep myself out of trouble. So far, I've managed. I don't want you thinking that I'm some sort of crook; I'm not. When I was younger, maybe. Not now.'

He's letting her think. She'll be thinking about herself first. How much can she trust him? Should she walk away from him now? Spare herself trouble. He's a competent liar; she'll fall for the talk of a reformed character. A bit of a chancer in the past, now living clean. It's what she wants to believe, so she'll believe it. Now that she's considered her own position, she'll get round to the rest of what was said. Process it. Dwell on what he said about the kinds of friends he has. Think about how that relates to her. She'll get to Emma eventually. In her own sweet time. George is still sitting there, waiting. She'll get there. Any second now.

'So you have some friends that are more involved in that sort of life?'

'Some, sure.'

'What about your friend Calum?'

Here it is. This is the moment he's been waiting for. Has to play it carefully. Don't lay it on thick. Start by not saying anything at all. Look as though you regret this turn in the conversation. Look as though you don't want to talk about Calum. Now say something. 'I don't want to get him into any trouble,' he's saying.

She's managed to look grave. 'Is he one of the friends you were talking about?' she's asking.

'Listen,' he's saying, 'Calum's a good guy. I like him. We're not terribly close, but we get on well. I know he's been involved in some stuff.' A thoughtful pause. 'I don't want to go into detail. I just know that he's been involved in some heavier stuff than I think is decent. That doesn't make him a bad guy, though. He's always been a good friend to me.'

'Serious stuff? What's that?'

'Look, I've said too much. I don't want it getting back to him that I've said stuff about him behind his back.' That sounds genuine. It is. 'He's a friend. I'm not going to gossip about him. I like him, I just wouldn't do the things he does for a living. I'd be way too scared of getting caught. That's all I'll say.' Another pause. Let her think about all that for a few seconds. 'Let's not talk about him, huh? Let's enjoy this lunch. We need to give ourselves a chance here.'

She didn't mention Calum again. She actually didn't say an awful lot. At one point she even seemed a little upset. George struggled through the next half-hour. It's a strange thing. He's done some rough stuff in his work. Beaten up people who didn't deserve it. Good people, too. He didn't feel as sorry for them as he does for Anna right now. They're walking out; she has her coat. Into the car and driving back to her flat. Silent, most of the way.

'Well, that was nice,' she's saying. They're outside the flat again. Saying it to be polite. It wasn't nice. 'You have my number. You can call me if you'd like.' Saying it with no enthusiasm. Like she already knows he never will.

'I will,' he's saying. He won't. 'I enjoyed that.' He didn't. She's smiling and going inside. He's back in the car. Hated every minute of that ordeal. Not because of her, but because of what he was doing. Hating John Young right now. Hating himself.

36

Picking up a car from his brother's garage. William's always happy to see him. Always looking out for his little brother, without going into unnecessary details. He knows enough about what Calum does to avoid awkward questions.

'I might need it for a while. Could even be weeks.'

William's nodding. 'I've got something you can use. Not a punter's car, one I bought. Got it cheap. Bit of a con job really, the guy was desperate to sell, so I sort of ripped him off.'

'Sort of?'

'He needed the cash quick,' William's shrugging. 'It's pretty manky. I'll need to tart her up before I sell her on.' He's leading Calum into his office at the back of the garage. 'I'll make good money from her, though.' Closing the door behind them. 'What sort of job leaves you needing a car that long?' he's asking. The concerned brother. Genuine concern.

'Nothing that's actually illegal,' Calum's saying. 'Don't worry, it won't get picked up.'

'It's not the car I'm worried about,' William's saying, handing over the keys.

He didn't ask about the hands this time. Calum went a

while without seeing his mother or brother after the David-son incident. Letting the wounds heal. The dust settle. Then he went round to his mother's for Sunday dinner. He spun her a yarn about helping a friend with some printing. Same yarn that served so poorly with Emma. Consistency is important. His mother bought it. Never one to ask questions she might not enjoy the answer to. William was there, too. He wasn't taken in, not for a second. He didn't ask how it happened, he knows better, but he checked on Calum a few times. William knows the business. He's on the outer fringes, his business making a little extra money now and then by helping out connected people. Providing cars, respraying and tagging. William probably knows Shug, has a rough idea of what's going on. He wants his little brother out of it, mostly for their mother's sake. Too late for that. Calum's in too deep. William wants his brother safe, but he can't stop helping him. Giving him vehicles when he needs them, no matter the risk. Never charging a penny. Always the brother.

Sitting outside an old man's house in a car that smells dubious. Spying on one of the few people you respect. The tedium of the watch. Sitting watching a front door that doesn't open. Halfway along the street. Far enough not to stand out. Far enough that there's minimal risk of Frank spotting Calum. He should know he's being watched. An old hand like Frank, he should guess he has a tail. Obvious that a guy like Jamieson will take every precaution. Obvious that the world needs to know what Frank does next. Which, right now, doesn't seem like much. Calum can only guess that he's in there. What he knows of Frank's routine says he's in there. Might not come out all day. Certainly doesn't need to go to the club any more. He should; he ought to make a point of going round regularly. Putting a little pressure back onto Jamieson. Make himself useful in any way. It might not be what Frank wants to do, but it's a form of protection. You go round, you do the advisory job you've been offered. You rebuild trust.

Frank won't do that. Not his mindset. Calum's seen it in a few of the older ones. They consider themselves to be apart from the rest of the industry. The mindset of experience. You spend decades as a gunman, which few do, and you think of the world from a different angle. It's all about secrecy and self-preservation. A lifetime of hiding the things you do. It changes you. It must have changed Frank, too. He'll consider anything that draws him into the open to be counter-intuitive, threatening even. A friend's offer to keep him earning past his sell-by date will be spurned. He's a gunman, and that's all he'll ever be. You spend so long teaching yourself to be that, you simply can't become any other kind of person. You become so tied to your work that it dominates your life. Destroys it.

How long does it take? Calum's thinking. Hardly watching the house now. Nothing to watch. How long before he himself won't be able to live any other kind of life? He's been involved in the business for more than ten years now. Been a gunman and nothing else for eight or nine years. Started young and found he liked the life. Few jobs, decent money, peace and quiet. The quiet life of the freelancer. Now he's been drawn into an organization. Working whenever he's told to work. Unable to walk from things he doesn't like. Won't be long before he's thinking like the old men. A gunman and nothing else. Any other offer of work an insult. Any other life unthinkable. Just the thought of being reduced to an adviser will sicken Frank. His role as a gunman should be respected. People should recognize that it's a speciality, that the skills can't be transferred elsewhere. People should recognize his value. Offering him a role that's often used as a cover is humiliating to him. That's why he'll say no. That's why this has to end badly. Calum can't see any other way.

In the afternoon, the door opens. An old man, huddled up in a puffy-looking jacket, steps out. Pulls the door shut behind him. Locks it. Moves off down the front path to the gate. It's Frank all right, but he looks so shrivelled. You see him at work and he seems different. Young for his age. Wrinkled, sure, but a man of obvious strength. Now he's shuffling and small. There's a slight limp from the hip replacement. Perhaps made worse from falling on the floor outside Scott's flat. He looks to all the world like a little old man. Which is how he wants the rest of the world to see him. Weak and vulnerable. A kindly gent with a gleam in his eye, who would do no harm to anyone. Calum gets it. He gets that you create a different image for people outside the business. A gunman never has to look tough. You don't have to look tough when you're doing a job. The gun looks tough enough for both of you.

Thank God he isn't coming this way. Frank's gone in the other direction, as Calum assumed he would when he parked here. He'll go to the pub. He'll have a pint. He'll come home. Does it every day, apparently. Every day on his own. Seems rather sad to Calum. He'd rather stay in the house. The only thing lonelier than being alone is being alone with lots of other people. Frank's walking along the street. It's raining and it's cold, but he's going through his routine. Calum's watching him get out of sight. Let him get round the corner. Give him a couple of minutes. Starting the car now. Moving along the street to the corner, he can see Frank well ahead of him. Calum's turning right, to go the long way round. He'll still get to the pub first. Watch Frank go in, watch him come out. Get back to the house ahead of him. It's boring. Much as he hates to admit it, it's insulting too. If Jamieson thinks Calum's so talented, why the hell is he doing a garbage job like this?

Sitting, watching Frank go in. Sitting, watching the sad sacks go in and out of the pub after Frank. Losers, every single one of them. Middle of a weekday and they're in a dingy bar. They look like they've seen the end of the world. They'll consider Frank to be one of them. If only they knew. Takes Frank more than half an hour to drink whatever he drinks. Then he's out the front door. Heading back the way he came. Hood pulled up over his head. He looks so small. Calum never noticed that before.

Starting the car when there's a safe distance. Going quickly back, the long way round. Back to the house. It must be a boring life for Frank. Probably only made bearable by the thrill of the job. The secret life now lost. Here he comes. Limping a little more than he was when he first left the house. He wasn't ready to go back to work. Calum can see it now. Jamieson should have realized. A man still limping from an operation is no gunman.

Frank's back in his house. It's got quickly dark outside. His living-room light is on. There's a skill to following someone. There's also a skill to being followed. Frank may have guessed that he's being tailed. Might even have spotted Calum. But he keeps playing the part. Doing all he can to prove what a good employee he is. All the time he could be in touch with another organization. If he knows he's being followed, then he knows his phone records are being checked. He's old, but he still knows the current tricks. He has to. All good pros do. He could be sitting in there plotting anything. Making a mug of Jamieson. Calum, too. Or he could be sitting in there, oblivious. That would be an indictment. A man of his experience, his knowledge, unaware of what's happening around him. Unforgivable. It's not a mistake he would have made in the past. Not when he was sharp. This isn't the past. It's dark now. Evening. Calum's done his work for the day. He's driving home.

37

He's spent most of the day looking over old case notes. Some date back to the Seventies. Some of them name Frank MacLeod. Some hint at his then-employer's involvement. None comes up with enough evidence for a charge. Not even close. Even now, decades later, it's obvious that Frank MacLeod was guilty. Not in all of them. Some of them it's hard to tell. Some of them he's probably innocent. Not as if he was the only murderer in town. There are even a few cases where people have clearly thrown Frank's name in there with no good reason. They were desperate. They had a victim and they wanted to convict Frank of murder. Unfortunately there was a big gap between those two facts, where the evidence should be.

Always the same two. Two cops who never worked together. One had retired before the other became a detective. Both with a bee in their bonnet about Frank MacLeod. Determined that they would be the one to nail him. The older one retired twenty years ago: Richard Whyte. Fisher remembers the younger of them. He was still around when Fisher started out. Guy called Douglas Chalmers. Very old-school. Good cop, though he never got close to Frank, either.

Fisher's at his desk, a slip of paper in front of him. Is he becoming those two old cops, or is he betraying them? Maybe the latter. They would definitely think so, but times have changed. Frank isn't the big fish he once was. Not if he's on the outside. Besides, catching him as a contact is a catch of sorts. Not the lifetime stretch he deserves, sure. That would be the ideal, but it won't happen. Frank was always too good for that. Then he got old, like everyone else. Had his hip replaced. Obviously isn't fit enough for it any more. Now he stops being the big catch and becomes the bait. He could lead to Jamieson. To all of Jamieson's people. That would be worth a guarantee of safety. Not one he truly deserves. How many people has he killed? He should be inside. It could still happen. Tell Frank he gets safety for info. When you have the info, arrest him anyway. Then forget about ever getting another contact in the business. Shit, it always has to be this bloody awkward. People like Frank MacLeod can never give you an easy ride.

He has the number on a piece of paper in front of him, daring himself to throw it in the bin. Go for the short-term prize of MacLeod himself. Tail him. Wait for him to slip up, now that he has no protection. Then get him in the dock. Wait for him to slip up – that's a laugh. Fisher's running his hand over the pile of case notes again. Not a single mistake in there. Not one. No reason why Frank should slip up now. Less reason, in fact. No safety net means more precautions.

Less work. A man like Frank MacLeod will adapt to suit his conditions. So the hope of an arrest dwindles. The hope of a contact remains. Talk to him. Offer an olive branch. Give him the only protection that can guarantee a prison-free retirement. Still might not take it. Free of prison, but an enemy for those he informs on. It would still be a life on the run. Hiding until death.

He's picking up the phone and dialling. Only one way to find out how this will go. It's ringing. Still ringing. No answering service. Fisher's hanging up. So either Frank isn't at home or he's not answering his phone. Might be better to go round there, but that's not how you cultivate a contact. Turning up on their doorstep scares the crap out of them. Fisher knows that. Seen it happen before. You turn up and put that sort of pressure on and they run a mile. First thing they do is look to their boss for protection. If, like Frank, they don't have a boss, then they go to ground. You've lost them forever as a contact. Subtle manoeuvres. Like trying to get a shy girl to go out with you. Slow and steady, nothing to frighten them away. Frank MacLeod isn't like other contacts, though. Nobody else has his experience. Experience of the business, the people in it, its relationship with the police. He must know so much. He isn't going to be frightened by the same things that normal people are.

If he's frightened at all. Sitting here in an office in the police station, dark outside, making assumptions. Any other

266

gunman would be nervous, surely. Out of one organization, looking around for somewhere to go. Old Frank might be different. Old Frank might already have a plan. He might already have been through this sort of thing before. Knows exactly what to do. Already contacted an organization that he knows will take him. A bigger one than Jamieson's. Sell your soul to another ageing scumbag like Alex MacArthur. Give him everything you know about Jamieson. Wouldn't be long before Jamieson's world fell apart around him. Frank's biggest threat would be gone, his safety almost assured. Don't kid yourself that there's loyalty amongst these people. They're all as fickle as the wind. They go where the money is. They go where they'll be safe from the consequences of their own actions. Greedy cowards, by and large. Just because he's old and smart, that doesn't make him any different.

Dialling the number a second time. He's let twenty minutes pass. Maybe Frank's back home. Or maybe he ignores strange numbers first time round, as a matter of routine. Perhaps he'll answer this time. It's ringing, again. Fisher hasn't thought about what he'll say. No point. These people can be very unpredictable. The only thing you can consider is your tone. Polite, but not friendly. You're not here to make a friend. Firm, but not aggressive. They have to know you're in charge, but they also have to know they're safe with you.

'Hello?' A wary voice. Clearly not young, but not feeble-sounding, either.

'Hello, is this Frank MacLeod?'

The slightest pause. 'It is. How may I help you?' If not old, certainly old-fashioned. Much too polite to be a modern gangland figure.

'My name's Michael Fisher. Do you know who I am?'

Another pause. This one longer. 'I do.'

Fisher's allowing Frank that little moment of silence. Let him gather his thoughts, question what this call means. Let him compose himself, so that he doesn't feel he's being jumped.

'Then you probably have a fair idea why I'm calling.' Matter-of-fact tone. Two guys who've been around the block, talking honestly to one another.

'Why don't you tell me why,' Frank's saying. Sounds a little like defiance. Probably a default setting. A cop calls you up, and you immediately get all defensive.

Fair enough, Fisher should have seen that coming. Frank might be smart, but he's had forty years of conditioning. At a time like this, his instincts will be taking over.

'I know you probably don't want to talk to me, Frank, but I have a few things I think you should hear. You're on the out-side now. I know it; so do you, so does everyone. It's common knowledge by now.' That's a little white lie, but it'll come true soon enough. 'I know where that leaves you. I want to make you an offer.' Pause, leave it hanging. Wait and see what reaction you get. For an uncomfortably long time, nothing.

He's thinking about it, which is a start. There are plenty of people who would have told him where to stick his offer, without even stopping to hear what it is. Not old Frank. He has more sense than that. How much more remains to be seen. He's still not speaking.

'I'm not going to demand anything of you right now,' Fisher's saying. 'I think a face-to-face would be a good thing. We'll both be better able to judge how this might go.'

There's a sigh on the other end. Sounds like exasperation, not disgust. 'I doubt it would go very well for either of us,' Frank's saying.

Time to put some cards on the table. 'Maybe not,' Fisher's saying. 'On the other hand, I can offer you something you won't get anywhere else. You're on the outside now. You'll become a target, no matter what you do. You know how these things work. I can offer you safety. Hide you; protect you – whatever's needed. I can keep you out of jail. I'm not asking for yes or no right now. But let's meet.'

Another pause. 'I have your number now,' Frank's saying quietly. 'Let me think about it. Call you back.'

It went better than expected. It wasn't no. It was a probably not – but that's something he can work on. Frank will call him back. Could take a while, but if he can get a meeting, then Fisher would be halfway there. Once a person commits to meeting, it usually means they've already made up their mind. There's a lot of risk in a meeting, so it's a commitment in itself.

There's nobody else in the office now. Couple of the guys from the nightshift have come and gone. God knows where to, probably the canteen. He doesn't care. For once, Fisher's not in the mood to chastise. This is his one chance. A chance to crack the Scott killing, maybe the Winter killing, too. Maybe a number of others. A chance to bring down Peter Jamieson. A chance to do something that would actually matter. So little of what he does matters any more. You round up some moron with a gun who thinks he's a gangster, and you chuck him in jail for ten years. Within a fortnight three other morons have taken his place. You arrest the attention-seekers, the ones who think they're celebrities and live accordingly. All the while, the people who matter stay hidden away. Safe. Then you get the chance. The once-in-a-decade opportunity to bring down an entire organization that matters. This might just be it.

38

His alarm goes off at half past seven. He always gets up at half past seven on a weekday, eight at weekends. It occurs to him now that he could ignore it. It occurs that he should have been ignoring it all his adult life. Never had a proper job. A job making something, contributing something. He's only ever been a destroyer. Destroyers don't need to get out of bed early. But he will. He's spent so long forming the habit, it's become impossible to break. When you live an unpredictable life, you need to form some sort of routine. It's comforting to Frank. You don't control your work. Your work controls the kind of life you're able to live. So you build routines, and you stick to them.

He's out of bed, into the shower, dressed, downstairs for breakfast. Now he's thinking about his situation. Where does he stand? All alone, it seems. He can't think of another organization he would want to go and work for. Plenty that would take him, there's no doubt. He could find work if he needed it. And protection, which he does need. People would give it, but they would want so much in return. He would have to deliver them Jamieson, and all his people. They would only take Frank because of what he knows. They would dismiss his skills as those of an old man, as Jamieson has. It wouldn't be progress. He doesn't want to give them Jamieson.

He's making a second cup of coffee. A little less milk in it this time. Looking round his house. Looking at his lifetime's accumulations. Nothing. At least, nothing that he couldn't live without. No family at all. No friends that he couldn't leave behind. A lifetime of gaining nothing. It didn't feel like that at the time, obviously, but you can see it on reflection. All that time, all that work. In the end you have nothing.

He's going to the shop. It's an excuse to get out of the house, nothing more. Buy a few things that he probably doesn't need. A loaf of bread that'll go green and be thrown out. A carton of milk that he'll use half of. He'll buy a news-paper and read maybe three pages of it. He has his coat on, and he's out into the street. A casual look around – nobody there he doesn't recognize. After a job he's usually very careful to check. You're on the lookout for reprisals, no matter who the target was. If it was someone in an organ-ization, then there could be a professional after you. Harder to spot a pro, but they're less likely to come after you anyway. Organizations don't go after gunmen; they go after the person who hired them. Different when it's a smaller target. Some guy trying to get rich on his own, steps on toes. Not connected to an organization, just trying to make money for him and his family. You can never predict the reaction of a family to a hit. People get emotional, pledge vengeance.

He doesn't think of the Scott job as a job at all. It wasn't his kill, in the end. Calum was the guy who did the job, not Frank. They're Calum's victims, another two notches for him. Hard to know how to feel about it. It's strange that he's still thinking about them. Scott and McClure. He's usually stopped thinking about a target this long after a job. You think about nothing else in the build-up, and then you do the job. The second it's finished and you're clear of the location, your life goes back to the old routine. You think and do the things that you usually do, and the victim is no more than a name in the newspaper. It sounds cold, he realizes, but you have to have that detachment. Can't spend your life thinking about all the jobs you've done, it's not a sensible way to live. As he's walking along the street, heading for the corner shop, he's thinking about Scott and McClure again. Two people he didn't kill. Should have. Didn't. They could be his last ever targets.

He's in the shop. Loading a few things into a basket, hardly even looking at them. He has to do something. He suddenly knows that he has to do something. He can't live this life. He can be the sad old man when he has work to keep him thrilled, but not without it. Without it, he really is just a wreck, waiting for the end. He's placing his basket on the counter; the woman behind the counter is adding it up. He sees her three or four times a week, but he has no idea what her name is. She must be in her mid-thirties, maybe a bit older. She looks a little worn, but she's not wearing a wedding ring. Twenty-something years his junior, but he's always thought of himself as a young man. In the past he would never have thought of asking her out. Too close to home. If he's not working any more, then why not? Because he's built the image of the sad old man – that's why not. This is the cost of the life you've led.

A single bag of shopping; walking back along the street. He knows what he's going to do. A mildly attractive woman in a shop, and he knows. If he's ever going to have the freedom to have that life, to be able to ask, then it needs to be away from here. It needs to be a life outside the business. Only one organization can make that happen. He has to call Fisher. It feels like a betrayal, but why should it? Jamieson pushed him out, not the other way round. Peter Jamieson threw him overboard, and now he has to find any life raft he can. He keeps telling himself that it's not a betrayal. He hasn't convinced himself yet, but he'll keep saying it. Into the house; the few items of shopping put away. Over to the phone. Going through the menu, finding the last number that called. Fisher's office number. Everyone in the business knows Fisher. They know he specializes in anti-organized crime. Tough. Respectable. A man they hate because they fear him.

Pressing Dial and listening to it ring. He might not be

there. Will Frank have the guts to call him a second time? Unlikely. He knows how hard this is.

'Hello.' Enthusiastic, expectant. Sounds like Fisher was sitting by the phone, waiting for the call. Nice to feel important, even if it is the police.

'Mr Fisher. It's Frank MacLeod. I've been thinking about what you said yesterday.'

'Good,' Fisher's saying. Now he's waiting for the follow-up, but nothing's coming.

Frank can't quite bring himself to say it. He's already made the decision, but until he says it, he isn't a traitor. Isn't the worst of the worst. He's told himself that a lot of other people have done it, but that doesn't help. Just means there's a lot of other traitors. Forty years of being told that it's the worst thing you can do is hard to overcome.

'I think we should meet,' he's saying at last. It sounds like he's forcing the words out, as if he wants rid of them. 'Soon, I think,' he's adding. It's hard to hide the nerves.

'I think soon would be best,' Fisher's saying. Good to get the agreement in, make it seem like they're on the same wavelength. 'Do you have any preference for where?'

Frank's thinking. Where the hell do you do this sort of thing? Where would be safe? Nowhere is totally safe, that's the truth of it. The location matters less than the cop probably realizes. If you're being watched, then anywhere is deadly. If you're not, then most places are safe enough.

'There's a house we can use,' Fisher's saying, impatient at the delay. 'Or I can come round to you, if that would make you feel safer. The choice is yours.'

He certainly won't have the cop round to his house. That's a dumb suggestion, Fisher should realize that. Meeting in public would be fine if he could be sure they wouldn't be spotted. 'I think this house of yours would be the best option. What's the address?'

It's not too late to back out. Go to Jamieson; tell him you've been contacted by Fisher. Tell him you have the address of Fisher's meeting house for contacts. Jamieson can have it watched; see what he learns from that. It might just prove that Frank's not useless, that he can still contribute to the organization. Nah, that's not how they would see it. They've got it into their heads that he's a decrepit old fart, with nothing to offer. If he went and told them about this call, they would view it with suspicion. They now see Frank as a suspicious character. He's seen it happening to others, he knows it's happening to him. Still not too late to walk away from this.

They set the meeting for tomorrow. Mid-morning. Quite possible to stay away. He's not truly committed until he turns up. Not a traitor until he goes through the door. All this because of Tommy-bloody-Scott. What a laugh! Scott's finally important, but only because he's dead.

39

Wasn't an easy place to find. Hidden away on a side street, the kind of little dump she expected. Calum had told her it was a small place, but that his brother manages to make an okay living from it. There are a number of cars parked along the street in front of the entrance, enough room left to drive cars in and out of the building. She can see someone inside, standing looking at a car that's up on a ramp. He looks too young to be William. It would help if she knew what William looked like. She's approaching the mechanic. He's stopped staring at the car for long enough to glance her way.

'Can I help you, love?' he's asking.

'I'm looking for William MacLean,' she's saying. No detail. Not to anyone else. Emma knows she'll have to be careful, even with her boyfriend's brother.

'Nah, he's busy, can I help?'

'No, it has to be William. Is he here?'

With a sigh the mechanic's disappeared to the rear of the garage. Into the office at the back. There's a window that looks down at the garage, and she can see the back of some-one's head inside. Must be him. What an introduction this is going to be! Calum always speaks warmly of his brother, which is something. The mechanic's coming back.

'You can go through,' he's saying, nodding towards the office.

Up a couple of wooden steps and into William's company. He's sitting at a small desk, a computer in front of him. It's a cramped, narrow little place. He's nodding hello, looking up at her enquiringly. He looks a little nervous. Worried that she's a customer with a complaint. Worse than that: a lawyer for a customer with a complaint. You can see the similarity with Calum. It's in the mouth and chin, especially. William's perhaps a little more handsome. Not noticeably older. Lacks the sharp expression that Calum always has.

'You're looking for me?' William's saying, trying to sound friendly. He's checking that his hand's clean before he offers it to shake. Some people can be sniffy about a little speck of engine oil.

'You're William MacLean?'

'I am.'

'Calum's brother?'

That got a reaction. A flash of the sharp look. The polite smile falling away. It's a look that demands that she is careful what she says next. He might not like what his brother does, but Calum's still his brother.

'I am,' he's saying gruffly. His hand had gone out a little, but it's being withdrawn.

'My name's Emma. I'm Calum's girlfriend.'

Okay, that got a reaction too. William's sitting back in his chair, looking at her. He looks suspicious. This is clearly news to him.

'I just wanted to clear something up with you,' Emma's saying. Be quick. Don't let the conversation become about the relationship. 'You remember a week ago. In the middle of the night.'

'Uh,' he's saying. She's stopped, waiting for a response. He doesn't know where this is going. Not somewhere good, he can guess. These aren't the things a brother's girlfriend should be saying. 'Go on,' he's saying.

'You called Calum, right?'

He's pausing. 'Er, yeah, I called him,' he's nodding, a little uncertain. Piecing it together. Calum's used him as an alibi. The girl's got suspicious, maybe thinks Calum's playing away. 'That's right, I did.'

He doesn't look certain at all. Could be because he was drunk on the night. Could be because he's lying. Seems more likely the latter. She doesn't trust him.

'You're sure you definitely called him? Do you remember why you called him?'

Now there's a hard look on his face. One that isn't going to go away in a hurry. She's asking awkward questions, and none too politely. 'I said I called him, didn't I? What exactly is

279

your problem with this anyway, Emma?' Saying her name like an insult.

'I didn't say I had a problem, I just want to know.' She's getting defensive. Getting a little aggressive. It's not helping. 'I'm just not sure you're being honest with me.'

Mistake.

'You're calling me a liar?' He's raising his voice now. 'You're saying I didn't call him. You're calling Calum a liar too, is that it? Saying my wee brother's lying to you. You sure you're his girlfriend?'

This is going badly wrong. She needs to bail out. 'Listen, I just want to know.'

'Yeah, well, why in the hell are you asking me? Ask Calum. If you don't trust his answer, you shouldn't be going out with him. If you even are. Jesus, you turn up here giving me grief when I've never fucking heard of you. Some girlfriend, when he's never even told me about you.' Shouting now. Getting up and holding open the door to the office for her to leave.

He's watching her walk out of the garage. Just the kind of girl Calum would go for. Smart and trouble. Getting his phone from his pocket. Screen's filthy. One day he'll get round to cleaning it. Ringing Calum. Nothing. Going through to voicemail. Telling his brother that he just had a visit from a woman claiming to be his girlfriend. Asking questions about some night a week ago. Telling Calum that of course he backed him up, but if she is his girlfriend, then he might want to be careful. Seems cute, but terrifying. Not the sort of girl-friend Calum should have. Hanging up. What's he supposed to do? William always tries to help his brother, but he knows it's not right. He wants Calum safe. Maybe a tough little nut of a girlfriend would be just the thing to force Calum to change his life. Or maybe not. Maybe it's not possible now. William knows how the industry works. Once you're in, it's mighty hard to get out.

Emma has another visit to make. Not likely to go much better than the last one, but she might get more info. This one can't bullshit his way out of it. Up the stairs to his flat and knocking on the door. It takes twenty seconds or so for him to answer. He looks rough, hung-over maybe. George is glaring back at her. Doesn't look shocked, just disappointed. He's running a hand through his curly hair. He's wishing she had enough sense to take the message. Worst thing she could do is ask questions.

'Can I come in?' she's asking.

'I suppose you'd better.' He's stepping aside to let her past. See, this is why he doesn't do relationships. The only woman he'd ever get serious with would be one with as many secrets as he has. Might be possible for him. No such woman in the whole city for Calum. He's closing the door behind her and following her into the living room.

'I know why you took Anna out for lunch,' she's saying, standing in the middle of the floor.

'That right?'

'Yeah. You took her out so that you could drop hints about Calum. Because you don't have the balls to tell me to my face. Well, I'm right here. Why don't you tell me now?'

What's the answer to that? Shit, it's like people gang up to make life more difficult than it needs to be. 'What are you doing?' he's asking. Seriously, and with a little bit of anger in his voice. He can't help it. 'You're not this stupid. The hell are you doing, coming round here asking things like that? You know. You just said you know.'

'I know all right,' she's nodding, and there are tears in her eyes. That's shut George up. 'I know that he went off in the middle of the night a week ago. I know that he says he went to pick up his brother, but he didn't. I know two guys got killed that night. Now his brother's lying for him, and you're trying to push me away from him.'

She's crying properly now, and George is standing there watching her. Two guys died that night. Scott and McClure. She can't know. Not really.

'You're just putting two and two together,' he's saying in a whisper.

'Tell me I'm wrong,' she's demanding.

He's pausing. Just a little too long. 'Of course you're wrong. You're being hysterical,' he's saying. Doesn't sound like he means it. Not one bit.

She's nodding. 'At least now I know.' She's making for the door, shooting a last dirty look at George.

'You are wrong,' he's saying loudly. 'Totally wrong.'

'Oh, don't worry,' she's saying as she's pulling open the door. 'I won't tell him that you're a grass. You'll be perfectly safe.'

George is moving to the door. He's going to go after her. No, he's not. He's stopping. Why make it worse? She's slamming the door behind her. It's not as though she's wrong. She's dangerously right.

40

As soon as he got Frank's call yesterday, he came round to the house and set everything up. Two small recording devices, one in the hall and one in the kitchen. They might not be of the highest quality, but they don't need to be. This conversation isn't ever going to be replayed in court. Fisher wants to have these on record, for his own use only. No other cop knows about this, or will ever be told. He needs to get every word he can out of a guy like Frank. You don't need this effort for the likes of Kenny McBride; you can demand that they repeat themselves. You don't push Frank. As a contact, he's A-list. He's A-list because of all he's seen, all he's done.

Therein lies the difficulty. How do you combat the itch to arrest him? There are some contacts, the low-level morons, that you can create a relationship with. Not friends, but comfortable. That'll never be the case with Frank MacLeod. Fisher will only ever see him as a killer. A man who's simply been too talented, and too lucky, to find himself in jail. That's if he turns up. A lot of them don't show up at the first meeting; their bottle crashes. They come the second or third time. Or, more likely, you never hear from them again. That'll be the case with Frank. For him it'll be first time, or not at all.

As it happens, Frank's sitting in his own kitchen, thinking much the same thing. If he doesn't go to this meeting, he'll never go. Hand himself over to the police, be at their mercy. He'll have to give them good info. Things they can use – no bullshit. They won't be interested in the old news of his early days. They might close a few cases from back then with his help, but they won't consider it important. It's the current generation that motivates them. It's not a moral question, not any more. The idea of the grass being the scum of the earth, so what? When you've been pushed to the outside, left adrift, none of the old rules matter. They can't push you out and then demand that you keep playing by their rulebook. He'll play the game his way now. There's a personal issue, though. If he wants to get out of Glasgow, set up somewhere safe, then he has to hand them Jamieson.

He actually met John Young first. Didn't have a great impression of the boy. A little cold, a little too vague. He came round to visit Frank. Introduced himself, told Frank that he was Peter Jamieson's right-hand man. Frank knew the name, of course, and he knew Jamieson was small. Not the sort of guy he had much intention of going to work for. At that point he was sure he could still get work with the best. Young urged him to meet Jamieson before he made his mind up. Frank agreed. Met him in a pub. Dingy little place, the only one Jamieson owned at the time. A pub, a couple of betting shops, some industrial property. Not much to shout about. He had plenty of ambition, though. Lots of energy, lots of personality. Lots of plans too, and that was what impressed Frank. This wasn't your typical climber, full of big ideas that would never happen. Jamieson was ambitious, sure, but he was sensible too. His targets were realistic; the things he had set up were detailed and plausible. He was the most impressive young boss Frank had met in decades. He agreed to work for Jamieson a week or so later. Never looked back. Best decision he made in his entire career. Jamieson's was the best-run organization he ever worked for. The fact that it wasn't a family business helped enormously. The fact that Jamieson had the best instincts in the business helped, too. It was a joy to work for him.

Now he's putting his coat on, getting his car keys from the phone table in the hall. Ignore all sentiment. That's the secret to being a good gunman. Dennis Dunbar taught him that. It's the key to being good at anything in this business. Frank learned that for himself. He thought highly of Peter Jamieson. Not as a son, maybe more a nephew. He loved the boy, if we're being honest. But that's all gone now. That Peter Jamieson doesn't exist any more. There's a new one, and he's a threat and has to be considered accordingly. Out the door, into the car. Looking up and down the street, not seeing anything that shouldn't be there. Heading for the address Fisher gave him. He doesn't need satnav, doesn't need to check a map. This is his city. Born and raised, he knows every inch of it. It's changed a lot, and you have to keep learning, but he never shirked that side of his work. No good pro finds himself lost in his own city.

He's parked a street away from the house. Sitting in the car, taking his time, thinking it through. He drove along the street once, saw the house. Terraced house, easy for neighbours to see you come and go. Not a great location. Still, if he's not being followed, then it doesn't matter. He hasn't spotted a tail. He's sure he would have seen one, if it was there. He's Frank MacLeod. He's tailed countless guys, knows all the signs. There's a nagging feeling, the sense that he should be followed. If the roles were reversed, he would have put a tail on Jamieson. At least for a little while, just to see what his reaction was.

Make the decision. Stop stalling. He's getting out of the car, pressing the button to lock it. Walking slowly round the corner. He's feeling his hip a little more today. The doc warned that he would feel discomfort for a little while. Warned him there would be days like this.

There's a knock on the front door. Fisher's moving quickly along the narrow corridor. He's looking through the peephole. It's Frank, and he's on his own. It has occurred to Fisher, more than once, that this could be a trap. Maybe if his work hadn't been going down the toilet of late, he would have believed it. If Shug's targeting Jamieson, then there's a link from Jamieson to the Winter, Scott and McClure deaths. A link that might threaten a man like Jamieson, if the investigations had been successful. Jamieson isn't daft. He won't target a cop unless that cop is on the brink of taking him down. It's always a last resort. This would be a good set-up, though. Send the driver round as a contact. That's all off the record. The driver feeds a line about the gunman. Fisher calls up the gunman, sets up a private meeting at a secret location. Just the two of them. Nobody else even knowing they're meeting. Good God, that would be a perfect set-up.

Frank's stepping in the door, all by himself. He looks small, old and ordinary. He looks like any old man who would pass you in the street. That's the point. Don't forget. He's nodding to Fisher, but not saying anything. The door's shut behind them. They're standing in the corridor, at the bottom of the stairs. It's gloomy and unpleasant. It sets a tone.

'Come through,' Fisher's saying. He's leading the way through to the kitchen. It's become a familiar meeting place for him. Prudence says it's time to find somewhere else. You keep meeting people in the same place, and someone's bound to work it out. Frank's followed him through. Fisher's gesturing for Frank to take a seat at the table. To his relief, Frank does. If this was a fix and he was going to kill him, it would have happened by now.

'Can I get you a cup of tea, Frank?' he's asking. Being friendly with this old murdering bastard.

'No thanks.'

He can see that Fisher's making an effort. He can see the strain it's putting on the cop, too. Fisher hates him. Of course he does. He's the enemy. They're not here to make friends. They're here to make a deal. The chance of a new life. The only chance of a new life. Even a job with another organization just means more of the same. The only racket that can protect him now is the police.

'I'm glad you came,' Fisher's saying. Sitting opposite him, looking serious. 'I know this isn't going to be easy. Not for either of us. We're from different sides of the fence, you and me. But I reckon we're both realists. Have to be. We have a chance to help each other. It's a chance that might not come along again.' He's pausing, waiting for Frank to speak.

'Maybe I will have that cup of tea.'

Fisher's putting milk in the cups. He knows what this is all about. Frank just wanted to shut him up. Typical of a criminal. Even the supposedly great ones – the ones at the top of the tree. They're all the same. The same little tricks, the same deflections, the same reluctance. They can't help themselves. It turns into an instinct for them, and it makes meetings like this an almighty chore. They know what needs to be said, but they prevent themselves from saying it until the very last minute.

'You take milk, sugar?'

Frank's shaking his head. Probably won't even drink the bloody tea. This is all about buying him time. More time to think about what he's done. More time he shouldn't need. Fisher's putting the cup down in front of him, sitting at the table again. No more delay.

'I'm led to believe that you're no longer working for Peter Jamieson.'

Frank's glancing at him. 'Not strictly true.' He's talking low, a little above a whisper. Forcing Fisher to listen close. 'My role has changed. Not necessarily for the better.'

Fisher's nodding. 'If you're being pushed out, then you only have one chance of a clean break,' he's saying. Frank's given him a knowing stare, then looked back to that spot on the table that he's been so taken with since he arrived. The stare was his way of saying that he has more than one option. He may only have one legal option, but they both know that's not a major consideration. 'I can give you a clean break. I can give you protection you won't get anywhere else. I know you could go work for someone else, but that can't be your best option. You already have a lot of enemies. Going to work for someone else makes that worse. It means I'll be keeping a close eye on you; see what you do for your new boss. A lot of people will be keeping a close eye on you. I can put you somewhere nobody will see you. Out of the city. Across the border, if that's what you want. You can have a normal life.'

He saved that line until last on purpose. Frank knows it, too. Fisher's seen members of the old guard like Frank before. Not many. Never personally handled one as a contact, not someone this high up the food chain. But they all have one thing in common. The desire to live like normal people. Just a few years of normality, when you're not looking over your shoulder. Most of them have gone decades without experiencing that. Some are stupid enough to try to live it without protection. Selfish enough to try to create normal relationships that put other people in danger. Frank doesn't seem like that guy. Too smart.

'You think you can guarantee my safety?' he's asking.

Fisher knows how to answer this one. 'We both know I can't guarantee it one hundred per cent. No one can. But I can give you a better chance than anybody you might work for can. You go work for someone else, you have to be seen working for them. That would be the whole point of hiring you. You have to stay here and be visible. Look over your shoulder everywhere you go.'

He knows how to sell treachery, this boy. Frank's looking at him. Not a boy. A rather rough-looking middle-aged man. A lined face, in need of a shave. Looks like he's had a lot of late nights. Bags under his eyes. Not a surprise that he's stressed.

'And from me you would want?'

'I would want as much as I can get. I'm not going to ask you to incriminate yourself. I'm not daft, I know there's a lot of things you'll want to hold back, for a lot of reasons.' Be reasonable with the man. Don't be demanding. Let him think it might not be as bad as he expects. Hard to fool a man like Frank, but worth a try. 'You know that I'll need something reasonably big. Something recent and big. Giving you a new life means a big investment. Hard to get that these days. I'd need something good to back it up with. I know you have some good stuff you could afford to throw my way.'

Frank's nodding, but he's not saying anything. Why do all these old men have such inscrutable faces? Fisher's waiting for the response. It's make-your-mind-up time.

Something big. Something recent. Something that doesn't incriminate him. Hard to think of any job Jamieson's done that Frank wasn't connected to in some way. Lewis Winter, perhaps. He even had minor involvement in that. It was Frank that Calum went to after the phone call from Glen Davidson. Still, all he did was pass on information. They couldn't come down on him for that. It might be suitable. Suitable. Yeah. And then what? They go arrest Calum MacLean. A young guy who's a carbon copy of the person Frank was thirty years ago. A talent. A quiet boy who knows how to do the job. How to live the life. They go arrest George Daly. A good wee boy, that one. Good muscle. The only muscle that's ever been likeable, in Frank's experience. Most muscle are unforgivably stupid and annoying. Not George. Then they go arrest John Young. Okay. He could live with that. Young's sole redeeming feature is that he's always been a good friend to Jamieson. Honest, smart and loyal. Then they go and arrest Peter Jamieson. Not that he doesn't deserve it. They all deserve it. But Jamieson. Shit! He did so much for Frank. Bent over backwards. Anything Frank needed. From day one. Always no questions asked. He wasn't just a boss. He was a friend. That's too rare to sacrifice.

Frank's standing up. Not suddenly. Not overcome with emotion. He's an old man who's accepted the situation.

'I have to apologize to you,' he's saying to Fisher. 'I don't doubt that you would have done your best for me. You're a good cop; it's why they're scared of you. You're persistent. They don't like that. I thank you for the offer, but I can't do this. I thought, maybe, I could. It's not me. I've been too long at this. Sorry.'

Fisher's standing up. Shit! So close. That fucking close. 'Look, you don't have to walk away from this. The offer's there. It'll stay on the table. Let me give you my mobile number. You can call me any time. Never too late.' He knows he sounds desperate. He doesn't care. A golden contact is about to walk out the door, and he's not the sort to come back.

'I don't think that will be necessary. If I need you, I can find you. But I don't think that's going to happen.' He's smiling sadly. 'There's nothing else you could have done.'

Frank's gone. Walked out, and he won't be back. It feels like Fisher's last chance has just walked out that door. The Scott investigation will die. The best they can argue is that

Shug was supplying to Scott. Which he wasn't. Not directly anyway. So that'll go nowhere. Another investigation gone. They'll close it. Call it murder-suicide and everyone moves on. Another failure for Michael Fisher. Another chance for those bastards to laugh at him. People like Jamieson and Shug, laughing behind his back. Fucking up this city from top to bottom and getting away with it. Getting away with it because he can't close a case any more.

He's thumping the table. Twice. Enough to bruise his hand. Doesn't make him feel any better. He's grabbing the two recording devices – little plastic things the size of a memory stick. No fucking use. He'll keep them; it might become profitable to prove that he had a meeting with Frank MacLeod. Getting his coat on, stomping out the door. Back to his car. It's cold and wet.

41

He's followed Frank to this random house. It's a little odd. Frank drove past once, then parked a street away and walked back. It would be nice if he was visiting a friend or family. Maybe even a love interest. Calum's not aware of any love interest that Frank's ever had. It would be nice, but who goes to these lengths to visit a girlfriend? Chances are it's someone from another organization. The thing Jamieson feared. This isn't what Calum wants to report. He's parked at the top of the street, car facing away from the house. When Frank leaves, he's likely to go the other way back to his car. When Frank leaves, Calum already knows he won't be following him. Frank had disappeared into one of the houses on the street before Calum parked. He's not actually sure which house, but it'll be easy to spot Frank leave.

It's taking a while. There is surely nothing more tedious than tailing a guy. You sit and watch someone else lead their boring life. It's reality TV with consequences. He's checking his phone. Two missed calls from Emma. Missed calls from William and George as well. They can always wait. He missed a couple from Emma yesterday as well. It's not like her to be this clingy. He wants to call her, but he can't. As soon as he dials, Frank will come out that door and he'll have to hang up. Sod's Law. However pissed off Emma is at him for not answering will be nothing compared to her wrath if he hangs up on her. Keep missing those calls. Keep watching Frank. As soon as Frank bothers to do something noteworthy, Calum can report it to Jamieson. With any luck, that'll be the end of it. Do your job. But, oh boy, is it a boring job. The drizzle's coming down on the windscreen. Nobody will get a good look at him now. He's watching his mirror, waiting. And waiting.

A door's opened and Frank has stepped out. He hasn't even bothered to look up the street. He's come out the door, pulled his hood up and walked back the way he came. You can see his limp clearly. Not even checking for a tail. Calum's shaking his head. He's getting sloppy. Easy to see now why Scott was able to jump him. Stop thinking like that. That's Frank MacLeod. For all you know, he's going down the street to his car to get a weapon. Might be coming back for you. Watch. Pay attention. Watch front and back. If Frank's spotted him, then he could be a sitting duck. Five minutes have passed. Ten minutes. Nothing. Frank must have gone home. Staying to wait and see if anyone else comes out of the house is a risk. Might be the other person lives there. Won't come out. Might be there is no other person. Frank might have been storing something, or picking something up. It's a risk he'll take, though. Better to find out.

Someone coming out of the house. Stomping to a car parked on the street. Looking aggressive as he drops into the driver's seat. Didn't recognize him in the mirror. Too much rain, too far away. Looked middle-aged. Dressed in a dark coat and trousers. Doesn't tell anything. Shit, his car's facing the other way. He'll leave by the other end of the street. Time to break a couple of rules. Calum's starting his car before the target car is out of sight. That's rule-break number one. Now he's trying to execute a three-point turn in a narrow street. Drawing attention to himself, if there's anyone around to see. That's rule-break number two. He has the car round. Off down the street, trying to play catch-up. He's lucky. He spots the back end of the target car turning up another street. He moves a little closer, has it in sight. From here it's easy enough. You tail carefully. You tail in a way that does nothing to draw attention. When you're used to looking out for tails of your own, this becomes easy.

He's an aggressive little driver, this fellow. Quick off his mark, pulling in front of people. He's drawing plenty of attention to himself. Something Calum can't copy. It's causing him to fall back. Don't push it. Don't be tempted. Trust the traffic to slow the bastard down and bring him back towards you. The traffic never lets you down. If you know how to use it, you can escape a tail easily, or catch a tail easily. You just have to trust it. His tail is a red car. Probably smells a lot better than the crappy little banger William's loaned him. Doesn't look in much better condition, though. He's as close now as he has been at any point. He'll drop back a little, but first he wants a better look. Not at the driver, but the car. Get the number, then he can ID the driver any time. Provided the driver owns the car. In this business, they often don't. Still, you take the number. They've been going fifteen minutes now. It's getting irritating. His phone's starting to rumble in his pocket. He has it on silent. Probably another call from Emma. Another one blanked.

He's slowing down. Got his indicator on. He's pulling in off the street. Into a little private car park, surrounded on three sides by high walls, one of them the back of an adjacent building. Calum's carried on round the block. He can see the sign on the front of the building as he drives past, but he doesn't need to. He knows it's a police station. Never been in it, but he has a good idea where most of them are in the city. Round to the back again, looking for the driver. Gone. Must have gone straight in through the back door. The tradesmen's entrance. This isn't the place a man like Calum should be seen loitering, so he's driving on. Frank, you dumb bastard. You met a cop. Did he even know he was meeting one when he went? He's in such shit now. Or he will be, if Calum makes the report. Maybe he should give it more time. Give the old boy a chance to prove that he's not in the process of pissing away forty years' good service.

He's gone back to Frank's house. Driven past. The car's

there. He was half-hoping it wouldn't be. Half-hoping it would be at the club, and Frank would be talking to Jamieson. Telling him that he has a cop in his pocket now. No such luck. He's gone straight home, putting his feet up, out of the rain. Calum's going to do the same. Nothing else he can do for now. Trying to think of an excuse not to report to Jamieson tonight. He should make the report. He knows it. That's his job. You find something interesting, you report. He's found something. Found Frank MacLeod spending twenty minutes in the company of a detective. Private meeting, just the two of them. All very hush-hush. But for whose benefit? Frank going to the cops. Jesus, it doesn't bear thinking about. If he crossed that bridge, shit – they're all finished. Calum will be wrecked. Jamieson and Young, and everyone else who ever worked for them. Frank knows so much. Too much.

He's back at the flat. He's not panicked. Calum doesn't really do panic. A little sad about Frank; mostly annoyed at the prospect of having to move home again. If Frank's blown his cover, then they'll all be on the move. Looking for an angle. A way in which he could turn this to his advantage. A chance to get out of the organization. Hell, if Jamieson's organization falls apart, then Calum's free. All he has to do is stay out of jail. That would be just about impossible if he stays in the city. Stays in the country. If this was their first meeting, Frank might not have spilled many beans. This might have been them agreeing on a deal. In which case there's still time to shut him up. If Calum reports tonight.

He's walking up the stairs, more slowly than usual. Thinking things through. Now he's seen her. Sitting at the top of the stairs, her phone in her hand.

42

She's sitting at the kitchen table, waiting for him to sit down. He doesn't want to. He knows what this is going to be. Or has a good idea. The sooner he sits, the sooner it happens.

'I've called you,' she's saying. She looks angry. Upset.

'Yeah,' Calum's saying. 'I was helping William at his garage.'

'We need to have a conversation,' she's saying. Here it comes. She looks serious. She's good at that. 'I want to ask you something.'

He's sitting opposite, watching her. Trying to judge her expression. This is unpleasant for her, he can see that. Not just sad, but horrible. 'Go on,' he's saying.

'I'm not going to ask you what you do for a living. I think I know. I mean, I'm guessing what you generally do, not the specifics. I don't really want to know. I'd rather not.'

Maybe she doesn't want to know because it would upset her more, but that's not what it sounded like. It sounded as if she wanted to maintain deniability. She knows there's a lot to be said for blissful ignorance.

'I want to ask you. Is there any chance . . . ?' She's stopped and she's laughing. Not the happy sort of laugh. 'This just sounds stupid. Would you be willing to stop what you do for me?'

That was unexpected. He's sitting there, thinking about it. She's asking him to stop his work, for her. A woman he's known for, what, two months? She's asking him to make an almighty sacrifice. She doesn't understand. That's the truth of it. It seems like a romantic notion to her. The idea of her rescuing him from his degrading life of crime. She doesn't realize what she's asking. To walk away from his work would be to put his life at huge risk. Hers, too.

'It's not . . .' How do you say this without making her think she's playing second fiddle to his job? 'That's not how it works. You can't walk away.' How much does she know?

'You can always walk away,' she's saying. 'If you really want to.'

She's so earnest. It's one of her greater faults. Thinking that she knows everything. 'I don't know what exactly you think I do for a living. Maybe, if I started planning it now, I could walk away in a few months' time. Although it wouldn't be walking, it would be running.'

'I know you've been lying to me,' she's saying. 'You lied to me not five minutes ago. I know you weren't with your brother today. Been lying to me since day one, I guess. Stupid me.'

Calum's sighing. 'I never . . .' Nope, can't finish that

sentence without lying again. He's a good liar. Better than his brother anyway. Better than George, too. 'I want to be as honest with you as I can. It's just . . . better that you don't know some things.'

She's nodding. She's taking a hankie from her pocket, balling it up in her hands. 'I'm not completely gullible, Calum,' she's saying quietly. 'I knew you were lying at the time. I just didn't look too deep. Didn't want to see the truth. Well, I've looked now.'

Hard to respond to that. 'Okay.'

'I know that when you went out of here in the middle of the night last week it wasn't to pick up your brother. I knew it at the time. I did. I knew it, but I let it go. I thought you were up to no good. I figured it was something I could overlook.' A pause. 'Do you know that two guys were found dead that night?'

Oh God, don't do this. Calum thought she was smarter than that. If she thinks there's murder involved, then she must realize that silence is her best option. Now he has to lie. No choice.

'Whoa, wait a second. I hope you're not suggesting I had something to do with people dying.' Sounded convincing to him. Careful not to add a single detail that she hasn't already offered. Sounding genuinely offended. Shocked.

She's shaking her head. 'I didn't, at first. But then I went to see your brother. He lied to me about that night, same as you. He's a bad liar, your brother. Takes him too long to think of an answer. I don't think he's as smart as you are. Then I went to see George. He tried to lie too. I mentioned those dead people. I saw his reaction. I know.'

He's trying to laugh. It doesn't sound right to him. Or to her. 'I don't know what the hell George said, but you have to know that's not me. Jesus, Emma, what are you saying?' *What are you doing?* That's what he wants to ask. *Why the hell are you setting off alarms all over the city?* Questioning George. A man she must know is involved in the industry, too. How does she think that's going to end? This is the problem with people on the outside. They really think they're untouchable. They think that, because they play by the law, everyone else will play nice with them. They think they're protected by their own decency. They're wrong.

'Look, I don't know how involved you were. I know you were involved, so let's not lie to each other any more about that,' she's saying, holding up a hand before he can protest. 'I just . . . I think you're a good person. Or – I don't know – capable of being one. If you want. All I'm asking is that you stop that life. Find a better one.'

He's closing his eyes. He can't make her understand. 'I'm sorry, Emma; it just doesn't work like that.'

She's looking at him and she's shaking her head. She

thinks it's a lack of will. The world seems that easy to her. You want to do something, so you do it.

'I'm going to make it really easy for you,' she's saying. 'You either quit what you do, or you don't see me ever again. It's that easy.'

He's smiling wryly, which, incidentally, is the wrong response. He's thinking about his work. What would her reaction be if she knew? There would be no ultimatums then. She would be gone, no matter what he promised her.

'If it was as easy as you think it is, I would have done it already. I just don't have that option.'

She's nodding her head. Not saying anything. Twisting her mouth, trying to keep her emotions in.

It's taken twenty seconds of silence. Then a big sigh. The sort that tells you that a mind's made up. She's getting up, pulling the strap of her bag over her shoulder. She's looking down across the table at him. Now it's just sadness.

'Goodbye,' she's saying, and she's making for the door.

He does wish there was something he could say. Something that would make her understand without making her hate him. Something that might rescue the relationship. Relationships are so rare in his life. Losing this one will hurt, he knows that. What's the alternative? Everything he thinks about saying sounds stupid in his head. She's opening the door.

'I don't want to do what I do,' he's saying. She's stopped,

and she's looking back at him. Now she's stepping out through the door and pulling it shut behind her. And he's back where he started. Back where he should always have been. Alone.

43

Staring out the window, watching the rain come down. The life of the loner. How did Frank do it all these years? Calum's been thinking about that for the last hour. Not thinking so much about Emma. He liked Emma, but it was only two months. She was great company, but anyone would have been welcome after so long without. Calum's twenty-nine. Frank's sixty-two. He's had thirty-three more years of it. Right up until the Scott job he seemed as if he was handling it all happily. He must have had moments like this, when the sacrifices didn't seem worth it. Maybe not. Maybe he was always stronger than Calum. It's not the sort of thing you ever get to find out. No gunman is ever going to tell you about an emotional crisis. Strange thing is, this has only crept up on him in the last six months. Before that, nothing. He was happy to go along with the life he had. As long as he had control of it, he could live with the sacrifices.

A bitter determination. Time to take action. Do some work. Frank's risking everyone's freedom to try to protect his own. Inexcusable. Jamieson has to know. Calum's pulling his coat on, picking up his car keys. No more messing around. This is the life you're stuck with; let's not make it any worse.

He knew what the sacrifices were when he started. They've never been a surprise to him. He has no right moping about it now. You have a job. You have money. You have a life. You'll have none of that if Frank talks to the plod. You don't have to like the life you live, but you still have to protect it.

He's out the door and down the stairs, out into the rain. Looking up and down the street. Moving slowly, not caring if he gets a little wet. It's more important to be careful than dry. Make sure there's nobody out there watching you. He's in work mode now. He's about to go and report to Jamieson. It's important. The sort of thing Frank would want to stop if he were aware of it. It's Frank he's looking for, but there's only an empty street looking back at him.

He's parked a street away from the club. He's walking briskly, but not too fast. The speed a person should walk in this weather without drawing attention. There's nobody outside the front of the club, so he's ducking into the alley. He'll go in the side door. None of the regulars turn and look at him. They know better. Not for them to crane their necks at people who don't want to be watched. A couple of people at the snooker tables look at him. Kenny's one. The driver. He nods a hello and doesn't say anything. The guy Kenny's playing is Marty. A pimp and loan shark. A real scumbag with a big mouth. Calum doesn't acknowledge him. He's popular, though, because of what he supplies. All the wannabe gangsters want to get close to the guy who organizes the private parties. And he's very profitable, so Jamieson and Young are willing to suffer his company now and again.

Marty's probably there for a meeting. He's probably sent word along the corridor to Jamieson that he wants to meet him. Doesn't matter to Calum. Queue-jumping is hardly the worst thing he's ever done. He's marching along the corridor to Jamieson's door. The security really is terrible, he's thinking. Knocking on the door, waiting for a response. It takes a few seconds, but he gets a 'Come in'. He's opening the door and walking inside. Jamieson's behind his desk. He's sitting facing Young, who's on the couch, as ever. They're both looking at him. Watching him drip water onto the nice carpet. Calum has a stern look on his face, letting them know that this is serious. He tends to look stern and miserable anyway – it doesn't require any effort. Perhaps they don't realize that this is anything special. Jamieson's turning back to Young, nodding dismissal.

Calum's sitting across the desk from Jamieson. Jamieson's good at doing the dead face, expressionless. He can do it whenever he wants to, which isn't now. Now he looks worried. He knows Calum's here to report, and that he wouldn't turn up in the evening, drenched and dripping, unless he had something worth saying.

'So what is it?' Jamieson's asking.

Worse than you think, Calum's thinking. He won't say that. That's for Jamieson to judge. 'I followed him yesterday and today. Yesterday, nothing. Today he went and met a guy. They met in a house out Renfrew way. I followed Frank in, followed the other guy out. The other guy drove back into the city centre. Stopped at Cowcaddens. At the police station. Parked in the car park, went in through the back. He was one of them.'

He's told Jamieson what he needs to know. Now Jamieson's saying nothing. Sitting there, staring at the top of his desk. It's like he's been asked a question he doesn't know the answer to, and doesn't want to admit it. He's gone blank.

'You sure he was a cop?' he's asking now. It's a stupid question.

'Wouldn't have gone in the back on his own if he wasn't.' This doesn't need to be said.

The wheels are turning. He's thinking that every investigation that's ever been done into his work has come from that station. He's thinking that if Frank was ever going to turn grass, that's where he would go. There are cops there desperate for Jamieson. They would protect Frank to get at the bigger fish. Frank could probably cut himself a handy deal.

'There must have been contact before this meeting,' Calum's saying. He's not going to sit in silence and play gooseberry to Jamieson and his brooding. 'Phone records, maybe.' If it was anyone else, Jamieson wouldn't need corroborating evidence. But it's Frank.

'Tell me about the cop,' Jamieson's saying quietly.

'Nothing special. Middle-aged, I'd say. Drove a red Renault. I didn't get much of a look at him, but I got his reg.' He's taking a slip of paper from his coat pocket and passing it across the desk. It might be useless, it might not. 'The only thing I noticed that might be something: when he came out of the house, he looked pissed off about something. He came out after Frank. Gave him a head start. When he came out, he pulled open the car door, slammed it shut behind him. Looked as if he threw something onto the passenger seat – I don't know what. He looked like a guy who didn't get what he wanted out of the meeting.' Offering Jamieson a crumb. It's no more than that. The fact that the meeting happened is all he needs to know. Frank couldn't gain protection without spilling a lot of beans. Not after everything he's done. There's no comfort in the suggestion that their first meeting wasn't a roaring success.

Jamieson's nodding. They both know the cop's mood means nothing. Frank has broken the golden rule. There are all sorts of bullshit rules in the business, most of which mean the square root of nothing at all. Most rules are never enforced. Most only exist because people want to look strong. Want to look like they're organized. Truth is, only two things matter. Money and police. You don't screw a senior out of money; that will be punished. You don't talk to the police; that will be punished severely. The rest of it's minor. All the talk about loyalty and honour, that's fantasy. Men have done appalling things and been forgiven because they were profitable. Money is god. Police are the devil. Frank's supping with Satan, and will have to pay the price. They both know it. Nothing gets done until Jamieson confirms that he knows it. Doesn't matter that Frank's actions affect everyone else. Calum could go and do something about it and get away with it. He'd be forgiven, eventually. But you don't do that. You don't make the boss look weak by acting without permission.

'Okay,' Jamieson's saying, 'I'm going to think about this.' It's said with finality.

Calum's getting up, making his way out of the office. He's opened the door, not expecting to hear any more.

'I'll probably be in touch,' Jamieson's saying. Quietly, with no enthusiasm. 'Soon.' His way of saying: Be ready.

Calum's out the door and down the stairs. Going out the side door, so that he doesn't have to face people. Happy people, going dancing. People looking for a good time. He doesn't want to have to look at them. Emma's gone from his life. With Frank out, he's the only gunman Jamieson has. His next job will almost certainly be deeply unpleasant. A job's a job. It detaches him from reality. It takes him away from all the boredom of his life. It gives him something to think about, every waking moment. Being in pro-mode is a relief. He's checking all around him as he drops out of the rain and into the car. There's nobody there. He's starting up the car. He has work to do.

44

Today's problem is Frank, and what a big problem he is. It means another conversation with Jamieson. More banging your head against a brick wall. Nobody's ever said it to Jamieson's face, but a lot of people consider Young the brains of the operation. Jamieson's fine with that, always played along. He and Young both know it's just playing.

Young's driving to the club. He might just catch Jamieson there before he goes home for the night, might not. He's trying to think of a time when he's ever been able to compel Jamieson to do something he didn't want to do. Something important. Sure, there have been times when Jamieson let a few minor things happen that he wasn't happy with. He'll always give Young a few little victories. Never anything that matters. The big things are always Jamieson's decision. Young doesn't kid himself. He's a strategist and recruiter; he's the right-hand man. But he doesn't call the shots.

Pulling up outside the club. Almost silent in the street. No bouncers at the door, but it shouldn't be locked. The cleaners will be in. Up the stairs, past the tables. One man sitting on his own in a corner, playing with his mobile. Kenny. Which means Jamieson's still here. Down the corridor. Into the office with a brief knock. Jamieson's behind his desk – where else? A glass of whiskey in his hand. He doesn't look like a man who wants to hear confirmation of his worst fear. This is going to hit him hard. He wants to believe that Frank wouldn't betray him. One of the few men he's allowed himself to trust. Frank gets pushed out and straight away goes running to the police. It's a blow. They have to act. Get over the disappointment and get on with the dirty work. Jamieson's looking up at him. He looks aggressive, but he always does when he's drunk. He's always either a mischievous drunk or a nasty one. It can be a fine line.

'What do you want, John?' he's asking. His voice is crystal-clear. He doesn't slur or fall around when he's drunk. You have to know him to see it. It's in the look.

'I just had a meeting with a contact in the police, the boy Higgins. The cop Frank met was almost certainly Michael Fisher. He's been in charge of the Scott McClure investigation. Been ignoring it to pursue something else on his own. Something like a golden contact.' That's enough detail. Jamieson should know what to do with that.

'Huh,' is all Jamieson's saying, and taking another swig from the glass. He's looking sideways, away from Young. 'You want me to hit him, don't you?' It's an accusation.

'No,' Young's saying, 'I don't want you to. But we both know you have to. I don't think he gave them a lot of info in the first meeting. He'll have to give them something the second time they meet. We can't let that meeting happen. We're fucked if it does. Every one of us. I'd like to do it tonight.'

'No,' Jamieson's saying. Making sure his tone doesn't invite any argument.

Young's gone. He spent a few minutes standing there, waiting for Jamieson to agree with him, then said he'd be back in the morning. He tried to sound disgusted. Jamieson doesn't care. He can easily win Young back around. Always been able to do that. But Frank. Frank's gone. Gone and never coming back. If Frank's talking to the police, then he's gone forever. You trust a person. Jesus, the things he's told Frank! The things he's had Frank do for him. Frank knows it all. Every fucking detail. The bastard! The complete bastard. Jamieson was going to bend over backwards to keep him involved. He was going to give him a proper position. Not a gunman. The old fuck can't handle that any more. But something else. Something that mattered. But no. Frank was just like all the other little bastards who swarm around, looking to get what they want for nothing. If he's not getting his own way, he stabs you in the back, front and side. Going to the police. Shit, if only it had just been another organization.

There has to be a mistake. A misunderstanding. Frank's old-school. He's not a guy who would turn on you. Not that easily. Some of the kids, yeah, but not Frank. Maybe Frank's been set up. Maybe he's playing the copper. That could be it.

Maybe he's gone to the copper to set him up. Fisher's been the pain in the industry's arse for a while now. Might be that Frank has something he's playing, to impress. To win Jamieson back round. Try to persuade him that he can still cut it as a gunman. No. Don't kid yourself. The only way Frank could use Fisher to persuade the world he's still a gunman would be to kill him. Frank's not that stupid. No gunman could be that stupid. Killing a cop is off the table. Always. It's pointless in anything but the most extreme circumstances. The dead cop gets replaced by a living one who's out for revenge. No, Frank ain't playing the copper. The only angle Frank's ever been able to play is killing a man.

So much of what he thought about Frank is starting to fall down around him. He's thinking about all the things Frank can't do. The things he could probably never do. Yeah, he was one of the great gunmen, but that's all. He was a specialist. No broad skills. And what is he now? Certainly not special. Look at the three jobs Calum MacLean's done for the organization. Winter was textbook. Frank couldn't have done it any better. Davidson was a minefield, and Calum got through it. Frank couldn't have done that as well as Calum did. Not nearly so well. Then the Scott thing. Reverse the roles. Frank probably wouldn't even have tried. He'd have struggled if he did. That was a big job. Would Frank have handled it so coolly? Hard to believe that he would. Maybe they're better off without him. Better off without a friend.

He's picking up the phone in the office. He knows Frank's number by heart. He's waiting. Is the old man in bed or out at another meeting? The phone's answered, Frank saying hello. He doesn't sound sleepy. He does sound old. He never used to. He always just sounded like Frank. Familiar old Frank. Now that you listen, you can hear the age.

'Frank, it's Peter.'

'Peter.' A slight pause. Might be nothing, but he's not the pausing type. 'Something up?'

'I just think we need to meet and chat. Discuss where we are now. You know?'

'Yeah, I guess.'

'Why don't you come round the club tomorrow morning, say ten o'clock? We can see where we are now. I think it'll do the both of us a lot of good.'

'Sure,' Frank's saying, 'ten o'clock. I'll see you then.'

He didn't sound nervous about it. Maybe he's not. Maybe he has nothing to be nervous about. Or maybe he's just a good liar. He's been in this business long enough. You get good at things like that, with enough practice. Frank couldn't have come this far in this world without learning how to hide his feelings. Jamieson's downing the last of the glass. Time to go home. There's no more work to do here. A bad day at the office. Had a few of those, but this one might take the biscuit. He's getting to his feet. No wobbles, which tells him he kept the drinking to the right side of stupid. It's a painkiller. He's smiling. Something Frank once said. You can tell a good gunman from a bad one by how much he wants to forget. A lot of gunmen fall to the drink. Not Frank. Not Calum either, apparently. They can live with what they've seen. What they've done. There's a warning. A man who can live with doing that for a living can probably live with anything.

He's switched the light off. Out into the corridor, along to the snooker room. Kenny's sitting looking bored. Always there, always eager to help.

'I shouldn't have kept you this late, Kenny,' Jamieson's saying.

'That's okay,' he's saying. Not going to say anything else, is he? They're down the stairs, out the front door. Along to the car, Kenny getting there a few paces ahead to open the door for Jamieson. Jamieson's never liked that. Riding in the back of the car. Having the door opened for him. Makes him feel like some old man.

'Let me ask you something, Kenny,' he's saying as they pull away from the club. 'Do you trust all the people around you?'

Kenny's making uncertain noises, shrugging his shoulders. He's nervous. Jamieson's smiling. Poor guy, doesn't want to give the wrong answer. 'I guess I do,' he's saying eventually.

'Shouldn't. You need to look out for yourself. Don't rely on other people too much. Becomes a bad habit. You're a good man, Kenny, you know that. You do a good job. I'm thankful for it,' he's saying, leaning back in the seat. He didn't realize he was this tired.

45

Frank didn't sleep much last night. A night spent thinking about that phone call. Peter sounded okay. Not too aggressive, not like he was scheming something. He sounded genuine. That doesn't stop you thinking about all the things this could be. It could be a proper meeting. Jamieson wanting to lay out what work Frank will be doing from now on. Giving him the detail of the future that he hopes will convince Frank to accept his new role. It could be a set-up. No, not a set-up. They wouldn't kill him in the club – that would be idiotic. Way too much of a risk. Could be the first step to a total removal. Frank knows too much. He's on the outside now. The old man who bungled a simple hit. Maybe Jamieson thinks it'll be easy to get rid of him altogether. Frank's getting out of bed, feeling his hip. Maybe Jamieson's right. What fight could he possibly put up? He's walking into the shower, getting ready for the meeting. He has to go.

Out of the house, heading to the car. Looking up and down the street. Nothing stands out. Driving to the club. Thinking of all the conversations he's had with Peter Jamieson. There were times when he was able to win Peter round. Persuade him that some things were a good idea, when Jamieson was unsure. Persuade him that some things were a terrible idea. There's at least one person alive today because Frank talked Peter out of the hit. That was then. Frank was a man worth listening to then. Now he's an old man on the outside, clinging on. He's out of the car, in through the front door of the club. It's quiet inside. Up the stairs, those annoying, treacherous stairs. Through the doors to the snooker room. The tables are busy. This is their time of day. The club's quiet, no music playing; they can pretend to concentrate on their game. Most of them are useless, no matter the distractions. A few faces he recognizes – the regulars. The driver is amongst them.

He's nodding to Kenny, a polite hello.

'You here to see the boss?' the driver's asking stupidly. Why else would he be there?

'Yes,' Frank's saying. Kenny's away down the corridor to let Peter know. Frank's noticed how nervous the driver is. Not a good sign. A driver's bound to hear things. There could be a good reason why he's nervous around Frank. He's coming back into the snooker room.

'Go through,' he's saying and immediately turning away from the gunman. Determined not to get into a conversation. Determined to avoid being seen with a condemned man. Frank's leaving him alone. No point in agitating the boy by talking to him. This is part of the process of being pushed out. You can't blame an expendable, low-level employee for avoiding him. If he could get his position back, people like Kenny would want to be his best friend again.

Along the corridor, knocking on the office door. A shout for him to come in. Jamieson and Young, in their usual places. Young's getting up, though; he's not going to stay. Not sure if that's a good sign or a bad one. Why does Jamieson not want his right-hand man there? Hard to escape the feeling that it's a bad thing. If this were business, he would keep Young there. Young has the more detailed business knowledge. He's always useful in a business conversation. Young's walking past Frank, not looking him in the eye. Could be a bad sign, but it's hard to remember when Young ever did look him in the eye. They've never been close. That's another good thing about Jamieson. He's never forced his men to pal around with one another. Some bosses do. They have a terrible tendency to mistake camaraderie for loyalty. Jamieson's always been smarter than that. Let people get on with doing their job. If they're good at it, that's enough. Young's closed the door behind him. Just the two of them, in the office. Been here many times before. Never with this atmosphere, though. Frank takes his seat.

'Good to see you, Frank,' Jamieson's saying. 'How are you keeping?'

'Fine.' A man of few words when he's on the defence.

'Will you take a drink?'

'No, I have the car.'

'Of course,' Jamieson's saying with a smile. The pros don't take risks. They're not going to allow themselves to get done for drink-driving. No minor offence that could lead to bigger convictions. He'll leave the bottle where it is then. Doesn't want Frank thinking he's being weak by drinking. 'We need to have a good talk about where we both stand,' Jamieson's saying. 'I'm not sure we parted on the best of terms last time round.'

Frank's nodding slightly. 'Perhaps not.'

'I want to know what you're thinking,' Jamieson's saying. 'I want to know what you'd like to do with yourself. What are your plans?' He can't say it any more bluntly than that. He was never going to come straight out and ask him. Frank has to tell him. He has to share the information willingly.

Frank's looking down at his feet. He's thinking of what he wants to say. This is the chance. Jamieson's laid it on a plate for him. All he has to do now is be honest. Tell him that the police were in touch. Tell him that he went to meet the copper, to see who he was and what he had to say. Pretend you went because you were hoping to find out where he got his info. Jamieson might not buy that bit, but he'll accept it. It's Peter; he'll accept the gloss as long as what's underneath is close to honest. There won't be another chance.

'I'm a gunman, Peter,' he's saying. Focusing on the wrong thing, and he knows it. 'I don't know how to be anything else.' That was a stupid opening. He's cursing himself. No wonder.

'Just because you haven't done other things doesn't mean you wouldn't be good at them,' Jamieson's saying. 'You have to give it a chance.'

Frank's nodding. Peter used the words 'have to'. That wasn't an accident.

'Look,' Jamieson's saying, leaning forward for emphasis. 'You and me go back a way. I think we know each other well enough not to bullshit each other. I can't give you work as a gunman. Not right now. You understand that, right? Shit, after what happened, I have to give you distance. It's not that I want to – I have to. That's how it is. That was a really bad night. Not just for you, but for all of us. I have to handle this carefully. I need to keep you away from the gun work. Maybe not forever, but for now.' A pause. 'So what are you going to do? You can stay with us, do other work. Maybe, eventually, I can get you some of your old work, if you still want it. You could go work for another organization, but do you really want to do that? I mean, there are a lot of complete shits out there. You know that. You know what it's like, going into a new organization. What else is there?' he asks. He can't make it any easier that this.

The only other thing is the police. All Frank has to do is chuckle and say it's funny Peter should ask. Say he got a phone call from a copper. The offer of protection. It's so easy. But it's impossible. It's about trust. If there was anyone in this business he should trust enough, it's Peter Jamieson. But he can't. He just can't. Forty years. All that time thinking one way, now you have to think another. You spend your whole working life being told not to trust anyone. Learning to be sceptical. You trust people up to a point, but never all the way. Doesn't matter how good a boss is, you hold a little back. Telling Jamieson about the meeting with Fisher would require complete trust. He doesn't have that. It would be nice to believe that Peter Jamieson would accept the info. Nice to believe their relationship could go back to the way it was. But that's not realistic. Jamieson would assume the worst.

'I guess what happens next is up to you,' Frank's saying. He's hearing the words come out and he's wishing he had the courage to change them. The courage to trust his friend.

'Aye,' Jamieson's saying, and he's slumping back in his seat. That wasn't what he wanted to hear. 'If that's how it's going to be.' There's silence. Awkward. Frank looking at Jamieson, seeing the sadness in him. 'I'll look around,' Jamieson's saying with no enthusiasm, 'try and find a few jobs for you. Something interesting, no bullshit. We'll talk about it, maybe next week.'

'Sure,' Frank's saying, and he's getting up. It's a relief to be leaving. It didn't go well, he knows that, and he wants out. Get away from Jamieson and stop pretending to be relaxed. Stop pretending this isn't the end of the world. He's at the door, glancing back at Jamieson. His boss. Sitting there, one hand on the table, his forefinger tapping it. Looking down at nothing at all. Looking depressed. Frank wants to say good-bye, but that would be admitting that this is the end.

He's stepping out and closing the door behind him. Through the snooker room, not looking at Young or Kenny or any of the others. Down the stairs, out into the street. Into his car. Still the hard look on his face. Always the hard look as long as there's a danger of being seen. Driving away, and softening. Cursing himself. Cursing Jamieson. Wanting to cry, if he only knew how. There's one last option. The chance to run.

Where to go? People would go looking for him. Jamieson wouldn't let him settle anywhere. If he disappears now, Jamieson will be convinced it's because someone's rehoused him. London? No, not safe. Nowhere in the UK would be safe. Couldn't even go abroad. Jamieson would follow. He'd have Frank hit, no matter where in the world. A high priority is worth the extra risk. Wherever he went, Frank wouldn't find work. Glasgow is his city. Always has been. He has no name anywhere else. He would just be an old man with a bundle of old glories. Plenty of old men like that around. Nobody would hire him. A life of poverty on the run. No. Maybe twenty years ago, but not now. Now, he has to stay. This is how it ends.

46

Taking a drink of whiskey. Switching on the TV behind him. Switching it off again. Hearing an everyday sound outside and going to the window to investigate. All distractions welcome. Anything to avoid having to make the decision. Anything to avoid deciding to kill Frank. Young's been in and out. He knew better than to stay. This is something Jamieson has to do for himself. Something new. It's never been like this. Never been so hard. Never been so real. How many times has he done this before? Jesus, too many. Ordering that someone be killed for the good of the business. Gets to a point where you don't even think about what you're saying. It's the right strategy for the business, so you do it. You tell someone to make it happen. Give him a target; let him get on with it. Nothing more than that. So easy. People you've never met. All he knew of them was their name and what they'd done to piss him off. Killing was easy.

He's thinking about the first one. Must be sixteen years ago now. That'll make him feel old. They didn't have Frank back then; they had to hire a freelancer. Some big, lanky bastard with a long face. Can't even remember his name. It seemed like such a big deal at the time, and now he can't remember the name. Remembers the name of the victim, though. Derek Conner. Fat little guy, who thought Jamieson was getting too big for his boots. Jamieson's network was small back then. No legit business to hide behind – living on the edge. It was exciting. Conner had his own network, no more impressive than Jamieson's. He started making trouble. There was a chance he could run them off the cliff. Young found a freelancer, hired him, the job was done. Messy, as Jamieson remembers. There was an investigation; it went nowhere. He and Young were terrified while it lasted. It seemed such a big deal. Then, with each hit that followed, it became less of an issue. The victims became forgettable, the investigations ignorable. It was so easy. Until now.

He's playing games with himself, and he knows it. Pretending that he has a decision to make. There is no choice. No alternative option. There's only one, and he's going to select it. It's Frank's own choice. That's what he keeps telling himself. The more he thinks it, the angrier he gets, and the more determined he is to make the call. Frank chose this for himself. He went to the police; he said nothing about it when given the chance. How could he not have guessed that Jamieson knew? He could so easily have been honest with him. Frank might be the only person that Jamieson would have let off the hook. He doesn't deserve leniency. Nobody who puts so many at risk deserves it. Frank's selling them all out to save his own skin. He shouldn't get away with that. He can't be seen to get away with it. The humiliation alone would ruin the business. The police would just sweep the remains away.

He's called Young into the office. They're in their usual seats. There's a little comfort in that familiarity. In knowing that he's doing the right thing.

'It needs doing,' Jamieson's saying quietly. 'Tonight, I think. We can't let them have a second meeting. Can you make that happen this soon?'

Young's nodding. 'Shouldn't be a problem. I'll call Calum.'

Jamieson's taking an abnormally long time to respond to an obvious point. 'Yeah,' he's saying, 'you call him. Let's keep this as normal as possible.' That's a laugh. Normal. When did making this decision ever feel like this before? When was the person on the receiving end someone worth caring about? This might just be a once-in-a-lifetime job. Yet you still have to present it as normal. Make sure nobody else involved knows how much it matters to you.

Young's left the office. He doesn't usually do that, but it feels right. Doesn't want Jamieson sitting there, hearing orders being given and regretting it. He's made the right call. Young wants to tell him that, but it won't help matters. Not right now. In the future, when emotions have calmed, maybe. Right now Jamieson will want to be alone, to soak himself in whiskey and sulk. That's fine by Young; he doesn't need anyone else interfering now. This is the bit he enjoys. Organizing, ordering and watching the result. He's found an office downstairs, towards the back of the club. Locked the door, checked to make sure nothing's out of place. Now he's calling Calum. Three rings and it answers. Little threat of the little girlfriend picking up. George called to let him know that he'd done the deed. Reckons they'll be splitting up, if they haven't already. Another successful piece of work.

'Hi, Calum, it's John Young. How's the hand?' Calum will already know what the call is really about. He's a smart one. You get some gunmen who are pretty dumb, if we're being honest. They go and do the job, but they don't have the brains to understand detail. To piece together the little things. Calum seems smarter.

'The hand's okay,' he's saying. Always sounds so bloody miserable. 'Fit for whatever.'

'Good, pleased to hear it. Listen, that thing Peter mentioned to you yesterday.'

'Yeah,' Calum's saying. He remembers exactly what that thing is.

'Any chance you could do it for him – say, tonight?'

He's put it so politely. Calum understands, though. It's not a request, it's an order. It has to be done tonight. 'Sure,' he's saying, 'I could do that.'

'Make it tidy,' Young's saying.

'Okay. Might need a little help on that. I can call George.'

'Do,' Young's saying. His way of telling Calum not to leave a body behind.

He is slow at his work. That's Calum's one big flaw. Good, but slow. That's what Young's thinking. He needs to do all he can to buy Calum time. Then he's thinking about Davidson and Scott. Wasn't slow then. Was lightning fast because he had no other choice, yet he did a fine job. Needn't worry about putting him on the spot.

'Try not to make too much noise,' Young's saying. 'Don't want to upset the neighbours in the early hours of the morning. I'll have an envelope put through your door with something useful in it.'

'Sure, no bother,' Calum's saying. He doesn't sound impressed. He's not a man who needs to be told to keep the noise down. Common-sense advice is no advice at all to the sensible. He'll cheer up when the envelope with a copy of Frank's back-door key arrives.

Young's making his way back upstairs. All his work is done. He'll be the point of contact if something should go wrong. He'll be ready by his phone, waiting. It's incredibly rare. Frank called once, to let him know that the target's house was crawling with cops. That was a scare. Turned out the police were raiding the address at the same time. Young still has his suspicions about that one. Maybe someone leaked the identity of their next target. Maybe Paul Greig decided to stick his nose in and score brownie points by pointing the finger at a dealer. Didn't matter much. Took their target off the street for three years. By the time he came out he had no network left to run. Still, you never know what might happen. Especially with a target like Frank. He has to trust Calum to be the better man. And trust's a horrible thing to have to rely on.

He's stepping back into the office. Walking quietly across to his couch. He's not saying anything. Jamieson knows what he was doing. Knows that if anything had gone wrong he would tell him. The silence means that everything's set up and ready. It means that Frank is going to die tonight.

'You making any progress on finding a replacement?' Jamieson's asking. You can hear a little misery in his voice, but he's making an effort now. Down to business. Keeping it friendly, trying to sound interested.

'My first thought was George Daly, but he's still not playing ball. No point in forcing him. The next obvious candidate is Shaun Hutton. When we squash Shug, he'll need a new employer. Contacting us about Scott shows that he's interested in us.' Careful not to mention Frank.

Jamieson's nodding. 'Leave him where he is for now. We can use him there until Shug's done. That won't be long.' Sounding like he's forgotten all about the man called Frank MacLeod.

47

Sometimes it feels like they don't want him to be successful. They want a result – not the right result. You can either chase statistics or you can be a proper copper. Only rarely and co-incidentally do those two styles of policing overlap. That's Fisher's belief, anyway. There's a uniformed cop downstairs who got a commendation for the high number of arrests he made. Fisher loathes the boy. Not his fault that he got the pat on the head from the bosses, but look at the arrests. Most were very minor, some the sorts of things he shouldn't have been wasting his time on. Sure, people like it when you arrest a vandal or a drunk-and-disorderly, but it makes little differ-ence to the big scheme. The big scheme means taking dealers off the street. They can't supply the junkies, who then don't go breaking into houses and mugging people to pay for the habit. You go for the big fish so that they can't corrupt further down the chain. That's what he's always tried to do. But they keep stopping him.

He's going to explode soon, you wait and see. Someone's going to say something that sets him off. It'll be a brief flash of anger, it always is with Fisher. Nobody in the office cares much for that; it's the couple of days of silent rage that follow that bothers them. There's a bit of bustle around the place, people in and out. A woman's been found dead in her house. Wasn't raped or burgled, and her on-off boyfriend is nowhere to be seen. Looks like the on-off boyfriend is going to be answering a lot of awkward questions when they catch up with him. That's why there's a bunch of cops buzzing all over that case. Of course they want to catch a dangerous man, but there's ambition there, too. It should be an open-and-shut case. They want their name on it. They know this will resolve itself quickly, and they want to be associated with that. Nobody wants long-standing open cases with their name attached. Nobody wants a case that runs away from them and is taken out of their hands. Nobody wants to be where Fisher is right now. No new evidence to suggest that McClure didn't kill Scott and then himself.

He was called into DCI Reid's office. He was told that the Scott McClure investigation was being wound down. Not officially closed, but essentially abandoned. Too many men wasting valuable time on a dead investigation. Their skills, such as they are, required elsewhere. This is murder-suicide. Put it to a coroner, present the evidence and he's going to record murder-suicide. Let him. End the active investigation; let the families put it behind them. Fisher didn't point out that they seemed to have already done that. The lack of family interest in both dead men was horrible. Unusual, although not unheard of. You pick up bodies that have no family to care about them. You find the next of kin and you inform them. Their greatest concern is the expense of a funeral. It can be unpleasant. The families won't care about this investigation shutting down. They'll accept the murder-suicide, and they'll get on with life. They won't put pressure on for further investigation. Neither will the media. No headlines for a couple of street dealers. It would take outside pressures to get a case like this energized again.

It won't get pressure from Fisher, either. Other priorities. Priorities like Frank MacLeod. The lying, cheating bastard Frank MacLeod. Fisher followed him. Followed him all the way to Peter Jamieson. A set-up, to either humiliate or endanger him. Or maybe old Frank is trying to keep all his options open. Play every string on the fiddle at once. That wouldn't be a surprise, either. Not with a guy like Frank. There could still be a chance. He just has to make sure Frank knows that he only has one option. It helps if Frank likes him, but it's not necessary. It helps if your contact wants to give you info, but forcing him is better than losing him. How do you play hard with a man like Frank? A man who's seen every hard tactic in the book. Anyone can be scared. That's the key. All those old guys are obsessed with holding on to life. The fear of losing it is the key. Make him believe that the only person who can keep him breathing is Fisher. Make yourself his only option.

He's in his car, driving round to Frank's house. No more

sitting outside the house watching the hours rush away. He has to take action or see this all fall through his fingers. He's not going to let another chance go. You spend years getting good results, doing your job the right way. You have a couple of failures, and people start to point the finger. They think you don't have it any more. He's been guilty of that himself in the past. He knows how it works. A cop getting older – you start to question their ability to close a case. Are they still in touch with modern crime and policing techniques? Do they still have the hunger? Some do lose it. They've done their bit, now they're looking towards the end. He's not that kind of cop. His ending will be forced on him, he knows it. The hunger's still there, but nothing is falling his way.

Sitting outside Frank's house. His car's there, which suggests the old man's still at home. Fisher's looking up and down the street as he gets out of his car. Doesn't seem to be anyone about. Nobody sitting in a car watching. Up to the front door, knocking. Takes about twenty seconds for Frank to open. His eyes have betrayed his shock.

'Hello, Frank.'

'Come in,' Frank's saying. There's a roughness in his voice. That betrays him, too. He doesn't want anyone seeing him meet the copper. Doesn't want Jamieson knowing that they've met. This suggests that it isn't a set-up, that Frank really is on the outside. He's meeting people to check his options. Now there's a real chance of landing him.

Frank's led him through to the living room. Fisher's taking a seat without waiting for an invite to do so. Frank's watching him, obviously trying to pick his words.

'Can I ask why you're here?' he's asking, sitting opposite Fisher. Always so polite. That's rather old-school, a charming generational difference. These days, most people would curse Fisher for turning up unannounced.

'I want to talk to you,' Fisher's saying.

'I thought I made it clear that I wasn't going to talk to you.' A slightly harsher tone this time. Making it clear that he doesn't appreciate the visit. He doesn't need to come out and say it, though. Fisher's not dumb; he knows the risk for Frank. Frank understands what this is. Lives at risk; pressure being piled upon pressure.

'I want to make it clear that you need to talk to me. I think you're out of options. You may not realize it, but you are. I'm the last show in town. I may not be much, but I'm it. You can go running to other people if you want. Try and ingratiate yourself with a new bunch of crooks. Maybe try and cling on to Jamieson, like some pathetic love-struck teenager. How do you think any of them would react if they knew about our meetings?'

Frank's laughing. Sitting there and laughing in Fisher's face. Not the response the detective was expecting.

'I didn't realize I was quite so funny,' Fisher's saying, looking for an explanation.

'Oh, you are. Don't think I don't know what's going on here. This is your last roll of the dice. You're desperate, so you're putting the pressure on. Coming here to lean on me. You're the police equivalent of muscle. You really think I can't see how desperate you are?' The laughter has gone from his voice now. More serious, more challenging.

Fisher's frowning back at him. Nobody wants to be told how desperate they are, even if it's true. A cop like him can't afford to have it be so obvious to others. 'This isn't a question of me. This is a question of you. I'm beginning to wonder if you realize the situation you're in.'

Frank's laughing at him again. 'You think I don't know where I am? I know. Trust me, I know. It doesn't look good for me. I understand that. You want me to think that you're the only person who can save me.'

This is becoming pointless. Fisher's standing up. 'Listen,' he's saying. 'I want you to understand what I'm going to do. I'm not letting you off the hook, no way. Not after everything you've done with your life. You have two days to call me and tell me that you want to get on board. You do that, and I protect you. I find you somewhere safe to live; I make sure you don't get prosecuted. You don't do that, and I make a few phone calls. I know I can't get you for myself. I'd love to put you in the dock, but that's not going to happen. Thing is, people like Peter Jamieson don't need the same weight of evidence I do. He can find you guilty on a whim. One call from me, and I'm pretty sure he will.'

Fisher's walking to the door, letting himself out. He feels like shit. He feels like a criminal. Threatening a man with murder. Doesn't matter what the man's done, who he is. You start lowering yourself to this level and you've lost. Maybe he's already lost. The Scott McClure case has withered and died in quick time. Frank's going to escape him, he knows it. He's going to lose again.

Frank's standing at the living-room window, watching Fisher drive away. Didn't think the little bastard had it in him. Ballsy thing for any cop to do. Desperate, though. Pathetically desperate. Fisher looks less and less like a man to be afraid of. The man to be afraid of is Jamieson. Maybe Fisher will call him, but Frank doubts it. Not that kind of cop. Maybe it doesn't matter.

The meeting with Jamieson has been on his mind constantly. It almost doesn't matter how much Jamieson knows. Their conversation was so awkward. It was more like two old enemies than two old friends. Frank's seen it before. Seen most things before. Never been on the receiving end, though. It's the talk you have when you're so far on the outside that you become a threat. The old employee who knows too much. Who has to be silenced. Seen that before. Done the silencing. He's been kidding himself, pretending that this wouldn't happen to him. That his relationship with Peter Jamieson was different from the rest. It was always going to happen. Gunmen don't get happy retirements. Nobody gets to walk away.

48

Walking round the flat, just going in circles. Getting some of the nervous energy out of the way before he sets off. It's actually nice to be able to do it. A relief, almost. If Emma was still here, then he could never prepare properly. Well, properly might be the wrong word. There is no properly. There's just whatever works. Pacing around the flat, planning what to do with each half-hour until you leave – that works for Calum. He'll get something to eat. Something light, nothing that'll play on his stomach when his nerves are running. The nerves are worst during this preparation. The two or three hours before you leave for the job. When it's under way you have so much else to think about. A good gunman's focus will crush his nerves. You have to think clearly. For now, he paces and plots.

It's after midnight when he leaves the flat. Black jeans, comfy black trainers, a plain navy-blue top. He picked up his gun from his usual supplier a few hours ago; he'll return it as soon as the job is done. An expensive rental, rather than a purchase. Got a silencer for this job. Rarely uses them. Expensive and awkward. You only take them on a difficult job that needs every precaution. Jobs like this.

He's taking his car to the meeting place agreed with George. They'll take the van that George is picking up to do the job. Another job that'll need a removal. He hates that. But it's Frank. Jamieson wants the maximum respect shown; have Frank treated as well as a murdered man can be. The removal has something to do with covering tracks, no doubt. Try to make it look like another disappearance. Too many awkward jobs in a row. The chances of something going wrong are piling up. It would be so nice to have a couple of simple jobs. This is the price you pay. The price of working for an organization. Things are never straightforward.

He's pulling up in the parking places outside a cash-and-carry. There's CCTV, but it won't be working tonight. The building's owned by Jamieson, or by someone who works for Jamieson. It's complicated, but Jamieson's on a percentage and George will have made sure about the security. This is where he has to trust someone else with his safety. George is sitting in the van already. Small, old, white, no markings on the side. Nothing that anyone could possibly remember. Getting to the point where its age might become notable. Calum may have to point that out to Young, make sure he has it replaced. He's leaving his own car unlocked, with the keys tucked inside the sun visor. A risk he has to take. Doesn't want to be found with his own keys on him. Doesn't want to be found with anything on him. On this job, it shouldn't be an issue. The target already knows him. Still, plan for every eventuality; make sure you have nothing about your person that could identify you. He's dropping into the passenger side of the van. Nodding a hello to George.

George looks more of a wreck than Calum's ever seen him. Looks like he hasn't slept for days. Looks like he's been out partying. It could be nerves. Frank has an aura about him. The greatest gunman in the city, so they all say. George should know better. People get reputations, but it's like Chinese whispers. A rumour starts, word goes round and, before you know it, people have reputations based on non-sense. People become known for things far removed from what they've actually done. Sure, Frank was one of the greats. Up until he walked through Tommy Scott's front door, Calum might have believed in that mystique too. Seeing Frank sitting on the floor, guarded by Clueless McClure, quickly broke that spell. Frank used to be great. Now he's not. Now he's problematic. That's the business. George can be as nervous as he likes. He's the driver and he'll help with disposal. Killing is Calum's job.

'You get everything we need?' Calum's asking. The collection of tools for a removal was left in George's hands.

'Think so. Couple of spades, big canvas body bag, couple of spare bags.' He's finishing with a shrug of the shoulders. Calum's meticulous about these things. Demanding, to the point of annoyance. George has done this sort of job with him before, though. No surprises here.

'Let's go,' Calum's saying. It's after half past midnight now; by the time he gets into the house it'll be after one. He wants this done quickly. Someone could be watching the front of the house, so it has to be quiet and has to be quick. Who's likely to be watching? Another organization. Maybe Shug's. Could be police. They could be killing someone else's target. Forget all that. He has to put it out of his mind, focus on his own job. Never mind what other people are doing. This is going to be hard enough.

George is driving. They're nearly there. It's a wet night, which is bad news. Soft ground means footprints, and no doubt George hasn't brought plastic bags to put over their shoes at the burial. Boot prints can be one more clue you don't want to give away. They won't drive along Frank's street to check for watchers. Frank's back garden looks onto the garden of the house in the next street, an alleyway in between. That's the entry point. George has parked the van on the street at the bottom of the alley. If anyone's watching Frank's house, they'll be close. Calum's looking at George. George is usually the talkative one, yet he's had nothing to say. It's that kind of job, Calum supposes.

'Give me ten minutes, then come in soft,' he's saying.

'Aye,' George is nodding. 'Good luck, pal.'

A little nod. Calum's pulling on his balaclava, opening the van door.

Trying to make as little sound as possible. Walking as

close to the wall at the bottom of the row of gardens as possible. Not a great place for a job. A group of occupied houses close together. Too many bedroom windows looking down on the alleyway. Going to be hard to move the body without some nosy bastard twitching the curtains. Especially if they hear a bang beforehand. The silencer will keep it quiet, but there's still the flash to think about. Closed curtains, hopefully. The victim can make a noise. Hell, even a silenced piece makes a sound. Better to use a knife for silence, but that would be messy. Blood everywhere. Could never hide what happened there. He's halfway to Frank's back garden. Counting the houses as he passes, making sure he gets the right one. Dodging bins and a lone bicycle optimistically chained to a rotting wooden gate. Silent so far, but now he's reached Frank's gate.

He's pressing down the latch slowly, not making so much as a scrape. Pushing it open, peering inside before he makes a step. There aren't likely to be any obstacles yet. They'll come when he gets inside. The only fear would be Frank standing there, waiting for him. Not a realistic fear, but this is no realistic target. He's stepped inside the gate and shut it behind him. Looking at the windows. Not for light – Frank would never be so sloppy. Checking for movement. Frank lining up a shot from an open window. No, he wouldn't kill a man in his own garden. Frank knows better. He can explain a bang from within his house, but not a body lying flat out on the grass with an extra hole in it. Put yourself in Frank's shoes. What would you be doing right now? He must have set up some sort of alarm. He can't be lying asleep in there, thinking there's no threat to him. Not Frank. He must recognize the danger, and he must be ready for it. That's what Calum's looking out for as he walks slowly towards the back door. He's taking the key from his pocket, placing it silently in the lock. Taking his gun from his inside pocket before he turns the key. This is where he starts looking out for traps.

49

He knew what he would do about ten minutes after Fisher left the house. It was actually liberating. It's the first time since he woke up on the floor of Scott's corridor that he's known exactly what to do. First time since then that he's felt in control. It's nice to have your focus back, even if it might not last long. He's in work mode now. Thinking about everything he'll need. Plotting, considering, playing out eventualities in his mind. If this was life, then everything would be okay. This he can do, and do well. He doesn't need a lot of equipment for this job. The only thing that's taken any amount of time to find was his passport. Frank, like Calum, is a very neat person. Everything in its rightful place. Things should never be hard to find. It's a useful mindset, always being able to reach out and grab whatever you might need. Only his passport wasn't in his bedside cabinet under his never-used cheque book, as usual. It was still in the side pocket of one of the bags he took to Spain with him. Recovering in the sunshine at Peter Jamieson's expense.

It'll be Calum. No great mystery in that. Peter will show enough respect to send his best man. Technically his only man, but he could have hired a freelancer. Young will have

347

Frank's replacement lined up. Probably Shaun Hutton. That's the obvious one. He was clearly the Scott leak, looking to ingratiate himself with Jamieson. He'll get the gig when the time's right. Wouldn't be Frank's first pick. Too flaky. Never held down a position before. Besides, they need someone who can work with Calum. When they're done with Shug, they'll be aiming at bigger targets. There will be jobs that require more than one armed man willing to pull a trigger. Frank's done a couple of those in his time. If you don't trust the other guy, it can be an unpleasant experience. Waiting for them to say or do something wrong. It could be hard to find another gunman that a guy like Calum will work with. Frank's smiling to think of Calum. All moody and silent. Just a little bit superior. Other gunmen aren't going to enjoy working with him. They'll accept it, though. They'll accept it because he's good.

It's because Calum's good that Frank needs to be better prepared. He'll come in the back. Logic says he won't use the front for a target like Frank. Too much risk. You knock on a target that doesn't expect you. They open the door and you barge inside. A good way of getting in without breaking doors or windows. Calum will realize that Frank is on high alert. He'll come in the back. Maybe wedge it with a crowbar; it is a thin, old door. A key. Jesus, of course. They'll have made a key up. Young will. That clever little bastard will have done it years ago, on a day when he knew Frank wasn't at home.

Something a lot of the big organizations do. Make sure they have easy access to their own people. Frank's at the back door. Clearing everything away. Making preparations. Making sure it looks like a house that's been abandoned by someone with no intention of return. Making sure his departure won't appear as sudden as it will actually be. Wiping surfaces, tidying everything away. Gathering up the few things that a man who wants to disappear should take with him.

Back upstairs to the bedroom. Not the best place for it to happen – it's just creating more work, being this far away from the back door, but it's where Calum will expect him to be. It's a small house, so there aren't many better options. The back door opens into the kitchen. That would mean firing on sight, and a gunshot with the back door open is out of the question. Better not to do it in a front room. Frank wants a little light to work with. More people could see light from the front. So the back bedroom. He's taking a spare pillow from the cupboard, placing it at the bottom of the bed. His passport, cheque book, credit card, wallet, mobile phone, driver's licence, coded contacts books and a few old photos he's placing neatly on the dresser opposite the bottom of the bed. Everything where it can be grabbed quickly and swept into a bag upon exit. The last thing to do, before the waiting. The curtains are closed, but, thick as they are, he's not going to risk putting the light on. He wants some light, though. He's pressing the head of his anglepoise bedside lamp downwards and switching it on. Not a lot of light escaping. Enough to see with, not so much that it can penetrate the curtains and be seen outside.

That's it. That's all the preparation done. It's not even midnight yet. Calum won't arrive until around one at the earliest. It would usually be after two – that's the busy hour for gunmen. Much less likely to bump into random drunks and lost souls if you leave it just a little later. They'll be planning a removal, though. This isn't a murder to send a message. They'll have a vehicle to move him in, a burial place planned. Frank's sitting in the chair beside the wardrobe, facing the open door. It's an old cushioned chair. A wreck of a thing, he's had it near thirty years, but it's the comfiest seat in the house. A good place to sit and contemplate things. With a removal, they'll come early. Desperate to make sure the burial is finished and everyone's back home before the sun rises. They'll be cursing the rain. Frank's thinking about a lot of things, a lot of people. Most of them involved in the business. It's been his life for so long. That and nothing else. He met some interesting people, did some things he can hardly believe now. There's a little smile on his lips as the clock goes past one o'clock.

He's in the back door. Hasn't made a sound yet. Closing it behind him, slow and careful. Breathing low and slow. Through the kitchen and into the hall. No lights. No sound.

No movement. He's gently pushing open the living-room door with his left hand, gun in his right. Nothing in there. Moving slowly across to the downstairs bedroom. Empty. In all likelihood he's in his own bed, but you have to check. The nightmare is getting to the bedroom, only to have Frank creep up on you. Leave no enemy standing behind you. Onto the stairs now. Pressing each downward step against the edge of the stair on the wall side. Stairs creak, more so in the middle. Even with this precaution they're creaking gently with each step. The first noise he's made so far. Grimacing slightly as he reaches the last few steps and turns the corner at the top of the stairs. Too much noise when you're trying to surprise a man like Frank. Now that he's round the corner he can see that it's much too late for that.

Frank's sitting in a chair opposite the door, looking out into the corridor. There's light, but not much. An old man, sitting in the gloom, staring back at him. He has a sad look on his face. Calum's raised the gun. First instinct, get him in his sights. Frank's smiling now, and raising his hands.

'You don't need to do that,' he's telling Calum. 'Come in.'

Calum isn't moving. Still pointing the gun, trying to judge this. Frank will know it's him, balaclava or not. What trap does he have in there? Might be safer to shoot from here, make sure that part of the job is safely done. He has a clear shot to take. There could be someone behind the door. Not likely. Frank wouldn't hire someone else. Not his style. Too much of a risk. Can't rule it out, though. A dangerous and desperate man. Clinging onto the edge of the cliff, hanging on by the last finger. Calum's stepping forward. It's two forms of caution clashing. His instinct to shoot, beaten by his instinct not to rush a job. He's in the doorway now. Can't see a trap.

Frank's getting up from the chair, hands still raised. Calum's risking a quick look round the door. Nothing there. Looking back at Frank. The low light. The vital belongings on the cabinet. He's starting to realize what this is. He's looking at Frank, puzzled. Even in the gloom, and with his face covered, Frank can see the disbelief.

'It's the end,' Frank's saying. He's getting up and moving to the foot of the bed, turning round. Now dropping to his knees, putting his hands behind his back. Making it as easy for Calum as possible. Being down on his knees already means he won't have far to fall. Should prevent, or at least reduce, blood-splatter when he goes down. Calum's seen the pillow. Frank's done everything to make this as clean and simple a job as possible. He really has given up. This is suicide by hitman.

Everything's there for him. The belongings Calum can take that'll make it look like a disappearance. The pillow that can both muffle the gunshot flash and reduce blood-spray from the entry wound. He feels he should say something, but he won't. Professional instinct. The moment arrives and you must take it. He's picking up the pillow. There's a twinge in his hand, the effort bringing his injury alive again. Standing behind Frank now. Pressing the pillow against the back of his head. Complete silence. Pressing the barrel of the gun into the pillow. Using his left hand to pull one side of the pillow around the gun. Pulling the trigger. A muffled whoosh. No blood-spray. Frank falling forward. Hitting the floor. Calum's automatically kneeling down beside him, pressing the pillow tightly against the wound. Not even thinking about it. Not processing that it's Frank who's just died. That it's Frank they're about to remove. Just thinking about the job. Thinking about how much he hates it now.

It's only a couple of minutes later when a wary George emerges at the top of the stairs. Calum, still holding the pillow tight, is glancing at him.

'Bring in the bag,' he's saying quietly, 'and a carrier bag for his stuff.'

George is standing there, looking at them. Looking upset. He's nodding, turning and going back down the stairs. Another one Calum can't trust. It could only have been from George that Emma got wind of his true profession. There's no one he can trust. Before, when he was freelance, he didn't have to trust anyone. A luxury then, a necessity now. Now he has to trust others, and he can't. You can't survive this way. It always catches up with you. Takes longer for some than for others. Frank lasted longer than anyone. Nobody lasts all the way to the end.

Calum's kneeling beside him, looking at the body of the man who used to do his job. Looking at his future.